In The Name Of The Mother

In The Name Of The Mother

John Broughton

Special thanks go to my dear friend John Bentley for his steadfast and indefatigable support. His content checking and suggestions have made an invaluable contribution to In the Name of the Mother.

For Suzy Rees, my dear lifelong friend and inspiration to write this sequel to Wyrd of the Wolf

Chapter 1

Cynethryth peered over the prow and gasped at the lashing foam that soaked her frock to leave it clinging tighter – if that were possible – to her swollen belly. The sea air, even on this mild late-summer's day, left her shivering as it added to the chill of the seawater permeating her linen dress and shift to the skin.

"Daughter, come down here, at once!" The rest of the warrior's words were lost to the breeze in an incoherent muttering but she caught 'in your condition'.

Little did she care for any discomfort, so her glance at the coast of her beloved Wiht more than compensated. Nearing her confinement – she was eight months into this pregnancy – Cynethryth had feared her child would not be born on the isle. Indeed, when she had followed her husband to Rome, she thought never to see Wiht again. As their ship approached the inlet to her birthplace at Cerdicsford, her emotions tumbled and whirled like the chopping waves where the tide met the river. She almost tumbled too as she picked her ungainly way to the steadying arms of her father.

The joy of beholding Wiht and the anticipation of reuniting with her dearest friend, Rowena, could not overcome the grief, still raw, of her loss of Caedwalla, whose child kicked mercilessly inside her womb. How cruel a wyrd had taken him from her after so few precious nights together, but at least she would see something of him again in the face of their offspring.

Aelfhere, concerned for them both, took off his cloak and wrapped it around his trembling, headstrong daughter.

"The ship'll not berth the sooner for all your staring over the bows, my angel."

He enfolded her in his strong arms and she snuggled against the man who had raised her in childhood. She had wounded him by disobedience over her betrothal, but their past differences, set aside, had brought them closer than ever. She basked in the fact that he had received the message of Christ in Rome, accepted baptism, and, without thinking, called her his *angel.* Aelfhere's emotions too, although less intense, were contrasting. His love of Wiht, no less strong than hers, and of Cerdicsford in particular, meant his spirits rose at their approach. But what would greet him? His possessions were now fallen into the hands of Caedwalla's – the conqueror's – man Guthred, from what his daughter had told him. Would he have to renew hostilities to wrest back what was his? He glanced down at the bedraggled red-gold hair of his only child and praised – who, the Lord Jesus or Freya? – who had blessed him with a grandchild for his old age. Ashamed at his spiritual ambivalence, he could not meet the adoring gaze of the dark grey eyes full of tenderness that turned up and scanned his face to gauge his sentiments.

"What manner of man is this Guthred?"

"A good man, father, a friend."

"No friend of mine."

She pressed closer to him, and the unborn child, as if to reprove him, kicked against his side. Cynethryth groaned and her father held her tighter.

"Yon's a warrior you're carrying, dear heart. He nigh on kicked me into the sea!"

"And what if he's a *she*, father?"

2

"In that case, she'll be as reckless, wilful and winsome as her mother."

Their laughter, precious in its complicity with the unspoken sense of forgiveness, broke off as the ship nudged against the wooden quay, causing Aelfhere to brace himself, tightening his hold on her.

"Home at last!" But there was an edge of unease in his voice.

He helped Cynethryth over the side of the ship where willing hands, belonging to familiar faces grinning into hers, hoisted her onto the quay.

"Cynethryth!" A woman's voice rose above the general stridency assailing her ears.

"Rowena!"

Island life suited her friend, who bore down on her in the full bloom of health. Rowena had always been pretty with her pale hair like burnished copper and almond-shaped eyes of sage green, but Cynethryth had never seen her so comely.

"Look at you!" Rowena rushed to embrace her. "Oh, you poor thing! You're soaked through. Come with me before you catch your death of cold! There's a fire in the hall and we'll get you some dry clothes. How many months is it? You must be due soon!"

Aelfhere smiled at their retreating backs. Had he lost her already?

Not that he had time to fret. In an instant, old acquaintances, bondsmen and friends surrounded him, all revelling in his unexpected return. Standing two hands taller than the tallest and keeping in the background, Guthred studied the reception of the returning lord of this homestead and formulated his own greeting. It was not long before the two men faced each other, aided by the insistence of Alric, a thegn from an outlying farmstead, who guided Aelfhere to come face to face with the new lord.

"So, you are the father of Cynethryth. Lord Aelfhere, is it not?"

Taken aback by the unexpected sincere friendliness of the tone and the title freely given, Aelfhere accepted the proffered hand and clasped it.

"Come! You must be weary and cold. Let us join the women-folk and drink together."

"Willingly."

This greeting exceeded Aelfhere's rosiest expectations. His spirits lifted but as he inhaled the familiar air of home and drank in the sights and sounds so much missed, his thoughts went to Baldwulf, Hynsige and Wulflaf, faithful comrades, each perished for love of him – how his heart ached at their absence, but he shrugged off morose thoughts as he stepped into the warmth of his hall.

"Father, wonderful news! Rowena is also with child!"

Aelfhere turned to Guthred and stared into the grinning face.

"It appears we have cause to celebrate. My congratulations!"

Two paces behind them followed Alric and Ewald, delighted to renew their old friendship. Aelfhere heard the thegn say, "I didn't know whether you'd survived the journey to Rome but we tended your woodland and your house is still in one piece!"

Amid the general festivities, prolonged into the evening when servants produced a splendid meal of shellfish and fresh crab, and much ale and recounting of tales, Guthred spoke in a low voice to Aelfhere.

"Lord, my wife and I have oft spoken about your likely home-coming."

Aelfhere's pulse quickened, so this was it! Was it to be war or peace? His eyes roamed over the bulging muscles of the Saxon, younger by many winters than himself. His gaze switched to the two redheaded women so happy and intimate and an icy hand clutched at his heart. Was happiness to be snatched from one or the other?

"I enjoy living here and have the respect of the folk." Guthred hesitated to gauge the effect of his words, but apart from a slight narrowing of the other's eyes, nothing. He pressed on, "The truth is, this is *your* home, these are *your* lands and *your* people, but I would not wish to leave the isle."

"What is to be done?"

Aelfhere was glad nobody was paying attention to their conversation.

This was not quite true because Cynethryth, from the corner of her eye, had noted the unease in her father's bearing and could see he was fighting to keep his temper under control. She prayed he would not ruin their heart-warming homecoming as she gazed into the sparkling eyes of her friend and tried to keep up her end of their chatter.

"I had thought, Lord, I could swear fealty to you, and in return, you might find me land for a home."

Aelfhere relaxed and in a spontaneous gesture took the hand of his new thegn. A mighty warrior in his service, what more could he have hoped for?

"The best farms are taken, Guthred. But I have an idea. Cerdicsford is an island within the isle and part of this island has another area as yet unclaimed. There is a headland to the west and it will need tilling but the land is fertile and easily defended. From the *tout* there is a clear view over the sea. It serves for an early warning of invasion: hence its name Toutland. You will be Thegn of Toutland, what say you? We can ride out to view it on the morrow. When you decide we'll have the announcement and another feast here. The menfolk will help you build your hall, and for sure, one or two will want to work the land."

Cynethryth's anxiety passed as she saw the two men in cordial agreement. How wonderful it was to be home! If only Caedwalla had been here to share it with her. For the thousandth time she cursed the sword slash that had never healed and that had taken him from her. But she swore she would keep his child safe and it would lack for nothing.

Chapter 2

October 689 AD

Having been brought up by her father, and in the absence of a mother's guidance, Cynethryth wasn't prepared for the agonies of childbirth. A few days before the delivery, the women of the village, when consulted, were of little help, offering vague comments like, "It was hard and tiring but worth it in the end." They meant well because they didn't want to scare her but thus they denied Cynethryth the mental preparation to face the ordeal. She knew that women died in childbirth, and so too did many babes, but she was determined this would not be the fate of her child or its mother, not if she had anything to do with it.

She went into labour unready for the pains of contraction and what followed were hours of utter hell. Afterwards all she could recall was the excruciating pain and the conviction that she would die. But as she stared at the wrinkled creature helpless on her breast, the small miracle, she forgot the suffering in a trice. She had a son and she adored him – her tiny princeling.

In the days that followed, Aelfhere reminded her that his grandson was, in fact, an aetheling. In reaction to her idea to name the child after his father, Aelfhere was adamant she must not.

"Caedwalla! Unwise! When he is older it will serve only to remind those in Wessex who mean him ill that he has a claim to the throne. Heed my words, it would be foolish and dangerous."

"Then, I will call him Aelfhere, after you." The dark grey eyes softened to tenderness.

"Better not. If they come looking for your child, they will hear of one named after your father."

Cynethryth folded her arms over her chest and glared, "Oh father, who are *they* who mean harm to my boy? You frighten me! What am I supposed to call him?"

"The latest news from Wessex isn't comforting. A youngster called Ine took the throne and, in so doing, bypassed his own father, Coenred. So, you see, there are other claimants and much unrest. While your little fellow is an infant, there's nothing to fear…but later…"

He left the rest unspoken and gazed anxiously at Cynethryth, whose usually serene countenance contorted into a mask of rage.

"Nobody will ever harm my son!" she cried, "Not whilst there's breath in my body!"

Tears threatened and Aelfhere, regretting his ill-chosen words, strode to comfort her.

"Of course, nobody will harm him – not with me and Guthred to protect him."

But Aelfhere knew too much about the struggles for kingship to believe his reassurances.

When Cynethryth spoke to him some days later about christening the boy, Aelfhere made no objection to her choice of name or rather, he bit off his demurral.

Instead, he said, "Aethelheard. It's a fine name. How did it come to mind?"

"I was chatting with Guthred and he suggested it."

"I see." *'That accounts for it.'* Cynethryth cast him a sharp glance and he added hastily, "Aethelheard is an excellent choice. *"Aethel-' is a royal prefix. I fear it gives the secret away.'*

"We must send to Wihtgarsburh for a priest as soon as possible. My little man must be brought into the faith."

In the small wooden chapel of the farmstead, hastily erected in Aelfhere's absence by Guthred, over the crude stone font, little Aethelheard gurgled contentedly in the priest's arms. The babe didn't react to the cold water splashed over his head so those present regarded the christening as auspicious.

The seasons passed on Wiht with plenty both on the farmsteads and for the fishermen. While unrest and political turbulence scarred the lives of the mainlanders, Wiht basked in the peace its geographic position afforded its people. It was of little import that Wihtred overthrew the King of Kent and invaded the land of the treacherous East Saxons or even that King Ine installed his kinsman Nothelm as King of the South Saxons, thus making him the overlord of Wiht. Cynethryth, more concerned with tending the grazed knees of her energetic five-year-old son, who was forever getting into scrapes, only sat up and took notice of major events when King Ine attacked Kent and extorted 30,000 pence in recompense for the murder of her husband's brother, Mul.

News of this episode and other Wessex matters brought Guthred to Cerdicsford to seek discussions with Cynethryth and Aelfhere.

"I have received a message from friends in Wessex," his blue eyes narrowed as he frowned, "Coenred died two moons ago."

"Who?" Aelfhere knew little of the Wessex royalty and, if he were honest, preferred to keep matters that way.

Cynethryth enlightened her father.

"Coenred was Caedwalla's cousin as well as father of King Ine who now rules Wessex."

"What concern is this of ours?"

"Well, it *is*." Guthred said, "Or more to the point, of Aethelheard."

"What has the boy to do with anything?"

"My friend Caedwalla, the boy's father, is a direct descendent of the true bloodline of Wessex." He recited, "Caedwalla, son of Cenberht, son of Cenna...and so it goes on, direct back to Cerdric, the founder of the dynasty. Aethelheard has a better claim to kingship than Ine and that ruler is becoming ever more the tyrant: he thirsts for greater power."

"But Aethelheard has only five winters behind him."

"I know that, Lord Aelfhere. But do you not see? The death of Coenred is a grave blow to the future hopes of the boy. There remains but one cousin of Caedwalla – Cuthred, the son of the late King Cwichelm, who might be willing to sustain the cause of Aethelheard."

"What cause?"

"The claim to be rightful ruler of Wessex."

"But he's only five!" Cynethryth's words were choked with emotion.

"Indeed," Guthred gave her an encouraging smile, "and Cuthred grows no younger and has no sons of his own. This is a chance to ensure Aethelheard's birthright. Will you not come with me to Cuthred? We should at least try. We owe as much to Caedwalla." Thus, he put forward his strongest argument and with satisfaction saw it drive home in the setting of Cynethryth's jaw.

"Father, I will go to Wessex with Guthred and see what can be done for Aethelheard."

"But the boy will remain here, where he is safe."

"I think not, Lord Aelfhere," Guthred spoke firmly, "our case is only strong if presented in the flesh. If you are worried, you too will come to protect the boy."

"And so I will. These are troubled times. We must tread with great care and you will need a wise head to save you from recklessness." This he said without a trace of a smile.

"Then it's agreed. We leave for Sussex and thence for Wessex. Will Rowena come too? I need a female companion and little Osburh will be a distraction for Aethelheard. They are such close friends."

"So be it!" Guthred smiled. I will ride to tell them of our plans. The weather is set fair, so we can sail to Selsey in the morning.

"Bring them here for the night, so that we may dine and discuss further our plans. I need to know more of this Cuthred," Aelfhere insisted.

What ought to have been a straightforward journey to Winchester was anything but. The crossing to Selsey was pleasant enough. Cynethryth passed it in conversation with Rowena and in keeping Aethelheard from perilous scaling of the ship's tempting structure. The road from Selsey to Chichester and thence to Winchester, remarkable for the women and children being endlessly jostled in their canvas-covered ox-cart, was slow and uneventful. The problems began in the town, when they at last reached it. Discreet inquiries led to learning that their bird had flown. Cuthred, on hearing of his cousin's death, despite initial opposition from King Ine had claimed the vacant sub-kingdom of Dorset. Having mustered sufficient support for his claim among the Wessex nobles, he was now enthroned in his new lands.

Aelfhere and Guthred discussed whether this was good news or not long into the night. In any case, they decided to continue their journey as far as Cuthred's court. They agreed to keep their movements a close-guarded secret, given Ine's fury at Cuthred's effrontery.

At the thought of having to cross through the dense Selwood, Guthred muttered, "We'd have come by ship to Wareham had we known."

Aelfhere, who had sailed the whole length of the south coast, shook his head, "The coastline in those parts has no safe landing place. We're better off by road, even though the way is arduous."

The worst part was going through the forest, owing to the poor trackway, its surface ruined by tree roots. Often, the men had to dismount and heave the cart over a tenacious obstacle. The constant fear of outlaws overwhelming the small number of men Aelfhere and Guthred had brought as escort troubled them both. Six armed and mounted men would be hard-pressed to withstand a band of forty club-wielding villains. Luckily, they encountered no such danger and emerged from the forest to cross an abandoned dyke before joining the rebuilt ancient road across the Chase, then striking south to the royal burh of Wareham.

Many days after their departure from Wiht, the welcome sight of the wooden defensive walls of the burh restored their cheer. Weary, Aelfhere raised his horn to his lips and blew two blasts to announce their peaceful intent. Nonetheless, when the gates opened, a group of heavily armed horsemen galloped out. Their leader, complete in mail shirt and a helm that hid most of his face, halted the riders a few paces from the small group.

"State your name, purpose and provenance," he called.

Aelfhere, in a strong voice replied, "Aelfhere of Cerdicsford seeking audience with King Cuthred, we come from Wiht."

The horseman nudged his steed closer and peered through the eye-slits of the helm at Aelfhere.

"You have travelled far. What is in the cart?"

"Women and children."

As if on cue, Cynethryth emerged from the canvas opening over the cart and rounding the edge of the waggon, demanded, "Why have we stopped? Oh!" she exclaimed on seeing the riders blocking their way.

In a gentler tone, the leader of the defenders said, "We will accompany you into Wareham where you can take lodgings, so I'll know where to find you should the king agree to your request."

Obeying the demand to follow, the travellers urged their exhausted mounts to one last effort, which took them into the small burh of perhaps fifty houses, a church and a hall that served as a royal palace. The burh also boasted an inn complete with stables. Saddle-sore, the men dismounted to consign their tired beasts to youths who led the horses to a drinking trough. Cynethryth and Rowena, each with a child in tow, followed the mail-shirted warrior into the inn and were soon joined by their menfolk.

"The king does not receive this late in the day but I will take your request for audience to him, Aelfhere of Cerdicsford. You will have your answer soon enough. Meanwhile, you should be comfortable here, Lady," he addressed Cynethryth with a slight bow. "The inn belongs to my kinsman, Eafa – ah, here he is!"

The innkeeper, a sturdy, slightly bow-legged figure, wearing a leather apron over a pale green linen tunic, greeted them. They soon agreed a price for the rooms and ordered a hot meal, of which they were in sore need. Eafa the landlord was married to a robust, ruddy-cheeked woman with curling grey hair poking out from under a grubby white linen headscarf. She was, Aelfhere considered, far less appetising than the delicious pork stew she prepared for them. The meagre dried food of the journey relegated to an unwelcome memory, everyone ate with a hearty appetite. Afterwards, chatting and laughing over beakers of passable ale, they were surprised when a stocky fellow, unrecognisable without armour except for his voice, interrupted their wassailing.

"King Cuthred will receive you, Aelfhere of Cerdicsford, after Mass tomorrow morning."

"I thank you, friend," Aelfhere bowed his head, "come, pray join us for a beaker of ale."

The fellow hesitated but Cynethryth bestowed on him a winsome smile to end his doubts.

"Do favour us with your company," she said, "there are so many things I wish to ask."

All resistance vanished in the face of such charm, and he took a place made for him on the bench across from the lady.

"We too will go to Mass tomorrow, will we not?" Cynethryth said to Rowena who gave her assent.

"We'll all go," Aelfhere agreed while pouring ale for their guest. Cynethryth, ever practical, began to question the thegn. She asked about the burh and its people, listening with attention to his fulsome praise of the decent, hard-working Dormsaete – the local Saxons, of whom he was one – now under the control of Wessex.

"Dorset was a hard nut to crack," the thegn said with no attempt to keep the pride from his voice. "The Britons defended their land as fierce as dragons. Their dykes were impenetrable for many years but King Cenwalh, in my father's time, broke through and won two great battles. He drove them back westward over the River Parrett after his second triumph at Peonna – and we've held the land ever since."

"We crossed one such dyke on our way here," Guthred said.

"Imagine its strength with the fortifications we demolished!"

"Is your king a great warrior?" Cynethryth asked.

"When he was younger there was no finer swordsman in Wessex."

"What age has the king?"

"I can't be sure but I'd say he's seen two-score winters."

"Your age then, father," she smiled at her sire.

"In that case," Aelfhere grinned, "I would not wish to cross swords with the king, for at such a young age, he will still be formidable."

The piping voice of Aethelheard chimed in, "Grandfather, you are *not* a young man!"

Everyone laughed, but Aelfhere leapt up, drew his sword and made a fierce face, "Come here boy and say that again. I'll have your head!"

Another boy of five might have crumpled and sought his mother's skirts but Aethelheard picked up a knife from the table and brandishing it, cried, "You are *not* a young man! I will not punish you *only* because you are my grandfather!"

"Put that knife down at once!" Cynethryth scolded him. "What use do you think it is against a grown man with a sword?"

"But mother, I can move fast, grandfather couldn't get near me." Aethelheard began to dodge and weave in imitation of a fighting man.

"One day, my wolf sword will be yours, boy," Aelfhere said proudly, "but you'll have to grow some muscles and learn to wield a sword first."

"Promise, grandfather! Promise!"

"The boy has pluck," the Dormsaete thegn acknowledged.

Aelfhere looked guiltily at his grandson. "I promise."

'*The boy and his mother must never learn that this sword struck the blow fatal to Caedwalla.*'

Chapter 3

King Cuthred, seated on a throne raised on a dais started at the sight of Cynethryth, standing behind Aelfhere. His countenance assumed a sudden anxiety. He stood, one hand holding the other arm at the elbow, before waving the same hand and thundering, "Out! All of you, out!"

Servants, guards and retainers all scurried to the doors. Cynethryth made to follow but Guthred took a restraining grip of her arm.

"I know you, Lady," said the king as soon as the hall returned to blessed silence after the noise of scampering feet died away. "I attended your wedding to my cousin. I never forget a face, especially one so comely!"

"I thank you, Lord King."

She curtsied and shot him a smile but noticed that it failed to allay the worry in his visage. Why the sight of her should alarm him eluded her. His next words made the matter clear.

"I recognised you at once, Lady Cynethryth. For all our sakes it's important nobody else knows who you are. God knows, I'm already in danger enough."

Aelfhere stepped forward.

"King Cuthred, I am Aelfhere of Cerdicsford, father of Cynethryth. We have travelled from Wiht to present Aethelheard," he gestured with two united fingers at the boy to indicate he should step forward, "son of Caedwalla."

Quick-witted as ever, the boy stepped forward and, recalling his mother's advice, made a deep bow to the monarch.

"The Lord preserve us!" Cuthred said, his hand covered his mouth, and with a slow disbelieving shake of the head, he murmured, "Look at him! The image of his father. You must take him back to your island, at once!"

"But we have brought him here for a purpose, Lord," Aelfhere protested. "We seek your protection for the boy."

"Have you taken leave of your senses, man?" Cuthred's face grew puce, with an unascertained emotion. Among them, only Aethelheard, in his ingenuity, stared at him slack-jawed and blatantly.

Cynethryth caught the boy by the shoulder and whispered in his ear, "Stop gawping, son."

The boy lowered his head and studied the crushed lavender strewn among the fresh reeds covering the paving stones. He looked up, mouth firmly closed when the king continued. "Have I not said that your presence places us all in peril? With the boy here, should his identity emerge, the danger is without limits."

"No-one can know who he is unless his mother is recognised," Guthred said in a respectful, reasonable tone.

"I know you too," Cuthred glared, "you were Caedwalla's man!"

"The same Guthred, Lord, and at your service." He bowed.

"King Ine wants me slain. If he learns I'm harbouring Caedwalla's son, his fury will know no bounds."

"I'm prepared to leave Wareham," Cynethryth's tone was conciliatory, "but wish to remain in Dorset near enough to ensure the wellbeing of my son. All I ask, as your cousin's widow, is that you offer protection and support to my son. For many a year, nobody needs know who he truly is. My son has but five winters behind him.

A series of emotions crossed the king's face as he stared hard at the aetheling before him. Brashly, the boy met and held his gaze, offering a timid smile.

The side of the king's mouth twitched and he said, "Protection and support, you say? I'll do better than that! By all the saints, I will! I'll adopt the boy and declare him my son."

Cynethryth gasped, clasped her hands in front of her and wide-eyed, stared at the King.

Aethelheard was first to react. He threw his arms around her thighs and gazed up into her face. "Mother, don't be sad. I'll be the king's son but I'll ever be yours."

Tears filled her eyes but she fought them back for his sake and hugged him, "Thank the king, your father, and promise to be obedient and studious."

"Thank you father. I promise to be all that you wish."

"Leave the boy and go with my blessing and hark! Not a word of this to anyone."

As they trooped out of the Hall, Cynethryth, straining to hear, caught the king's words to her son: "...and I'll make of you the finest swordsman in Wessex..." She smiled and wondered, *'Will my life forever be such sweet sorrow?'*

Back in the inn, they sat over a light meal to discuss the morning's events.

"It went well." Aelfhere was concise in his judgement.

"Better than we could have hoped," Guthred agreed. "Cuthred will raise him as his son and I approve of the king's wariness – it will ensure no harm befalls Aethelheard.

"I will miss my boy terribly. I'll have to find something to occupy me, for I cannot be seen in court. Cuthred was clear on that and I agree with his decision – whatever is best for Aethelheard." Her mind was quite lucid about what was right but her heart protested fit to break.

Aelfhere took her hand.

"It's for the best, my angel, but will you not come to Wiht with me?"

She shook her head. "I need to feel close to him even if I can't see him."

'I'll find a way to catch sight of my boy.'

"Rowena, do you wish to return to Wiht?" Guthred asked.

The green eyes, full of concern, switched to Aelfhere. "Forgive me, Lord, but I wish for little Osburh to grow up with Aethelheard. There's a chance that Guthred can enter King Cuthred's service so that we can attend the court. Forgive me, for you have been a generous Lord. We leave our homestead only for love of Cynethryth."

"I understand, and will keep you all in my thoughts. Come to Wiht when you can. What will you do, daughter?"

She was moved by the sadness in his tone. Her decision meant he was losing daughter and grandchild in one blow. She bit her lower lip and stared at the table. Whatever she said, she would not make this harder for him.

"I must find a useful purpose, father, and to that end, I will away to see the priest at Saint Martin's church. When will you depart?"

"My horse will be well rested by the morning, so I'll inform Ewald and the others that we leave at first light. I have to find the scoundrels first. I'll wager they're supping and wenching in some foul hovel while my back's turned."

"Then I will rise early to bid you farewell. Now, I must seek the priest."

They watched Cynethryth glide out of the tavern, straight-backed and elegant as ever.

"What do you think she means to do?" Rowena nudged her husband.

Guthred shrugged and teased, "What man ever knows the mind of a woman? She seeks a priest, so maybe she means to marry."

Rowena gave his arm another nudge, "Never! She loved Caedwalla too much to do that!"

"A man must watch his limbs when a swan starts to hiss!"

He grinned at Aelfhere and received another shove for his troubles.

"Father, why does mother keep hitting you?" The voice piped up from under the edge of the table.

"Because she's an aggressive little swan!"

"Mother, you *aren't* a swan! Tell him!"

They stayed together for an hour, expecting Cynethryth to return at any moment. When it became clear she would not, Aelfhere decided to search for his men. As he pointed out, Wareham was not so big and he would soon find the layabouts. When they had arrived, he had noticed a small harbour off to the east. If they could find a ship willing to take them and their horses to Wiht, it would save a repeat of the sapping journey they had undertaken. He was willing to trade passage in exchange for the ox and cart, but he needed to talk it over with Ewald, preferably while the rascal was still sober.

Cynethryth, warming to Father Feran, confessed the nature of their visit to Wareham, secure in the inviolable secrecy of the sacrament. At last, when she had revealed everything and had satisfied the old man's curiosity regarding her lineage, she proceeded to bare her soul. The need to offset the loss of her only child with a worthwhile occupation had driven her to him.

"Father, I am thinking of taking the veil. I seek no husband and wish to dedicate my life to the service of God. What do you counsel me?"

The priest frowned and lapsed into thought. Of course, the fact that this beautiful young woman wished to become a nun filled him with joy, but her royal connections meant he would have to move astutely. He bent his head in prayer and enlightenment came at once.

"My dear lady, I don't know why I didn't think of this straight away," he smiled and said, "it must be slowness due to my advancing years. But the daughters of our late, lamented King Coenred are still in Wareham. They returned for the funeral from Barking where they studied the scriptures under the Blessed Hildelith. Unless I err, Cuthburga was a cousin of your late husband. Who better to counsel you, Lady? I am but a humble priest."

"How will I find Cuthburga?"

"Nothing easier. She will come here. As on every day, she comes in the early afternoon. You will not mistake her if you wait. She brings fresh flowers to the altar before she immerses herself in prayer. You will know her by her regal presence, I am sure. Bless you my child." He sketched a cross with his hand over her head. "I will leave you to pray for guidance." With that, he departed and Cynethryth chose to follow his advice, kneeling and bowing her head in prayer.

Time hung heavily in the silent church but Cynethryth had much to think about, quite apart from formulating prayers seeking guidance. Her thoughts kept returning to little Aethelheard: would he cope bereft of his mother? She knew the boy had great inner strength and she believed it would do him no harm to endure a tougher upbringing than she would have provided. This, she knew, was a hard world for men of noble birth. She remembered the king's words she had overheard and smiled. If he made Aethelheard the best swordsman in Wessex, she need have no fears for his safety.

When footsteps along the nave alerted her to another person she did not raise her head but peered from under her brow to see a woman, small but with a presence that seemed to fill the church.

Judging by the lines on her face, she had seen two-score winters, but the few wrinkles were gentle and added to her beauty. Cynethryth caught the shrewdness in the deep eyes, weighing her up as she passed. The woman was clutching a bunch of red marigolds. She stepped up to the altar and replaced the flowers. There was no trace of wealth about her in spite of the regal bearing. A wimple covered her head and a hood draped her shoulders. Under it, a burgundy cloak overlaid a grey tunic. At the waist, a wooden cross was tucked into a belt. Stepping down from the altar, the nun genuflected and came toward Cynethryth. Cuthburga smiled and a dimple formed.

"You wish to speak with me, child?"

'*Can she read my innermost thoughts?*'

"I do, my Lady."

The nun sat on the pew next to her and took her hand. She listened patiently to Cynethryth's tale and only at the end when the younger woman expressed fear of King Ine did she react. Her tone was sharp, "You *do* know that Ine is my brother?"

Cynethryth did not and her sharp intake of breath betrayed as much. She should have known. Guthred had informed them weeks ago that Ine had bypassed his father to take the throne and she knew Cuthburga was Coenred's daughter. How foolish she felt! Had she betrayed Cuthred's secret on the first day?

She need not have worried for Cuthburga squeezed her hand and said, "So you are Caedwalla's wife? I was his cousin, more correctly, his second cousin. There are many in Rome who would have Caedwalla made a saint, you know. Now, I'm sure we'll be friends and work together for God's glory. Do not worry about Ine. He is not a wicked man, just a little too ambitious. He has seen that I and my sister Quenburga have devoted ourselves to the service of God and wrote me a letter that I received but two days ago. He desires to build an abbey hereabouts for the good of his soul and the advantage of his people. It must be near the royal residence so that he can worship when he comes. He wishes for me to be its first abbess. You will be one of my first nuns, I'll train you myself throughout your temporary vows. If you complete your training to my satisfaction, I will oversee your final vows. does that suit you, child?"

"It does, my Lady."

"The first thing to learn is to call me 'Mother.'"

"Of course, my L– er, Mother."

They both laughed but then Cuthburga put her hand to her mouth, bowed to the altar and made the sign of the Cross.

"We must not be frivolous in the sight of God. Tell me, do you ride? Do you have a horse?"

"I do, Mother."

"Good, then fetch it. We must set about the Lord's business. It will be good to have a riding companion. Meet me outside the church as soon as you can. Make haste, child!"

"I will, Mother."

For the first time since her separation from Aethelheard, Cynethryth was cheerful. She was grateful to have a purpose and as she strode towards the inn's stables, she wondered whither Cuthburga meant to ride and to what end.

She reined in her horse in front of St Martin's Church and looked in vain for the nun. Moments later, a rider rounded the side of the sacred building on a fine black mount at least two hands taller than her own.

"A fine creature," Cuthburga nodded towards Cynethryth's horse. "Come, let's away so there's time before nightfall."

They rode through the well-guarded gateway along a causeway raised above marshland, Cynethryth breathing the sea breeze, exhilarating her. She realised they were heading away from the sea, maybe in the direction that had brought them to Wareham. Cuthburga slowed her steed and leant near to her companion.

"If we are to follow Ine's instructions we can't go too far. So look out for a suitable place."

Before Cynethryth could ask 'for what?', the nun had urged her horse forward out of range. Cynethryth shrugged and geed up her willing animal in pursuit. As she tried to catch up with her new friend, she thought hard – look out for what? What had she said in the church? Ine wanted a new abbey not far from Wareham. That was it! She had to look for a suitable location.

They rode on until they came to a river. They followed its course for a mile or more when Cuthburga leant close to her and said, "This is the Stour. The name means 'the fierce one' because it flows many long leagues and draws on other rivers. It is fierce when it is swollen by the winter rain and snow. The river will be a useful source of fish and medicinal leeches." They pressed on until Cynethryth called to her companion, "Mother! Look there! That's the place! It's wonderful." She pointed to a confluence with another river where the land was level and green.

"The Lord has spoken through you, Cynethryth. You have said well. *That*'s where we'll build our abbey. It can be only three leagues to Wareham, we should be heading back. Praise the Lord!"

Chapter 4

If anyone had asked Cynethryth to describe her new friend, especially in the early days of their association, she would have had difficulty. Each day revealed some new aspect of Cuthburga's personality, such was her complexity. An austere appearance with assiduousness in fasting and prayer belied the kindly nature of the nun. Cynethryth, flattered to be accorded so much attention and to have secured the confidences of the holy woman, remained captivated in her presence. Gradually, she confided her innermost emotions and Cuthburga gave serious thought to her protégée's desire to serve the sick and infirm. Astute as she was, she did not separate this revelation from Cynethryth's oft expressed yearning to see her son. It was therefore some time before Cuthburga took any decision, assessing the intellect of her cousin's widow and considering the genuineness of her desire to take the veil. She did not find her wanting on either score; therefore after two months of their acquaintance she tackled the situation.

"Cynethryth, I have come to a decision regarding your future."

She said this with an authority and conviction that made the younger woman repress her natural tendency to object and assert herself. Instead, she gazed into the dark grey eyes, so like her own, and knew in an instant she would obey whatever this charismatic woman ordered her to do.

"Mother, what is it?"

"I find, child, that your wish to serve God is founded on the rock of true faith, which is most laudable and must lead to your taking the veil."

"Oh, Mother, I cannot hide my joy!"

"Nor should you, Cynethryth, but I have not finished," she said and the severity of her tone made the younger woman squeeze the fingers of one hand with the other and bite her lip. "Taking the veil will mean renunciation of your desires, relatives... of... your *son*..." She paused to gauge the effect of her words and pursed her mouth at the wretched expression on the would-be postulant's face. "The new abbey will be able to make use of a competent infirmarian, but you are far from attaining such competence–"

"Why–"

The nun held up a hand and frowned, "Do not interrupt! That is why I have decided to send you to Barking. Its abbey contains a vast library and I recall seeing volumes with titles like *Leechbook, Herborium* and *Remedies*. I have written to the Abbess Hildelith, a devout and saintly superior, who will be your spiritual guide. Pay close attention to her teachings, child, and in your free time frequent the library and learn all you can about the art of curing the sick. You will leave as soon as you can and bear the letter to Abbess Hildelith yourself. Now you may speak."

"I thank you for what you wish to do for me," the first spark of resentment flared in her breast, "but Barking is so far away from Wareham and I resolved to stay here, near Aethelheard. How long must I be away?"

"Until I send for you. There is time, for building has not yet begun on the abbey. I will ensure when it does, they construct an infirmary with a number of beds for the sick. You see,

Cynethryth, the sick will come to you. It would not be seemly for a nun to roam freely in the town."

The acid tone dripping from the last word, *town*, made it clear that her plan to use excursions to visit the sick as an excuse to see her son would never be permitted.

'*I will do as she bids, but first, I must see Aethelheard one last time.*'

"Of course, Mother, it will be as you say."

The grey eyes scrutinised her for the slightest trace of insincerity but then a sweet smile put her at ease.

'*I wanted a useful occupation. Well thus it will be!*'

"Clearly, you cannot travel to Barking alone. It's a journey of forty leagues fraught with peril. I'll arrange an armed escort with a guide to accompany you."

"Mother, you are kind. But I wish to see my son once before I depart."

Cuthburga frowned, "It's unwise. The boy's beginning to settle. Father Feran keeps me informed on his progress. Until ten days ago, he was fretful and missing his family, but now he is studious and it appears he is the king's delight. He has taken him to his bosom, instructing him in 'the ways of kings'. I believe they rode out for falconry together."

"B-but Aethelheard can't ride!"

"Oh no, he sat on the king's mount."

"How he will have enjoyed that!"

"You should do nothing to unsettle the boy."

"You are so wise, Mother."

"You too, Cynethryth. Now away to your lodgings and gather together only what is necessary for your journey. Sleep well tonight and ride to me in the morning. Your escort will be arranged." The nun scrutinised her face again, "Make no attempt to see your son this evening!"

'*She can read my mind but maybe she's right.*'

Cynethryth thought hard about this on her way to the inn. If only her father had not returned to Wiht: he had a way of consoling her with a mere pat on the hand. She resolved to set aside her selfish desires. Cuthburga was being so kind to her and it would be wrong to cause her displeasure.

After listening to and absorbing Cuthburga's recommendations for her time at Barking and placing the letter in her saddlebag, the company of horsemen set off across the embankment on the first stage of the journey. Cynethryth rode without gazing at the surroundings. There was much to think about, not least how much she would miss Cuthburga.

'*Is it possible that each time I grow fond of someone my fate wrests me away?*'

Occupied thinking over what the nun had counselled her, Cynethryth barely noticed a rider detach himself from the others to urge his horse beside hers.

"Do not brood so, my Lady. You are sure to like your new home."

Cynethryth started. She knew the voice.

"Guthred! What are you doing here? You should be looking out for Aethelheard and Rowena!"

"Do not scold, Lady. I should indeed be here. I'm in the king's service and my orders are to escort you safely to Barking. I sometimes wonder, it is true, whether I'm in the king's service or in Rowena's, for she gave me the same command!"

Cynethryth laughed. It was good to have Guthred's companionship on this long ride.

"How is Rowena?"

"Sad to see you leave. Did you not see her on the ramparts when we rode through the gates?"

Cynethryth's good humour, just restored, evaporated at once. Had she been so wrapped up in her thoughts, she had none to spare for others? She had not bothered to look around her and must have displeased poor Rowena.

"And what of my son?"

"The only danger he is in, my Lady, is of being spoilt by the king, who dotes on the boy. Only yesterday, Cuthred taught him how to defend himself with a wooden sword. I think it's a little soon. The sword was nigh on as long as the small fellow but to hear the king, Aethelheard will be the greatest warrior who ever wielded sword!"

"It would be treason to gainsay the king, my friend!"

They continued in friendly conversation as the horses carried them along the easy-going of the ancient roadway to the confines with Hampshire. Guthred, whom Cynethryth realised with surprise was the captain of the escort, called a halt within sight of the great forest. He gathered his men and gave instructions, sending two riders ahead, one a guide and the other a warrior, with orders to find a suitable place to refresh the animals – "and ourselves," he added with a laugh. Two others were delegated as flanking outriders. "You can't be too careful in the forest," he said ominously.

Cynethryth was not afraid. They had come untroubled through the great Selwood to arrive in Dorset, why should the Andersweald be less safe? Her reasoning proved mistaken after less than an hour among the trees. All of a sudden, the distant sound of a horn – three blasts as arranged for warning – alerted them.

"Swords!" bellowed Guthred and each man drew a blade. Cynethryth had only a small dagger in her belt. For the moment, she left it where it was, knowing it to be useless against a violent outlaw. Guthred led ahead at a canter, urging the others to keep together. She had no trouble keeping the pace and felt more secure that she was in the midst of an armed escort. That is, until the man two horses in front of her flung up his arms, dropped his sword and toppled from his saddle with a black-fletched arrow in his chest. Another horse reared, an arrow piercing its flank.

Its rider sprang off its back as it sank, screaming pitifully, to the ground.

"Gallop!" Guthred cried, and setting the example urged his mount at speed through the trees. Cynethryth drove her horse faster after the warrior in front of her and exchanged grins with two other riders who edged alongside her steed, keeping her exact pace.

What happened next was bewildering to her, but she heard screams and shouts from among the trees. The rider on her left seized her reins and drew her horse and his own to a halt.

"This way, my lady. We must seek refuge. My comrades will deal with the foe."

Keeping hold of her reins, the warrior led her horse at a gentle pace in among the trees to the left of the trail. As soon as he felt the undergrowth was dense enough and provided enough cover, he dismounted, tied his horse to a slender trunk, helped Cynethryth down and secured her horse.

"Sssh!" he whispered, "We must not be heard. Pray the horses stay quiet," he said, casting an appreciative glance at the animals grazing contentedly on the luxuriant foliage.

"How will we know how our comrades are faring?" Cynethryth whispered.

"Let's hope there's only one archer," replied the warrior. "We'll know when they come searching for us."

In spite of straining to hear for any indication of activity, Cynethryth remained bemused. Her guardian reached into a pack slung across his horse's back and returned, treading silently, with a leather flask. This he offered with a shy smile and she accepted gratefully but noticed how her hand trembled as she raised the water to her lips.

'*What will become of us if Guthred and his men are slain?*'

A single long blast of a horn answered her unspoken question although she did not know the meaning. Her companion did.

"My lady, the danger is over. We can leave."

He helped her remount and untied the horses.

"Follow me!"

She obeyed as they regained the trail and proceeded at a trot. She noticed that her guardian did not re-sheath his sword but carried it ready for action. Fervently, she hoped it would not be needed.

The horn blared once more, one sustained note. It was difficult in the woodlands to ascertain its whereabouts but within minutes they spotted a group of horsemen in a clearing ahead.

Her companion hailed the group, and one rider, whom she recognised with gratitude to be Guthred, detached himself from the group and rode to meet them.

"My lady," he bowed his blood-streaked face, "the vermin will bother us no more. Alas, we have lost three men and one horse. I'm sad to report, among our losses was the guide I sent ahead."

"Are you hurt, my friend?" Cynethryth looked at the crimson-stained sleeve of his tunic.

Guthred followed her gaze to his arm and laughed, "Nay, Lady, I thank you, 't is not *my* blood. We must find a stream to water our horses and make ourselves more presentable."

"How will we reach Barking without a guide?"

"Ah! We have a guide."

"But I thought–"

"I told you ours was slain, but we took one of them alive and the wretch knows the way to Lunden, which fact saved him from my blade. We have him trussed like a capon fit for the pot!"

Guthred laughed but she saw no humour in his eyes. Cynethryth shuddered and gladly followed when the warrior wheeled his horse. She felt queasy at the sight of blood as it brought back memories of the piled corpses at Kingsham when she had searched in vain for the body of her father. Little did she know that those memories would come flooding back, along with others, later in the day, for to Kingsham was precisely where they were riding.

She averted her eyes from the bodies strewn along the trail but saw enough to realise they were ragged, half-starved wretches living outside the law on what little they could gather or steal. There was no wonder that the well-armed and trained warriors had defeated them. She felt pity for a second but remembered the warrior brought down by the black-feathered arrow and curbed such thoughts. Clubs and staves against horsemen with tempered steel blades was no match – only the bowman had inflicted death. She hoped that he lay among the slaughtered. It would only take one arrow from an archer hidden among the trees... it didn't bear thinking about.

They came to a stream and Guthred called a halt. The horses drank their fill and began to graze on the lush grass bordering the watercourse. The men took their turn to refill flasks and to wash the blood from their hands and faces, cursing the iciness of the water, some looking with embarrassment at the lady for the ripeness of the language used. Cynethryth smiled to herself, recalling the coarseness of her father's words whenever a task did not go smoothly. How she missed him!

Outside the wooden walls of Kingsham, thoughts of Aelfhere returned to her. Here, by these gates, the men of Wiht and Sussex and those of Kent had lost their lives to Caedwalla's war band. When the gates swung open to admit them, she gazed with awe at the two burial mounds just within the palisade. Interred there were people she had grown up knowing. A tear came to her eye and Guthred, now riding next to her, understood.

"Remember, Lady?"

"Oh how could I ever forget?"

"It was here that I chose Rowena."

"Ay, and here Caedwalla chose me!"

She swallowed hard and blinked away the tears. It wouldn't do to make a spectacle of herself. She glanced at the hall and almost repeated some of the language she had heard by the brook:

sweet-sorrow once more! In the bedroom there, she had lain with her husband for the first time and failed to shift the shoe of subservience thanks to his strength. How she had laughed at his face when he had found the same shoe pinned over his side of the bed. She missed him, she missed Aelfhere, Rowena, Cuthburga and she missed Aethelheard. What was she doing here? She remembered her purpose. She had decided to devote her life to the service of God.

"The church! I must go to the church," she told Guthred.

"First, the horses, lady. They must be tended, for the journey ahead is still long. Then I will accompany you myself."

In the face of such reasonableness, she could only agree. But when they stepped into the church and she saw the great wooden bar that hadn't served to keep Caedwalla and his men at bay, she nearly swooned.

"My lady, what ails you?" Guthred, attentive, caught her around the waist and then begged her pardon.

"Nay, all's well. It was a passing moment, nothing more. I must approach the altar and pray."

"Are you determined to be a nun?"

Cynethryth looked at him sharply, what was he implying?

"Do you not approve?"

Guthred sighed, "It seems a waste..." he looked disconcerted, "I mean, for one so young and beautiful."

Cynethryth flushed, fought back the desire to slap his face and instead, said coolly, "It is no waste to serve the Lord, my friend. Do not dare express such thoughts in His House."

He looked abashed, "No, of course not, my lady. Foolish of me." He bowed his head.

Moved, she placed a hand on his arm, knowing him to be a good man.

"It's all right. I know you mean well."

She sidled to a smooth wooden bench and prayed for the souls of those who had died in the woodland, and she begged that nobody else would be hurt conducting her to the abbey. She gave up prayers for her family and friends, and then she asked the Virgin to give her the strength to fulfil the destiny the Lord had inspired her to follow.

Chapter 5

Barking Abbey, Lunden, 694 - 695 AD

The open road across the South Saxon downs made for easier and safer travelling. The Abbey at Barking, a wooden-palisaded enclosure near the great river containing many structures, made a welcome sight to Cynethryth. This was no unimportant backwater but, as Cuthburga had promised, the most important nunnery in the land.

It cannot have been a welcome sight to their guide, who having fulfilled his task, was no longer of use to his captors.

"Kneel and prepare to meet your Maker!" Guthred shoved the wretch to the ground.

"I beg of you, Lord Guthred," Cynethryth intervened with formal tone, "show mercy to this miserable creature, in the sight of God."

"What and let him return to his ways of killing and thieving? Maybe if we blinded him or cut off his hands..."

"Let him go un-maimed and the Lord will guide him to righteousness if it is His Will."

Guthred replaced his sword and expelled air through narrowed lips, and a swift kick to the ribs of the bound and kneeling man sent him over on his shoulder, where he lay groaning, still and terrified.

"On your feet, cur! You can't thank the lady for your miserable skin whilst writhing like a worm."

After garbled gratitude and blessings from the reprieved man, Guthred cut his bonds and the unfortunate scoundrel fled.

"I was wrong," Guthred said, and Cynethryth looked at him askance, "I mean, about what I said back there in the church. It's not a waste, Lady, you are a nun already – but without a veil – the best kind!" He gave her a wry smile, "Best get you to your nunnery so you can complete the mission."

Guthred and his men left her at the gate of the abbey.

She watched them disappear from sight before urging her horse through the gates. Her sense of being alone in the world oppressed her to the point of tightening in her stomach. The first surprise was to be met by a monk. Monks in the nunnery! Cynethryth was not aware that Barking, like many convents in the land was a double house.

"Welcome, Lady," he said, helping her dismount. "What is it that brings you to us?"

"I have a letter for the mother superior." She groped in her saddlebag and took out the folded document with its red wax seal.

"Then I'll take you to her quarters and see that your horse is tended to. He's a beautiful creature, aren't you boy?" He stroked the horse's velvety muzzle.

Cynethryth smiled at the monk's ignorance.

'*This boy's a girl.*'

But she did not enlighten him as it seemed rude and pointless. Instead, she said,

"I would be most grateful."

Abbess Hildelith, a formidable figure as austere as her quarters, which offered the minimum of comfort, almost as if she had furnished the chamber with chairs and table salvaged from the poorest hovel in Lunden, greeted Cynethryth with a deep voice. Two things about the voice disconcerted her visitor: the accent, indicating the woman came from a distant land, and its resonance, in so slight a frame. The abbess was tall but startlingly thin. Did the woman actually eat? White hair pinned under the edge of her wimple told their tale of advancing years. The piercing pale blue eyes, having scanned every inch of Cynethryth, transferred to the wax seal.

"My dear child, do tell me, how is my beloved Cuthburga?"

"She is well enough, Mother, and full of enthusiasm for her new venture."

The piercing gaze returned and settled on Cynethryth's face. "New venture?" The abbess's voice betrayed her confusion.

"Perhaps she explains in the letter, Mother. The Lady Cuthburga will found an abbey in Devon and the king commands she will be the abbess."

"Your king could make no better choice," Hildelith broke open the seal and read the contents of the document with a twitch of a smile.

"Typical of the woman," she said, gazing into Cynethryth's curious eyes, "she makes no mention of herself nor of her 'venture' as you call it, but only speaks of *you* with fulsome praise. We are to make you ready to serve God and your fellow man, Cynethryth. Are you ready for this life, child? It is one of abnegation and sacrifice." The eyes demanded a response.

"Oh yes, Mother, there is nothing I wish for more."

"Then we'll set about it at once!" The elderly nun reached for a small brass bell and shook it vigorously. At once, the door opened and two young women dressed in loose-fitting black gowns, their hair hidden by wimples, came into the room.

"Sisters, find this novice a gown and take her to the dormer. Make sure she has what she needs and show her the church and..." she added with a bright smile to Cynethryth, "in particular, the infirmary."

Outside the mother superior's quarters, one of the nuns asked, "Sister, what is your name?"

"Cynethryth, and yours?"

"Leofwen. We'll be friends," she smiled shyly taking Cynethryth under her arm.

"Wynflaed," said the other but her tone was sour.

'*She's jealous of her friend.*'

"The abbess seems very kind," Cynethryth sought confirmation.

"Ay, but she's a stickler for timekeeping and behaviour. Did you know that the founder of this house, a bishop, brought her here to instruct his sister Aethelburh, our first abbess. When she passed away, Hildelith took over. She's very learned and she has brought the bones of many saints to our church."

"Ay," said Wynflaed, "and but six weeks past a blind man regained his sight in our church of St. Mary. A miracle!"

"Did you witness this yourself?" Cynethryth asked.

"Why, do you doubt my word?"

"Forgive me, sister. I did not mean... it's just that miracles leave us all astonished."

"It is so!" Leofwen said and squeezed her arm.

Cynethryth worried that she might not settle in these strange surroundings, but this tiny act of kindness reassured her. At least, she would have one friend to count on.

Settling into the monastery routine was far easier than Cynethryth had feared. A day governed by bells, calling her to services, suited her sense of order. A free spirit as a child, she now appreciated the regulations that enabled her to explore her spirituality. She regarded it as an adventure and absorbed the wise teachings of her mentor who responded with equal enthusiasm to her burning thirst for knowledge, correcting her sharply on the few occasions she erred. What the abbess did not see for herself, she learned from the many eyes at her service: Cynethryth was making copious notes in the library on parchment she provided at her own expense.

Such was Hildelith's favourable impression that exactly a year after the novice's arrival, unbeknown to Cynethryth, the abbess wrote to Cuthburga. Summoned to the abbess's quarters, Cynethryth worried that she had in some way strayed and was about to receive some scolding. instead, when she entered the room, she encountered the warm embraces of her friend Cuthburga and her sister Quenburga.

"I am so pleased for you, Cynethryth," Cuthburga began, "Mother Hildelith has fetched me here for the ceremony."

Cynethryth, usually swift to understand, wondered to what she referred. "Ceremony?"

"I'm delighted to act as your godmother and Quenburga will be your other sponsor."

"I'm to take the veil?"

Cynethryth could not hide her pleasure, it showed in the flush of her cheeks.

"You are more than ready, my dear," Hildelith said. "Now, you may have a few minutes to talk with your friends but no more, because you must retreat to the church to meditate on your spiritual future. Your identity will be transformed."

With that, the abbess abandoned her quarters and the three women, left alone, sat on the rickety chairs.

"Our church is built and consecrated at Wimborne, Cynethryth."

"Wimborne, Mother?"

"Ay, it's the name of the place we chose for the abbey."

"I'm pleased to hear it."

"But there is much more to do before we can open our doors to a community. I have written twice to my brother, the king, for more money but..."

"I'm sure King Ine will provide when he can, Mother."

Cuthburga smiled. "He'd better – if he cares for his soul! Talking about souls, I'm pleasantly surprised you haven't asked me yet."

"Forgive me, Mother. I'm so full of this surprise but of course, I yearn to know about Aethelheard."

"Your priorities are right, they must be with the Lord, child. But He is a loving Master and would want you to know that your son thrives but suffers for the loss of his kind father who bestowed only love and encouragement. I believe the boy reads well and thirsts for learning – like his mother!" She smiled at Cynethryth whose bright eyes were wet with joy. Only after glorying in the achievements of her son did the full meaning of the words strike home. Her expression changed.

"King Cuthred is dead?"

"He has gone to a better world, sister, may God bless his soul."

"What of Aethelheard? Will he become sub-king?"

"No. My brother wishes to replace under-kings with ealdor-men. He has done so in other parts of his kingdom and Dorset is no different. Have no fear for your son. He is admired and befriended by the most important men in the region including the new ealdorman."

"Are you not going to tell her?" asked Quenburga.

Cynethryth looked anxiously from one to the other.

"You tell her."

Quenburga smiled and said, "Your friend, Rowena..."

Cynethryth looked worried, "Is she well?"

"Very well, it seems. She has given her husband another boy. What did she call him – ah, yes, my memory sometimes fails...she called him Aelfhere – not a common name in our part of the world.

"It's well known on Wiht," Cynethryth's heart leapt with joy. What a happy day!

"And that's not all, may I tell her, sister?"

"You may."

"The infirmary at the new abbey is built and there are a score of beds set out as well as a room for the preparation of medicines."

Cynethryth's face clouded and her lip trembled.

Quenburga looked at her in alarm.

"Is something wrong? Are you not pleased at the news?"

"Forgive me, I'm indeed pleased. But I'm not ready. There's so much I still have to learn."

"As to that," Cuthburga smiled, "Bless you child, you have all the time you need to perfect your knowledge. Sadly, we cannot yet open our doors. I believe it will be three more winters before the abbey is ready. I have spoken to Mother Hildelith and she is prepared to make an exception in your case. After you have taken the veil, you will be allowed to assist the brother infirmarian where you will gain invaluable experience, for he is renowned as a healer.

"Oh Mother, you are wonderful! You think of absolutely everything. How can I thank you enough?"

"By doing exactly what you are doing. You make me proud – although Heaven knows it's a foolish sin – when Hildelith speaks so highly of you. She is the severest judge but you please her. Now, go! You must obey her and ponder your spiritual future in the church. Tomorrow morning, you will take the veil. Ah, I nearly forgot. I brought you a white gown. You will wear it for the service.

Kneeling before the altar, Cynethryth thanked God for the blessings she had received and prayed to be worthy of them. Prayers over, she thought about her future. The significance of the white gown was clear: she would become the bride of Christ – an honour. With Caedwalla departed this life, she wished for no other man. In this way, she hoped Caedwalla, in Heaven, might gain favour with the Lord through her actions and prayers. The privilege she had received of working with the infirmarian thrilled her and though she was loth to admit it, the absence of male company weighed on her. She, who had been raised by a man and whose relationship with her father was so strong, missed the challenge a masculine mentality offered. She hoped the infirmarian would be kindly and intelligent and open to having a female assistant.

First, there was the enormous matter of taking the veil. All she knew about it was what Leofwen had told her, she would have to avow many renunciations and...her lower lip trembled again...Wynflaed had added spitefully, she would have her lovely locks shorn. She hoped this was not true, it might just be the malice of the petty girl. She was unsure because the sisters all dutifully kept their heads covered as the abbess required. Some of the monks were tonsured, others not. She stopped herself from thinking of trivial matters. Perhaps she should pray for guidance on how to ponder!

Her limbs were becoming stiff and numb when a hand shook her shoulder, it was Leofwen.

"Come, Cynethryth, the abbess wishes to speak with you."

She rose with difficulty, rubbed her knees and followed her friend out of the church, blinking in the bright, early summer light. She loved the month of June and not just because it was the month her son first saw daylight but also for the plentiful flowers, leafy trees, butterflies and bees.

The abbess wished to tell her what she already knew, that she would be accorded the privilege of working with the infirmarian to begin the day after the next. This came with a long discourse on responsibilities, which to Cynethryth was simply a matter of common sense. Even so, she took the advice to heart and was flattered but concerned that the nun thought she might turn male heads. She promised to give any such stupidity short shrift.

She walked down the nave the next day, wearing her white gown, between the congregated nuns. Cuthburga walked beside her and a pace behind, Quenburga with a thick lighted candle to symbolise the wise virgins. A priest awaited her at the altar and he took her through the list of renunciations. When she had vowed to renounce them all, the priest invited her to retire into the vestry 'to shed her clothes and dress in Jesus Christ.'

She reappeared wearing the simple habit of the nuns and now, blessed by the priest, realised, to her horror, that Quenburga was holding a pair of shears. Cuthburga, instead, held a silver platter with a crucifix. The former seized a lock of her hair and snipped. Cynethryth shuddered and watched helplessly as the tress of red-golden hair, her pride and joy, was laid on the platter Cuthburga held forth to receive it. This act was repeated until a heap of hair covered the Cross. The priest declared the work, representing the rejection of the body, done. Cynethryth, glancing at the congregation, had the misfortune to glimpse Wynflaed, whose sneer of satisfaction made her eyes prick with tears. Distracted, she needed a whisper from Quenburga to receive a wreath of flowers from her, whilst Cuthburga handed her a wreath of thorns. As she held them, a veil was placed over her head and face and the congregation burst into song, sweet and lilting; joy at her new status replaced the sorrow at the loss of her crowning glory.

The ceremony over, Cuthburga took Cynethryth in an embrace and kissed her forehead.

"Now I can call you Sister," she said. "Come, let's find you a wimple, you can't wear that veil forever."

That evening, at Vespers and later at Compline, Cynethryth took her place among the nuns, next to Leofwen and no longer with the novices. The last words of the priest in the ceremony came back to her, *'be dead to the world, your parents, to your friends and to yourself.'* She understood the meaning and was prepared for great sacrifice but could not help but be comforted by Leofwen's friendship. The nun's welcoming smile as she took her place next to her on the bench meant so much.

The next day, she made her way, as requested, to the abbess's quarters straight after Prime.

"You are pleasingly punctual, child," Hildelith said. "Follow me, we'll go to the infirmary together. By the way, you are excused Terce and None every day. What use would you be in the infirmary if you keep coming and going to church?"

"As you wish, Mother."

The infirmarian, a tall, round-shouldered monk with a hooked nose and thin lips but lively, sharp eyes, left off preparing a potion to attend to his visitors.

"This is the sister I spoke to you about, Brother Nerian, she will assist you as you require, but never lose sight of her main purpose, which is to learn your skills. One day, we hope in the near future, she will have her own infirmary. I will leave you now."

"Not too soon, I hope. I have so much to learn." Cynethryth addressed the retreating back of the nun.

The monk looked at her with respect. "I like your modesty, you will absorb much here."

The first impact of Nerian pleased Cynethryth too and she was not mistaken. As he showed her around his small realm, he displayed no impatience at her close questioning and praised what little knowledge she disclosed.

The weeks ran into months and Cynethryth grew in her role, taking immense satisfaction from healing and curing the sick. Brother Nerian was a fine teacher, above all by example. He had no truck with amulets or superstitious cures, the kind of white magic prevalent among the country folk. Neither did he attach too much importance to the power of prayer, preferring to search for a remedy. The concept of weakening a patient by bleeding disgusted the monk.

"It may be regarded as the solution to bad humours, Cynethryth, but do not swallow any of that nonsense. How can a person fight off a disease if we drain off his lifeblood? All nonsense!"

His greatest strength that she admired was his humility. One day, they had a patient with sores over her body that neither of them had seen before. Except, Cynethryth had a vague recollection of having read about something similar in the library. She begged leave to return to the dormer to consult her notes and permission was granted. Impatiently shuffling through her many pages, at last, with a cry of triumph, she found what she was looking for and bore it to the infirmarian, who read with interest.

"You could be right. The wounds are ulcers but the cure is a problem. I have no wild garlic bulbs in the infirmary."

"Brother, give me permission to leave the abbey and I will procure them. They will be plentiful at this time of year."

At first, he was reluctant to let her go out alone, but faced with the worsening situation of his patient, he contented himself with stern recommendations.

Cynethryth knew wild garlic could be found in marshy woodland, so she made her way down towards the river and entered the first copse of trees she spotted. Glorying in the freedom to wander away from the confines of the monastery and revelling in the birdsong, her heart leapt with joy when she chanced upon the bunched, six-petalled white flowers on their long stalks. Quickly, she pulled at the stalks and the bulbs came easily out of the soft ground. Shaking them to remove surplus soil, soon her basket was filled with sufficient bulbs to treat the woman for days. She decided not to take more than required; it would be an excuse to come back if more were needed.

The success of her expedition was only surpassed by the healing effect of the garlic solution on the ulcers.

"The merit is all yours, Sister," Brother Nerian said when the grateful patient thanked him.

"Not so, Brother, the merit lies with he who wrote the treatise. We did but follow it."

He gave her a radiant smile, "I liked you at once for your humility."

"And I, you, for the same reason, Brother."

She also liked him for his complete lack of jealousy. He was prepared to share his knowledge and encouraged her to make notes of anything that captured her interest. There were many of these occasions because Cynethryth had a voracious appetite for knowledge. Nerian teased her that she would need a train of ox-carts only to carry her notes to her new abbey.

Her liking for the infirmarian was matched only by her dislike of Wynflaed. At first, she blamed herself for provoking the nun's spite by being friendly with Leofwen but soon realised that the problem lay in the nature of the woman.

On her first day in the infirmary, Wynflaed noticed and reported her absence from Terce. This earned her a rebuke from the abbess who had given Cynethryth permission to miss the service. The reprimand only increased her bitterness and in the dormer she vented her resentment.

"It didn't take you long to wheedle your way into the abbess's graces, did it?"

"I don't know what you are talking about."

"Oh, you do! Privileges here and privileges there – and you've only been a sister two minutes!"

"Wynflaed, let it be!" Leofwen pleaded.

"Of course, you *would* take her side, wouldn't you? Little Miss too-good-to-be-true. She thinks she's so much better than us because she's wormed her way into the abbess's favour – goodness knows how. Did your father bestow money on the abbey?"

"Leave my father out of this and don't forget to *love thy neighbour* as the Lord commands. I forgive you, Wynflaed," she smiled sweetly. But she knew she was only stoking future trouble.

Leaving the abbey, when the time came, would be like the rest of her life, under the emblem of sweet-sorrow.

Chapter 6

Barking Abbey, Lunden, 695 - 705 AD

When life is led by the intermittence of bells, the seasons pass and lose their importance in favour of daily chores. Thus, Cynethryth lost count of the winters by which she numbered the passing years and yet she, more than her sisters, referred to the seasons. A knowledge of plant growth determined by the weather conditions was essential for an infirmarian. The revelation from the lips of the mother superior that nine years had passed since the visit of Cuthburga shook Cynethryth. A rapid calculation told her that her son would now be a youth of ten and five years – almost a man. How she ached to see the changes in him. But the abbess's sharp tone brought her back to matters in hand.

"Are you paying attention, Sister?"

"I'm sorry, Mother. I-it's that I had no idea that so long had passed."

"I was saying that you have spent it well, Cynethryth, but the time has come for us to part." She reached for a letter on her table. "This arrived from the Abbess of Wimborne, your friend and new mother superior, Cuthburga. She writes that the abbey is now open, as is the infirmary, but without its infirmarian. She requests your presence at the earliest opportunity." The abbess smiled kindly, "There's something else you should know, Sister. Under our present circumstances of overcrowding, I have acceded to Cuthburga's request for nuns to help her establish the new community. In this way, we solve two problems with a single solution. You will be pleased to have the company of ten of our sisters and ten and two novices on your journey. Bearing in mind your sisterly relationship, I have chosen Leofwen and Wynflaed to transfer with you. It will help you settle in Dorset."

Cynethryth met this well-meaning arrangement with a smile that did not reach her eyes and murmured thanks. *'Typical – bitter-sweet news!'*

The abbess continued, "Brother Nerian tells me you have many documents to remove to Wimborne and he wishes to contribute to your infirmary with diverse potions and powders. All these items will require careful packing and a means of carriage, so I have arranged for chests to be taken to the infirmary and a cart to be made available for the journey. In a matter of days," she exchanged sorrowful looks with Cynethryth, "your escort will arrive from Wimborne and we'll part, probably forever. But you depart with my blessing and I have the comfort of knowing that a skilled healer leaves our house where a raw novice entered the gates."

"Mother, I thank you for all the kindness you have so freely accorded me."

"God has guided us both, child. I ask only that you remember me in your prayers."

Cynethryth attempted her sweetest smile, "How could I not, dearest Mother?"

The days until the arrival of her escort flew by, filled with the necessary packing of chests, nursing of the sick, and prayers, including the oft repeated plea that it would be Guthred who led the company sent to fetch her. When the time for farewells came, saddened to leave Brother Nerian, who had become a close friend, she was, however, buoyed by the knowledge that he was more than a capable healer and her departure from Barking would do no harm. Her new adventure beckoned and filled her with joy. As usual, Wynflaed found a way to dampen her gladness.

The first time they passed in a corridor alone, the resentful sister confronted her.

"This is *your* doing! Why are you so full of spite?"

"What is troubling you?"

"You know full well! I'm to be dragged to the ends of the Earth thanks to you." Her lips trembled and her eyes filled with tears. "I like it here!" she wailed.

"Wynflaed, it's nought to do with me, in God's name."

"Liar! How can you utter God's name with deceit on your tongue?"

"Listen, Sister, if you have no wish to come to Dorset, tell it to the abbess. I feel sure she will heed your plea."

"She will not! I've already spoken to her. She says I must learn to befriend *you*."

"Is it so difficult, Wynflaed? I mean you no harm."

"No harm, you say?" Her face reddened. "Since the day you came through the gates, you have hated me."

Cynethryth stared at the tear-rivuleted face, aghast, "Nonsense, if anything it's the other way round. I beseech you, let us be friends." She moved forward to embrace her but Wynflaed shrank away and pushed out an arm to keep her at bay.

"Friends with you? Never! You'll pay for taking me away from..." her lips trembled "...my *home*!" The last word came forth distorted as a shriek and Cynethryth made the sign of the cross before turning away. She reflected on the encounter continually and could not pretend to herself that the malice in the other's eyes had not shaken her. What should she do? She could confide in Nerian but he was likely to give her platitudes. Nor did she feel free to go to Hildelith for fear it seemed either she was challenging her decision-making or that, in spite of all the kindness bestowed upon her, she was still dissatisfied. She therefore resolved to treat Wynflaed with kindness until her resistance to friendship was overcome. No sooner had she made this decision than she was able to complete all the tasks she had set herself, free of distraction.

The escort, led by none other than Guthred, to her delight, arrived late in the afternoon. This was perfect for an early departure the next day. But Cynethryth had to swallow her impatience. For reasons of propriety, she could not seek out Guthred in the monks' quarters and would have to wait till the morrow to greet him.

Before she could do that, she had to say her farewells. First, correctly, she went to the abbess and received recommendations and her blessing. Then, sorrowfully, she parted from Nerian with his wise words locked in her heart. He referred to the work of the infirmarian but they were appropriate for her whole life:

"Remember, Sister, the winds will blow from all quarters but 't is the steersman's hand on the tiller that sets the course the ship must follow."

In a spontaneous act, he broke the rules of his order when he took her in his arms and kissed her brow. Cynethryth was taken aback by this effusion but also delighted, especially because no-one had seen it happen, since they were alone in the preparation room.

Outdoors, at last, contenting herself only with a nod and a smile at Guthred, she mounted her horse, the creature having greeted her with a happy whinny and a toss of her head, and took her place in the procession through the gates toward her new life. She was aware and did not approve of the giddiness of the novices at their new adventure nor of the glances some of them cast at the mounted warriors of the escort. At the same time, she noticed the resentful glares of Wynflaed directed her way. It did not help that she was on horseback and the nun was on foot. It promised to be a long march for the sisters all the way to Wimborne.

After a mile or so out of Barking, Guthred brought his horse next to Cynethryth's.

"It gladdens me to see you well, my lady."

"Seeing you is the answer to my prayers. How fares Rowena?"

"Well, I thank you. We have another son, a brother for Osburh, his name is Aelfhere, who has eight winters to his name. Instead, Osburh is grown into a sturdy fellow, surpassed only by your own son."

"Aethelheard is strong, then?" There was a catch in her voice.

"A great brute of a youth and to hear the king, the finest swordsman that ever lived. To tell the truth I wouldn't care to come up against him in combat."

Cynethryth grinned, "His father was no mean warrior, as you'll recall, Guthred."

"I do, Lady. He was a hardy fellow too." He looked stricken, swallowed hard and muttered, "We'll talk again later, my lady."

A sudden sadness gripped her. She felt guilty at having mentioned Caedwalla to his friend Guthred, who must miss him sorely. Foolishness, because as the widow, her sorrow must be deeper than any other's. So, she reflected, Aethelheard took after his father. She must see that for herself.

The ground was firm under her horses' hooves and this meant the ox-cart trundled along at a steady pace without interruptions. The first of these had nothing to do with the state of the road but was due to Cynethryth. She had spotted little blue heads bobbing in the breeze in the turf on the downland. *'Haewenhnydele, I must gather it!'* She rode to the head of the company and drew next to Guthred.

"We must rest, for the sisters are unused to marching and are over-weary."

"Very well, my lady, but just a few minutes, otherwise we'll not reach our overnight stopping place before dusk.

"Agreed."

She waited in her saddle whilst everyone else sat on the springy turf by the road then urged her mount towards the cornflowers she had spotted earlier. Drawing a small knife from her belt, she dug up the flowers, making sure not to damage the roots. When she was satisfied, she soaked a bandage in water from her flask and wrapped it around the roots.

"There," she muttered, "you'll survive fresh enough to Wimborne and until we can cultivate cress, you'll help treat scurvy."

'*Ah, what's this, toadflax? I must gather that too.*'

She was bending over the false toadflax when a familiar voice behind her made her start.

Leofwen was holding the reins of her horse. "Cynethryth, what are you doing?"

"Collecting medicinal plants that do not grow on the land where we are going. See these clusters of creamy flowers?"

"They're like tiny purses that open into little stars."

"Pretty are they not? But useful, Sister. This plant helps sick people sleep and can take away headache or ease sore eyes."

"It is a wonder."

"Ay, a wonder of God's creation. Now, I must make haste and dig some up before our worthy thegn becomes fretful."

Cynethryth might have stopped more times to add to her treasures but mindful of the lengthening shadows, curbed her eagerness and told herself that the next day would bring more opportunities if she stayed alert.

Before twilight, the company crossed a river and found an ancient Roman roadway. Guthred told her its name was the Stane Street. Not far along this road they came to a monastery.

"This, my lady, is where you and your sisters will spend the night. They are expecting you, for it is all arranged by Abbess Hildelith. The abbey here was founded by the same Bishop Erkenwald who founded Barking Abbey."

"Bless the mother superior. She thinks of everything! My sisters are footsore – how many hours they have walked!"

"Some nine, I'd say at a rough reckoning."

"Then we must enter and let them rest. But what about your men, Guthred?"

"As usual. We'll pitch camp here outside the walls. It's a good place – the monks chose it well."

Fed and rested, the sisters soon recovered their high spirits, except for one. Wynflaed let everyone who would listen know how wicked was the high and mighty Cynethryth, who made sure she was on horseback, for marching them to *'the Lord knows where'.*

Her grumbling and malicious glances did not escape Cynethryth but she made sure the nun and Leofwen were invited to sit near her and the mother superior at the high table. This honour, even the sour woman had to acknowledge with something approaching a good grace. With it came the privilege of wine with the meal and honey-based sweets that the nuns in the main body of the refectory did not receive.

The improved humour of Wynflaed might not have lasted had she known what route Guthred had planned for them on the morrow. He meant to reach the monastery at Aldingbourne – a matter of twice the distance they had covered this day. The women would rise and depart at dawn immediately after Lauds. This was the only way to reach the house founded by King Nothelm for his sister Nothgithe before nightfall. Given the good road and the long day, it could be achieved. Cynethryth had misgivings about blistered feet and general weakness among the younger women, but to her way of thinking, a roof over their heads, food and beds compensated.

Doubts began to assail her after three hours of the tramping. The weepiness of some of the younger women, their limping and snatches of grumbling she caught, induced her to react. She made Guthred halt the march and spoke to him in little more than a whisper.

"But can they ride?" he asked.

"Many of them come from noble families and learned in their youth."

"So be it."

"Wait until you see a nun mount my horse, then give the order."

Guthred looked puzzled but agreed.

Cynethryth rode back to the nuns, sitting on the grass, many of them massaging their feet, and dismounted.

"Sister Wynflaed," she said, "you will mount my horse, you must be weary."

The nun gaped at her and looked around at the envious, disbelieving faces with a smug smile. Without a word of thanks, she hurried to the patient animal and eased herself into the saddle.

Cynethryth addressed the others, "Who among you has never ridden?"

Six hands raised in reply. She looked at the slight build of the women and smiled.

"It is not a problem," she said, "you six will double up with an experienced rider. The men will march, it is arranged."

The joy on the faces of the women raised her spirits. They would now reach Aldingbourne before nightfall with ease. She did not turn to meet the eye of Wynflaed; just as well, she would have seen loathing in her eyes, her privilege had been diminished at once.

The monastery at Aldingbourne received them with the same hospitality as received at Chertsey the night before. In reality, it was obligatory for a religious house to show hospitality to travellers, but the welcome offered to a party of nuns was warm indeed.

Cynethryth, weary from the march and footsore, spoke to Guthred before retiring within the walls.

"My soul quails at the thought of the long march through the Andersweald. What if the forest shelters outlaws and we are attacked again?"

"My lady, my warriors are well-armed."

"But they are equipped to fight on horseback. It means another long march for my sisters. Heaven knows, I have only tramped today but my feet cannot endure another such ordeal."

"Go and rest, Lady, tomorrow is another day! We can set off after Prime."

Did she notice something strange about his smile? Why set off later? She struggled to find an answer.

It became clear on departure the next day.

"Lady, we have but three leagues to travel."

"How can that be?"

"All matters considered," Guthred smiled, "including, above all, the settled weather, we can take a ship from the quay at Bosham. From there, we sail directly to Wareham."

"The Lord be praised!" Cynethryth resisted the urge to embrace the thegn. It was still a march of three hours but they could refresh their feet in the seawater. She would travel on horseback and let the sour wretch trudge to the quay.

When they reached the harbour, Cynethryth spoke to the thegn, "Tell me," she said, "was it always your plan to take a ship from Bosham? It seems more than good fortune that a vessel is available to us."

"You are astute, my Lady! All of this is the work of the two abbesses."

"I might have known!" She frowned. "Maybe if you had told me, we could have spared some ill-humour among the nuns."

"In my experience, my lady, people bear suffering better if they are not thinking of its ending."

"Well, I believe the opposite, Lord Guthred. Henceforth, keep nothing back from me."

"Very well," he acquiesced and re-joined his men.

The ship, rowed out of the creek by strong armed warriors, picked up speed with wind-filled sails in the open sea and Cynethryth's heart sang when she beheld her beloved Wiht. Again, her head was filled with sweet-sorrow. She could not help thinking about her decision to leave her birthplace for the sake of Aethelheard's heritage. What if she had stayed there? She would have brought up her son and enjoyed the company of her dearest friend in the place she loved the best. She peered hard, squinting against the sunlight reflected off the waves, in a vain attempt to distinguish a cove or a headland familiar to her. She sighed and pondered the life she had chosen: one of sacrifices, but to the advantage of her son and likely to that of her soul. She loved tending the sick and healing. Was there a calling higher than doing God's work? Yet, she missed her father and her son. But now as the ship ploughed through the waves, she was drawing ever nearer to him and about to start a new life. Would the time come when he was free to seek her out as she hoped and prayed?

Chapter 7

The end of their journey offered Cynethryth a glorious, uplifting sight. She remembered the day she had pointed out the confluence to Cuthburga as suitable for the abbey. Eleven long winters had passed since then, even if it seemed much less. How strange that this lovely corner of Dorset should be enhanced by the construction of the buildings the abbess had overseen. Embraced between the arms of two rivers, the structure nestled in the valley. Any doubts she might have had about being happy in Wimborne were swept away in an instant and her mood was shared by the sisters who talked and pointed excitedly at their new home.

Before her longed-awaited reunion with Cuthburga and her sister, Cynethryth had to bid a fond farewell to her late husband's friend, Guthred.

"Beseech Rowena to visit me as soon as she can for I must remain within the walls of the abbey."

Assurances given, Guthred turned his horse and led his men back to the royal vill of Wareham. She gazed after the departing riders and smiled, for Guthred had discharged his duty with flawless precision, and yet he had irritated her. Did she demand too much of others? She drove herself so hard, but could she expect others to be as diligent? The abbess Cuthburga certainly set high standards, surpassed only by Hildelith. Accustomed to the standards of the latter, Cynethryth supposed she would have no problem settling at Wimborne, but would it be so with the others?

They rode through the gates and it became evident at a glance that this abbey, like Barking, was a double house. Over to her right, she saw monks tending a garden and another drawing water from a well. On the left, a group of nuns gathered to stare and discuss the new arrivals. That did not last. A sharp voice rose above the others and the gaggle of curious sisters dispersed at once obeying the orders of the abbess.

Cynethryth dismounted and handed the reins to Leofwen before striding – she wanted to run but contained her impulse – to greet her friend.

"Finally! You are here, my dear child. Welcome to Wimborne."

"Mother, it is good to see you well."

"I must address the new arrivals in due course. First they will refresh themselves before Sext."

"Thank the Lord, the last part of the journey did not weary them, Mother."

"But the first part was hard, was it not? A little suffering will have uplifted their souls. Come to the dormer with the group, even though you will not sleep with the sisters. Provision is made for you to sleep in the infirmary."

"That is a splendid arrangement, Mother. It is true that you think of everything!"

Apart from being on hand if needed in the night, there was another benefit: Wynflaed would have Leofwen to herself and hopefully, this might make her less resentful toward her. Wynflaed was up to her usual petty tricks. Whenever within hearing of the nuns already established at Wimborne, she was full of praise for the abbey and its organisation, but once they were out of earshot, she would complain about and criticise everything.

Her resentment reached new heights at the end of Sext, when the abbess called for attention.

"Sisters, although the person I am about to introduce will be a new face to you, I assure you she was at Wimborne before any of you. She has been away for many years perfecting her skills. This, sisters, is our infirmarian, Sister Cynethryth. If in His wisdom, the Lord sends sickness to test our faith and forbearance, it is to our infirmarian we must turn. You will give her the respect her learning deserves. Should the infirmarian demand anything of you, I expect your full cooperation. In the name of the Father..." she brought the service to an end.

As a reflex action, Cynethryth looked at Wynflaed, who was whispering to a nun next to her. Their eyes met and the face of her detractor flushed with guilt.

'*She's already spreading her venom against me.*'

As the sisters filed out of the church, Cynethryth deliberately stared at Wynflaed and when the nun glanced back furtively at her, made sure she knew she was being scrutinised. It could not harm to let her know she was under observation.

The first days were ones of toil for the infirmarian. She unpacked crates and set out potions on the shelves carefully planned by Cuthburga. Her parchments and volumes followed. She hung bunches of dried herbs from nails driven into the roof beams and only when satisfied with her preparation room, did she inspect the sick room, mindful of the abbess's promise to supply anything she had overlooked. At the moment, without patients, it was difficult to know whether any essentials were lacking. The cupboards were full of bedding, ranging from linen sheets to woollen blankets and wolf-pelt covers for the coldest weather.

Satisfied, Cynethryth transferred her attention to outdoors. She could see that the monks had a well-tended garden, including an area reserved for culinary herbs. She needed a similar area devoted to medicinal plants. Feeling that she could not simply dig up the abbey grounds without consulting the mother superior, she hastened to make her request.

"Of course you must have a garden. But I won't have you toiling over it as it would create the wrong impression. Come, we'll gather a group of sisters to do the heavy work. You'll direct them."

Cuthburga first led her to the monks' garden.

"Brother," she called to an elderly monk, who straightened with difficulty from bedding in a plant. "We need to borrow six spades," she turned to Cynethryth, "make a list of tools you'll need for gardening and take it to the smithy. You'll find it beyond the church by the outer wall."

They took two spades each from the monk.

"Follow me, Brother, with the other two."

When they came to the ground near the infirmary, the monk spoke, "Begging your pardon, Mother, but the soil here is loamy and sandy. It'll need plenty of compost working into the top few inches. There's compost near the kitchen and a manure heap by the stables."

"Bless you for your concern, Brother, we take note of your words."

The monk bowed and hurried away and they laid their implements next to the ones he'd left before going in search of nuns for the digging.

Cynethryth paced out the area she wanted for her garden and marked it with sticks. They commandeered twelve nuns and set half of them to work digging down to a depth of one foot. When she judged the sisters were tired, she substituted them. By the time the bells rang for Sext, they had dug half of the area. The service gave the opportunity to rest. At the end of the service, Cynethryth decided to choose a new group of sisters to share the heavy work. She went to the nuns from Barking and told them, including Leofwen and Wynflaed, to come with her.

This time, she did not have the authoritative abbess next to her but was pleased that nobody challenged her orders. Indeed, to her surprise, Wynflaed was the first to pick up a spade and set to work. Cynethryth was quick to seize the chance.

"Come on, sisters, take a spade and follow the example of Sister Wynflaed!"

If only the sullen girl always showed this goodwill, they might even become friends, Cynethryth mused.

Leofwen leant on her spade and blew out her cheeks, "Phew! The soil is heavy, it will need compost if herbs are to grow."

Cynethryth smiled at her friend.

"I know. But first we must finish turning over the plot, ridding it of stones and weeds. So stop slacking, sister!"

Leofwen grinned and returned to her labour.

"Wynflaed, you two, come with me!"

She led the three women to the monks' garden where she found the elderly gardener still bedding in plants.

"Brother, we have no means of transporting compost. Can you help?"

"Of course, Sister. This way."

He led them to a shed and from within brought a wheelbarrow and fork.

"This should do, Sister. But heed me well, when you've finished, bring them back where they belong."

Wynflaed gave him a withering look, "We sisters ain't thieves, *Brother*! Mind how you speak to the infirmarian!"

Cynethryth was shocked by her support, but none too pleased because she did not approve of using an acid tone with a monk who was being helpful. She sought to calm the situation.

"Of course, we'll return them, brother. Soon, I hope we'll trouble you no more for we must obtain our own tools. Meanwhile, accept our thanks."

The brother bowed but glared at Wynflaed, who returned it threefold.

At the rear of the kitchen, they found a large compost heap.

"Take only from the bottom, where the leaves and roots are rotted," Cynethryth ordered.

They wheeled the loaded barrow over the bumpy ground to the new plot and threw the organic material over the freshly dug earth. Several more journeys and Cynethryth ordered the nuns to take the barrow to the stables, as fertiliser was needed.

"Notice Sister Posh isn't getting her hands dirty!" Wynflaed whispered to Leofwen whilst looking and smiling at Cynethryth.

She did not hear what was aimed against her but Cynethryth did not need to, she knew all about Wynflaed's methods and responded by giving her a sweet smile. The nun's narrowed eyes in reaction made her smile broader.

Having dug in all the organic matter, the nuns' work was done. Cynethryth was delighted. A herb garden right next to the infirmary was exactly what she had set her heart on. She would transfer some of her treasured plants, temporarily in vases, to the garden.

"Thank you sisters for your precious toil. Take the tools and the barrow back to the monks with our thanks. Oh, Wynflaed, I'm grateful to you, but I implore you, do *not* offend the brother gardener."

"I will not, sister, but he should learn respect."

With that, she hurried after the other nuns.

'*So should you, viper!*'

In the following days, monks and nuns with minor ailments came and went. Dealing with diverse aches involving the head, stomach and teeth was nothing new to her, but to be provided with this service was a novelty for the community. Soon her patients, their aches relieved, began to laud her efforts to anyone willing to listen. Sprained ankles and bruising were also dealt with but Cynethryth feared other worse diseases sooner or later would visit the Abbey and she had to be ready for such circumstances.

Whenever she had time, she concentrated on preparations. The trip to the smithy solved the problem of tools but she had to see to their storage and had an outbuilding made for the purpose. A visit to the abbess regarding the acquisition of plants for the garden obtained only a veto against leaving the Abbey grounds, which she half-expected. In vain, she argued that Abbess Hildelith had let her roam the countryside around Barking. Here, the problem, unexpressed by Cuthburga, was the proximity to Aethelheard. At least the mother superior had not actually spoken the words, 'You'll have to manage without the plants.'

The solution came in a most gratifying way. Rowena came to visit her. A discreet cough made her look up from preparing tincture for sprains to behold the pale copper-gold locks framing the familiar oval-shaped face beaming at her.

"Rowena! You came. Come, be seated and tell me about your boys."

Of course, she wanted to hear about her own son but manners required she listened with growing interest to an account of how the brothers were progressing, especially Osburh, who was but slightly younger than Aethelheard.

"They're inseparable," Rowena said, "it means Osburh gets to see the king every day. He rides out on the hunt with them and boasts of the compliments Cuthred gives – *er* – *gave* him for his prowess with the bow. His arms are like the branches of a tree, Cynethryth, hard and knotted, but so are Aethelheard's, they are two young warriors. They're always scrapping, having mock battles, wrestling and the like. When Osburh loses to Aethelheard, there's always some excuse – but you know what lads are!"

"I'm afraid I don't."

Rowena glanced sharply at her, trying not to show pity in her face.

"You *do* know what Aethelheard is like. Think of a young Caedwalla."

She pressed Rowena for as many details as possible before making her promise to deliver a message to her son. Her friend waited patiently whilst Cynethryth's pen sped across the parchment. When she had finished, she threw a white powder across the writing to dry the ink, then shook the dust onto the floor. She folded the letter and sealed it with a drop from a stick of wax passed through a candle flame.

"See he gets it this very day," she pleaded with voice and eyes.

"I will," Rowena reached to squeeze her friend's hand.

"I have another problem and don't know how to deal with it."

Cynethryth explained her need for woodland and riverside plants and the prohibition on her leaving the abbey.

"I wish I could help you, but I know next to nothing about plant lore and I have little time to wander the woods and meadows. But wait!"

Her green eyes lit up and Cynethryth admired her friend's beauty, undimmed after eleven winters.

"What is it?"

"There's a woman in Wareham – a strange cross-eyed creature – little children run after her calling her names and the folk she passes cross themselves because they say she's a witch. There are rumours that she 'solves' young girls' unwanted problems. But I know not if it's true or simply the malice of those who shun her. This woman is steeped in the lore of plants. Many a wench has left her hovel clutching a love potion, although I do not believe in heathen practices. I'll seek her and send her to you. You can tell her what you need, Cynethryth, but I dare say, she will press you for coin."

Cynethryth leapt to her feet and embraced Rowena.

"This could be the answer to my prayers! Oh, Rowena, how clever of you."

"I have to pass her house on my way home. I'll visit her before nightfall."

Cynethryth found it hard to settle to her work in the next two days. Her thoughts were forever drifting to the two tasks she had given Rowena. Had she delivered the letter? If so, when would her son come to pay her a visit? Had she spoken to the woman with a squint? Both were so important, she could not choose who she wished to see more – probably her son. But he did not come. Three days passed before a nun came to the infirmary trailing a wretched-looking woman in dirty ragged garments.

"Sister, this... person... says she has business with the infirmarian, although I cannot imagine what one such as she–"

"Thank you, sister, you may go. I was expecting her. This way, my dear, do not be afraid."

The woman drew near, timid in her approach.

Cynethryth looked at her, giving an encouraging smile, which faded as she failed to meet the woman's eyes. The unfortunate creature was, indeed, cross-eyed and it disconcerted the infirmarian. She recovered quickly from her embarrassment and asked, "Is it true what they say about you?"

The woman recoiled and looked stricken.

"That I'm a witch? 'T ain't true, Lady!"

"I didn't mean that. People are so stupid! I meant that you have a knowledge of plants."

"Ah, that be true, mistress."

"You should call me sister. Let's see, do you know what the verbena looks like?"

"That depends, sister."

"On what?" Cynethryth pursed her lips.

"On whether you be wantin' the pink or the purple one. They both be pretty enough."

The infirmarian relaxed, "I see you know your plants."

"If I make you a list will you collect the plants for me? I'll want you to take them up without damaging the roots."

" 'T ain't no good mist – Sister."

The woman looked embarrassed.

Cynethryth understood. "You can't read, can you?"

She shook her head and pleaded, "But if you tell me, I can remember up to five, sister."

"Well then, five at a time but you will have to do this many times for me. I will give you a coin for every time you fetch me a basket of the plants. I'll be wanting ten of each without the roots damaged, is that clear?"

"Ay, 't is, sister."

"Right then, verbena, fennel, chervil, wild garlic and sanfoin."

"Verbena, fennel, chervil, wild garlic and sanfoin…verbena, fennel, chervil, wild garlic and sanfoin…verbena, fennel, chervil, wild garlic and sanfoin," the woman repeated, like a child, and hurried away.

The woman reappeared the next afternoon, with a wicker basket crammed with plants. Cynethryth inspected them with a satisfied smile, noting that the roots were undamaged. She emptied the contents on a large table and returned the basket to the woman with a coin.

"There's another of these when you bring me ten of these…" She asked for five different plants as before and the creature began to recite them repeatedly.

"Before you go," Cynethryth caught her arm, "wash your hair in the river and when it's dry rub this powder into your scalp. It will destroy the nits." With wrinkled nose, she pressed a small package into her hand.

When she had gone, Cynethryth sorted through the plants, grouping them by type before taking them to her garden and planting them in a row for each species. As she worked, she wondered why Aethelheard had not come to see his mother.

Surely he must be curious to see her after all these years. When she had left him, he would have been too young to have a strong memory of her. She tormented herself with worry. Why doesn't he come? She repeated it over and over, like the woman with the plants. Unless... she straightened from her planting and rubbed her back... unless he was soured by resentment that she had left him behind. They would not have explained that she'd done it for him.

Cynethryth wiped a tear from her eye with her sleeve. She swallowed hard and told herself, *'of course, he will come.'*

Chapter 8

Wimborne Abbey, 706 AD

'*Why doesn't he come?*' the refrain tormented Cynethryth for weeks but the worry about the non-appearance of her son was not her only cause of anxiety. Wynflaed surpassed herself by spying on the comings and goings at the infirmary and seeking information about the strange woman with the wicker basket. It didn't take many inquiries to discover her reputation as a witch in Wareham. Insistent questioning also revealed the woman's use of pagan rites for her 'dark arts'. As soon as Wynflaed felt confident enough, she asked for an audience with the mother superior.

"These are grave accusations, Sister. But as far as I can see, all based on hearsay and supposition."

The fierce light in the young woman's eyes dimmed for a moment and her mouth became a thin line. This did not escape the astute abbess. For unknown reasons, the nun standing before her wanted to harm the infirmarian. Whatever her problem, it most likely dated from Barking Abbey. Cuthburga decided to make her own discreet inquiries. Nonetheless, she would not tolerate the presence of a heathen in her abbey. She dismissed Wynflaed with assurances that she would pursue the matter and summoned Cynethryth.

"I have received a complaint that you are receiving a practitioner of pagan rites in your infirmary. I sincerely hope this accusation is unfounded, sister."

Cynethryth's nerves jangled. What was this? She swallowed hard and clamped her jaw to prevent herself from gaping at the mother superior.

"Mother, whilst I was in Barking Abbey, my teacher, Brother Nerian impressed upon me to have nothing to do with superstition and 'magic' in healing, a principle to which I've faithfully adhered. I abhor pagan practices and will have no truck with heathens."

"You say this, but there are witnesses to the visits of a woman accused of witchcraft in Wareham."

"My lady... Mother, the woman does not instruct *me* in anything. On the contrary, I tell her what plants I require for the infirmary, and she, able to recognise them, brings them to me for our garden. Our relationship begins and ends there."

"Sister Cynethryth, the reputation of this house is of the greatest importance. Only the highest standard of sanctity will enable us to benefit from the generous donations our continued existence depends upon. I cannot allow the good name of the abbey to be sullied by association with pagans. Can you not find a good Christian to replace her?"

"Of course, Mother – she stands before you now."

Abbess Cuthburga narrowed her eyes and her hand tapped against her thigh, "Do not test my patience, sister! You know full well I have forbidden you to leave the abbey grounds."

"Which is why I had to resort to this woman, Mother. The alternative was to let my patients suffer for lack of medicines to treat them."

"The next time this woman comes to the abbey, tell her never to enter these gates again."

"But, Mother–"

"Enough! You will obey. Out of my sight!"

Shaken, Cynethryth backed out of the chamber and hurried back to the infirmary. Was it possible that her friend and mentor had spoken to her so harshly when she had only the welfare of her patients at heart? She wondered who had complained to the abbess and it did not take her long to think of a name. She knew when Abbess Hildelith sent Wynflaed to Wimborne it would only lead to trouble – and here it was. She pondered her problem. She could not leave the abbey and her supplier could bring plants only this one last time, after which her stock would dwindle to nought. What then? She needed to pray for guidance.

With this intention, she knelt before the rough cross she had made and nailed to the wall, clasped her hands, closed her eyes and asked the Lord for a solution. It came at once. She leapt to her feet, bowed before the cross and hurried back to the abbess's quarters delighted at the simplicity of the plan.

"Mother, I have prayed for guidance and the Lord has answered my prayers."

"I too, child. But first, let me hear *your* words."

"What say you, Mother, if I take a novice and train her in plant lore? A young girl of good character, naturally, who can be trusted to leave the grounds."

"Cynethryth, my dear child, this is the same answer that I received before the altar. The Lord be praised! I have an oblate in mind. Come, we'll find and instruct her."

In an unexpected gesture, the abbess took Cynethryth under her arm and escorted her out of the chamber.

They found the postulant in question receiving instruction with a group of other oblates from the sacrist, who was explaining the correct ritual accoutrements in relation to the liturgy. She broke off abruptly when she noticed the presence of the abbess. The novices rose politely to their feet as they too became aware of the mother superior.

"Excuse this untoward interruption during your invaluable teaching, Sister. Now, girls, who among you is the constable's daughter, Sefled?"

A girl in the second row, stared at by the others, timidly raised her hand, "Me – I mean, *I*, Mother." She flushed to the roots of her pale blonde hair.

"Come, child, you are needed at the infirmary, at once."

The sacrist resumed her instructing without objection and the two intruders left the church with the girl.

On the way to the infirmary, the abbess spoke to the postulant.

"Hark, Sefled, I have chosen you to be assistant to the infirmarian. It is an honour I bestow on you because of the excellent reports I have received from your teachers. Sister Cynethryth will need your quick mind and if you learn well from her, one day you too will become an infirmarian. I also expect you to take your vows very soon, so you must allow her to attend her usual lessons, Sister Cynethryth."

"Of course, Mother, early afternoons with me will be sufficient until Sefled takes the veil."

When the abbess departed, Cynethryth made her assistant take a seat and explained the importance of aiding the sick and infirm. She was gratified to note the eagerness of her new acolyte. The girl was bright and cheerful, exactly what she needed. Not for the first time, she blessed the abbess for her thoughtfulness.

"Come outside, Sefled. I wish to set you to your first task. This is the infirmary garden, where all the plants have healing properties. What is it?"

"Pardon, sister, but those nettles…"

"Ay, what of them?"

"Well… *er*… aren't they weeds that grow everywhere?"

Cynethryth laughed. She was pleased with her assistant's questioning curiosity.

"Just because a plant is common and can sting you, doesn't mean it's useless. The nettle has many properties. I use it to treat patients with problems of the bladder. It's a diuretic," she noted the puzzled look, "that means it encourages urination," the confusion returned, "*pissing*, child, to put it plainly. It helps free sufferers from kidney stones, which can be a terribly painful complaint. I use it to treat diarrhoea and to stop bleeding. So you see, we need the nettle to hand even if it means the odd sting."

The girl understood and with pleasing eagerness, said, "My grandsire had such an ailment a few winters back. I remember him crying out with the pain. Mother gave him a lot of water but she didn't know about the nettle cure."

"There you see, you've already learnt something new but you have to show me what a clever girl you are. Your first task is to learn the names of all the species in the garden. Nay, do not fret. Five at a time! These are the first five." Cynethryth pointed them out. "Repeat the names. Good! Recognise them, Sefled, for tomorrow after Sext, you'll come here and I'll ask you to describe one of them and you will be indoors, unable to see the plant. Later, when I judge you ready, I'll explain the properties of each. For now, learn to identify these five. Take your time and then be off when the bells call to Vespers."

The next day, the novice appeared straight after Sext, with the flushed cheeks and heavy breathing of one who has been running.

"Whoa!" said Cynethryth, "when I said after Sext, I didn't mean for you to risk an ankle in your haste to be punctual! But bless you, child, I'm glad of your keenness. Come inside and I'll put you to the test."

Indoors, the girl's eyes roved anxiously over the nun's face and the worry only cleared from her countenance, giving way to a broad smile, when Cynethryth said:

"Describe the chervil for me."

"Sister, its leaves are very similar to parsley and its flowers are small and white and in a group like five fingers, like this." She held up a hand and bunched the fingers slightly.

Cynethryth smiled, "Well done, Sefled, we'll make an infirmarian of you, you'll see."

The novice flushed with pleasure, something she did often, the nun mused.

"I can tell you the other four too, sister." There was no halting her, "Sanfoin's got long stems, with small leaves in pairs and..." she continued until she had exhausted her knowledge of all five.

Delighted at her pupil's intelligence, Cynethryth led her to the garden and showed her five more plants. The next day she repeated the test but asked about sanfoin to be greeted by an objection.

"But Sister, sanfoin was the other day!"

"Nonetheless, you will describe it."

And she did, to perfection, then followed it with similarly accurate descriptions of the latest five plants.

This went on for the whole week and not once did Sefled make a mistake.

"You will be wondering why I need you to identify plants, child." She explained how only the day before she had been forced to send away the woman who supplied her plants. It had been hard to tell the woman her services would never again be needed at the abbey.

"So that's where all the plants on the table came from," Sefled said brightly.

"Ay, and from now on, you will be my supplier," she told the girl.

"You mean I'll go out of the Abbey?"

"Ay, into the woods and down by the river. It's not all learning about names, you'll collect them too. Did you see those on the table came with their roots unharmed? That's how you will bring them to me."

The novice was almost bouncing with joy, "Wait till I tell the others," she murmured. Luckily for her, and unluckily for Cynethryth, the latter did not hear these words as she was back inside the infirmary taking up the new plants to demonstrate bedding plants in the garden to her pupil.

The abbess, meanwhile, was dealing with the agitated sacrist.

"Mother, you have taken away my best pupil. I had high hopes of the girl, Sefled. I learnt you have placed her in the hands of a half-heathen."

"Are you referring to Sister Cynethryth with those derogatory words, sister?"

Across the sacrist's countenance flashed a series of emotions from abashed to, in the end, resolute.

"Mother, I'm reliably informed that our infirmarian consorts with a pagan from the town."

"And would this reliable source be Sister Wynflaed, by chance?"

The sacrist looked disconcerted.

"Ay, the sister told me about the cross-eyed witch who brings plants to Sister Cynethryth."

"But, I suppose she did not tell you that young Sefled replaces the heathen in the infirmary."

The sacrist's jaw dropped.

"She did not, Mother."

"I thought not. Do not give credence to the words of an envious creature. I'll deal with her myself. As for you, sister, you'd be well advised not to question the decisions of your mother superior. Lest you forget, I am the embodiment of the Lord in this abbey."

The sacrist flushed a shade redder than ever achieved by Sefled and stammered.

"F-forgive me, mother, I didn't mean–"

"I know, child. We are blessed to have an excellent sacrist but also an equally exceptional infirmarian. If only we were endowed with peace, love, and harmony! You are dismissed, sister."

Once the door had closed, the abbess frowned, sighed, and knelt before her portable altar.

When she rose, as usual, her ideas were clear. With determination, she strode to the infirmary, where she found Cynethryth instructing Sefled with planting.

"How is your pupil coming on, sister?"

"Better than my highest hopes, Mother. I thank you."

"Splendid! Then, you can entrust her with the task in hand. There's something for which I need your presence. We must hasten to the church."

"Are we to disturb the sacrist again, Mother?"

"I *do* hope so, sister!"

"For it is her hour of instruction in the liturgy with the nuns."

"Ay, so it is."

There was something afoot, Cynethryth could sense it in the mother superior's determined tone.

Inside the church, Cuthburga went to the altar and brought the infirmarian to stand beside the sacrist.

"Fear not, sister," she said to the sacrist, "my interruptions will not become a habit, you have my word. Accept my apology and allow me to take this opportunity, with the sisters assembled, to make two announcements. First, I have Sister Cynethryth here with me for a purpose. Our infirmarian has been the subject of uncharitable and unfounded gossip," she stared hard at Wynflaed in the second row, who lowered her head to stare at her feet. "I will not tolerate calumny, especially against a *good* Christian and exceptional infirmarian. This is a House of God, based on the precepts of 'love thy neighbour'. Anyone who behaves otherwise will be punished. Secondly, on a happier note, I have become aware of the excessive workload of our Prioress Quenburga. After much prayer and reflection, I have decided to provide her with a sub-prioress. This person must have at least seven winters since her profession," she paused and her eyes ran over the congregation and halted again on Wynflaed. "Moreover, she must be of unimpeachable character, one who eschews pettiness and gossip and fulfils her duties righteously before the sight of the Lord. Such a person I have chosen. Step forward Sister – or rather I should say, sub-prioress Leofwen!

Cynethryth caught her breath, what a pleasant surprise! She looked at the joy on the face of her friend and she couldn't help but check the envy on the contorted face of Wynflaed. Her own mind was in a whirl. The abbess had devised a double punishment for the sly wretch, first, by shaming her in front of all the sisters and then by rewarding the constancy of her best friend.

"After your lesson finishes, Sister Wynflaed, I wish to see you in my chamber."

So, the abbess had not finished with the miscreant.

They left the sacrist to resume and conclude her lesson and as they walked out of the church, the abbess said, "I presume you approve of my choice of sub-prioress?"

"Indeed, I do, Mother. Sister Leofwen is a loyal and trustworthy sister and a dear friend."

"As you are to her. I have not finished yet, sister Cynethryth. I require your presence when Wynflaed, the wretched woman, comes to my chamber."

Cynethryth did not wish to be present but was too wise to question Abbess Cuthburga's decision. As ever, there must be a good reason.

They were sipping mead when a knock came at the door. They finished the drink before the abbess asked Cynethryth to open it. She did so and came face to face with the shocked, then baleful, countenance of Wynflaed.

"Enter!" Cynethryth gave the command with some satisfaction. Wynflaed glared, walked in and lowered her head to the abbess.

"Sister Wynflaed, you will know why I summoned you."

"Ay, Mother."

"Then let us hear it from your mouth."

"Because of what I said about Sister Cynethryth?"

"And what did you say about her?"

The nun looked desperate but her eyes blazed with suppressed anger.

"Only the truth, Mother. The infirmarian has been meeting with a heathen."

The abbess looked at Wynflaed with pity.

"Answer me this, Sister... how does a priest convert the heathen without meeting him?"

The nun shook her head.

"I don't know, Mother."

"It appears there's a lot you don't know, child. For example, you don't know what was the reason for our sister's meeting with the pagan woman. Yet you felt free, first to come running to me with your tales and then to anyone else who'd listen to your spiteful tongue. To attempt to destroy the good name of an innocent person is a sin. What if I told you the person responsible for the presence of the heathen woman is your mother superior?"

Both Cynethryth and Wynflaed stared at the abbess with shocked expressions.

"Then I was wrong."

"You were, child and you'll beg forgiveness of the sister, here and now."

"Please forgive me, Sister Cynethryth."

"Of course, I pardon you," the infirmarian smiled.

"But you must serve penance, Sister Wynflaed," the abbess enjoined. She took a pen and dipping it in ink, scribbled on a piece of vellum: *James 4:11; Proverbs 30:10; Proverbs 10:18; Matthew 12:36.*

She handed the scrap of parchment to the nun.

"Get you to the library. Find and learn these passages by heart and tomorrow you will recite them to the congregation at Sext. If you cite them correctly, the matter finishes there. If you make the slightest error, you will recite them again in front of everyone at Nones and so on through Vespers and Compline – forever if necessary, till word perfect."

"Ay, Mother."

The nun gave Cynethryth a withering stare, but recalling her situation, she replaced it with a weak smile.

When the door closed, Cynethryth turned to Cuthburga and the abbess saw her infirmarian was pale and distraught.

"Why, Mother, did you say you were responsible for bringing the wretched heathen woman to the abbey?"

"Because before God, it's true. If I had allowed you to leave the grounds, you wouldn't have had recourse to her. So I'm responsible. However, it's in the past. Come take another glass of mead before you dash off to check on your pupil. I must keep a close eye on Wynflaed – the girl is driven by the Devil."

Chapter 9

Autumn had arrived and still Aethelheard had not come to find his mother. Almost as if to compensate, Cynethryth threw herself wholeheartedly into her work. With the help of her assistant, the infirmary became so well ordered and stocked that she felt capable of facing any emergency. Sefled was proving to be invaluable. The girl fulfilled her tasks willingly with never a word of complaint and Cynethryth had to refrain from overworking her.

Surprised to find her assistant in the infirmary in the morning, Cynethryth asked:

"What brings you here at this hour?"

The novice beamed.

"Wonderful news, sister, I'm to take the veil on the morrow! I wished to share my happiness and seek a boon."

"I'm pleased for you, Sefled, for soon I will call you 'Sister'. But what is it you need?"

The girl flushed as was her wont when her emotions overwhelmed her.

"*I*-I need a godmother to sponsor me in the ceremony. Who better? You are like a mother to me. Please say you will, sister."

"Of course, Cynethryth smiled. It will be a great pleasure."

'*Am I like a mother to her because she takes the place of my son?*'

The ceremony brought back the joy of her own profession of faith and the happy occasion was twofold for Cynethryth. Sefled would now be able to work all day in the infirmary without the distraction of having to attend lessons. Her learning of medicine would now begin in earnest. The only cloud over the occasion were the sour looks the sacrist continually shot at Cynethryth. But she rebuffed them each with a smile of pure joy. Evidently, the sacrist had never accepted losing her best pupil to the infirmarian.

Such was the mutual respect between the two infirmarians that their relationship became more sisterly rather than that of infirmarian and assistant. Their closeness brought Cynethryth to address a moral dilemma – a notion that continued to gnaw at her. Sefled was at liberty to leave the abbey grounds, so why not give her a message to take to her son?

She resisted writing the note because the risk of getting Sefled into trouble was too great. It was clear to Cynethryth that she had enemies within the walls of the abbey who would seize any opportunity to harm her: the sacrist and Wynflaed, who had never forgiven her for the public humiliation of reciting, '*He who conceals hatred has lying lips, and he who spreads slander is a fool.*' No matter how much she wanted to see and hold her son, she must not lose Sefled's privilege of leaving the abbey, nor the good reputation of the young woman – she had only just taken the veil.

This torment would soon come to an end although she had no way of knowing it at the time.

A fortnight after the ceremony, a litter arrived at the infirmary door, dragged by four men from Wareham, accompanied by a monk indicating the way.

"In the name of the king! We have urgent need of treatment."

Cynethryth and Sefled peered at the figure of a young man lying on the litter. His face was bloodied and swollen, his right eye lost in a discoloured swelling. He seemed more monster than human.

"Bring him inside! Sister Sefled, prepare the bedding."

"What happened to him?" Cynethryth asked one of the men.

"Combat, sister. He took a mighty blow to the face. Lucky for him, it was a practice sword and not steel else there'd be no need of your ministrations."

Once settled in bed and the men sent away, Cynethryth bent over her patient. Judging by his fine tunic and the jewel on his ring, this was a young nobleman. She inspected the injury – it was severe. If the youth was lucky, he might not lose his eyesight. She was looking at a fracture of the cheekbone but it was too soon to tell whether the orbital socket had been harmed.

"Prepare a cold compress, sister, change it every time it warms. Be very gentle when placing it. When you're done, I'll prepare a draught to relieve the pain for when he regains his senses. Come and learn."

When the patient finally groaned, Cynethryth placed a hand under his shoulder, raised him enough to place a beaker of the potion to his lips.

"Drink, it'll ease the pain."

The effort of opening his mouth the fraction needed to imbibe the potion and the pain it caused, made Cynethryth blanch. But she was pleased to see him swallow the concoction. It would numb the pain and send him to sleep. In a matter of minutes, he was asleep. She replaced an icy cold compress over the damaged area with great care.

"The bones will need resetting in their natural position but the swelling must reduce first," she explained to Sefled who was peering over her shoulder.

"It's a pity, he's a good-looking youth, under that mess."

"Sefled! Repeat the ingredients of the potion I gave to him, instead of mouthing your silly thoughts!"

The assistant flushed and repeated the preparation, word perfect.

"Good, now off you go, prepare it. When he wakes, he may need it again although I pray not."

The next day, Cynethryth inspected the injury but considered it too soon to intervene. Her patient had slept through the night and her constant changing of the cold compress was taking effect. The swelling had halved but the eye, blackened and swollen, was still closed.

To her delight and surprise, Rowena arrived with a young man.

"This is Osburh," Rowena introduced her son, a handsome muscular fellow, who looked more like his mother than Cynethryth had imagined.

"Welcome, Osburh, I haven't seen you since you were this tall," she indicated knee-height.

"As you see, sister, I have grown, but tell me, how is Aethelheard?"

Cynethryth almost swooned. What was he saying? She groped for the table top to prevent her knees from giving way.

Rowena rushed to embrace her.

"You didn't know, did you?"

Cynethryth's chest heaved, the sobs repressed, she felt ill.

"His poor face!"

The words were barely audible. She broke free of Rowena and dashed into the sick room.

The young man was awake and peering out of one eye. Cynethryth bent over him and kissed the left side of his brow.

"Aethelheard, I'm your mother!"

She straightened and scrutinised his face to gauge the effect her words had had on him. A barely detectable twitch of the left side of the mouth produced a groan.

"My poor boy," she said and long-repressed tears rolled unashamedly down her cheeks. Suddenly aware of movement behind her, Cynethryth wiped her eyes with her sleeve and turned to see Osburh staring at his friend.

"What have I done?" he muttered.

"You?"

"Ay, sister. We were practising swordsmanship, as we often do. Aethelheard is better than me but he let his guard down unexpectedly and I struck. I didn't mean... will he be all right? Will it mend?"

Cynethryth took his arm and ushered him out of the room, marvelling at the strength of the muscular limb. No wonder her son's face was so frightful, and she wouldn't spare Osburh's feelings.

"It's too soon to say whether he'll lose his eye."

"My God! Is there that risk?"

"There is."

"Can you do nothing, sister?"

"I will do all I can, but for the moment, time is all."

Osburh looked wildly at his mother.

"I didn't mean–"

Rowena glared at him. "How many times have I told you not to fight so hard in practice?"

"Mother, there's no point in practice unless you fight as if there's a foe in front of you. Aethelheard would have it no other way."

"He's right, of course, Rowena." Cynethryth said. "In battle a man must give his all."

Osburh gave her a grateful smile.

"I must go to him, to give him words of comfort." Osburh said.

"Ay, but be quick. Do not weary him – he cannot talk."

Rowena and Sefled gazed at her but it was Cynethryth who spoke.

"The shame of it. I have prayed every day that he would come. But not like this. I didn't recognise my own son!"

The tears flowed freely once more.

Both women stepped forward but Rowena gently pushed Sefled away and took her friend in her arms.

"Do not blame yourself. How could you know him, Cynethryth? You haven't seen him since he was a little boy and with his face so disfigured – what shame is there?"

She stroked her friend's hair as the head buried into her shoulder.

She continued, "What better way to get to know him, than to restore him with loving care?"

The infirmarian straightened and offered a brave smile to her dearest friend.

"Of course, you are right. Thank the Lord I had a good teacher in Barking and I can use the skills I learnt there."

"Thank you, Cynethryth, for not being hard on Osburh."

"It was an accident not caused through malice."

The two women settled to exchange news. Cynethryth, whose life inside the abbey was not full of interest, told Rowena about having to do without the cross-eyed woman, the petty jealousies that surrounded her, and about her good fortune in Sefled.

Rowena, instead, living between the court and the town had more to relate. To Cynethryth's surprise, she began with politics, relating how Wessex had come close to war with the East Saxons. King Ine had averted it at a synod held in Brentford by extracting a promise from the joint kings of those people that they would no longer shelter certain exiled rivals to his throne. In exchange, he swore not to invade Essex.

"So, King Ine has his rivals," Cynethryth mused. "What was King Cuthred's position?"

"Since Ine let him rule in peace, Cuthred maintained loyalty to his overlord."

The infirmarian frowned, "It is as well. The time is not ripe for Aethelheard to move against the throne."

Rowena gazed, astonished, at her friend.

"What talk is this? Aethelheard must bide his time."

"Your advice is sound, Rowena. In any case, the most important thing is to restore him to health. Does the ealdorman know he's here?"

"It was he who sent him."

And now, Cynethryth, in turn, gaped.

"Does the ealdorman realise *I* am the infirmarian?"

"I think he knows only the high reputation of the infirmarian, not who she is."

"Ah, that accounts for it. Grant me a favour, Rowena, let it be known to him that Aethelheard must stay here for six weeks."

"Why so long?"

"Once I set the broken bones, they must not be subjected to sudden movement else they will un-knit. But if the eye socket is broken it will be terribly difficult. I pray all the time it is not. His state is delicate so he must lie still here."

"It'll be an ordeal for one so active."

"Yet, it must be so."

"I'll inform the ealdorman."

It was three days before the swelling was gone and the blackened right eye opened the smallest amount for the first time. Knowing it was time to intervene, Cynethryth prepared a drug to render her son insensible. This was necessary because she had to manipulate the bones by pressing the damaged area. Without sedation, he would have been in agony. The infirmarian explained every phase to her assistant, from preparation of the narcotic to the movements of her skilled fingers. Once, in Barking, she had performed this under the direction of Brother Nerian. A monk had slipped in the cellar, dislodging and pulling down a barrel on top of himself, breaking his cheekbone. She hoped the outcome would be as positive as in that case.

A preliminary check told her that the jawbone was intact although bruised. When she ran her fingers lightly over the cheekbone, she tut-tutted.

"What is it?" whispered Sefled.

"No need to whisper, sister, he can't hear us. It's the fracture, the bone's shifted over itself, I have to work it back. The good news is the floor of the eye socket is undamaged. He will not lose his sight. If I'm skilful enough, I will not have to cut him. In worse cases, the cut can be made here, or here or inside the mouth at the top of the gum. I hope to avoid cutting so there will be no scar." Carefully and slowly, she moved three fingers over the flesh of her son's face, pulling downwards. She sighed and repeated the action several times, finally massaging the area with a circular motion. She straightened and smiled at Sefled, "Sister, thank the Lord, it is done and easier than I hoped. It should knit back within two weeks. Our task is to make sure he doesn't turn to lie on that side of his face or chew solid food. He must survive on chicken broth and vegetable gruel. Whenever he has eaten, his mouth must be rinsed with salt water. He cannot clean his teeth in other ways."

"I'm so pleased for you both!" Sefled beamed at her friend, "but sister, I'm not sure I learnt anything." She looked downcast.

"Come here."

Cynethryth put a finger on the nun's cheekbone.

"Here was the fracture."

She removed her hand.

"Luckily, it was just one break, so that the bone had been raised like this, and rested on itself." She demonstrated with two fingers over the other hand. "I worked it back through the skin with the pressure of my fingers, like this."

"Now I see, and did you feel it go back in place, sister?"

"Ay, the circular massage was to ensure everything was smooth. Without the sedative, he wouldn't have resisted the pain. It's back to cold compresses. Prepare one, sister."

That evening, Cynethryth, who was taking stock of her medicines, hurried into the sick room at Sefled's urgent call.

"Sister, he is conscious and asking for you."

Cynethryth stared anxiously at her son, bent over him and asked, "How do you feel?"

The reply was weak and no more than a whisper.

"Sore...can't move jaw...numb...water."

"Sister, fetch a beaker of fresh water!"

She took the beaker from her assistant and with Sefled's help raised Aethelheard into a half-raised position, propping him with cushions.

She took the beaker and admonished him. "You will drink in sips but do not try to open your mouth wide. It will be days before we try that. Your face bones are delicate, like a broken vase. Once repaired, it must not be touched till it is whole again. Do not turn and put weight on that side."

Refreshed, Aethelheard slipped into sleep.

"Watch over him, Sefled. See that he doesn't turn to his right."

"When are you going to tell him, sister?"

Cynethryth looked sharply at the young nun.

"Tell him what?"

"That you are his mother."

Cynethryth's nostrils flared and her eyes flashed.

"You were eavesdropping on my private conversation with my friend."

Sefled's face crumpled, "Sister, I didn't mean to but I did over-hear. I mean, I wasn't spying."

"Can I trust you, girl?"

"Of course, sister, I'd do anything for you."

The infirmarian's face softened, "I believe you would. So, promise you will not breathe a word of this to anyone."

"I swear it!"

Sefled meant it at the time, but without malice since she loved to gossip, and from an unguarded Rowena, she discovered who the father was. She let the knowledge slip to her friend Leofwen, who told Wynflaed – and this, much later, would have dire consequences.

Cynethryth ended, "I've already told him but he's not in any state for conversation."

The next morning, Aethelheard woke to find his mother seated on his bed staring at him. He smiled and her heart leapt with joy. She bent close to catch his whispered words.

"For years I dreamt of you. At night I'd see your face and your golden hair." His 'good' eye looked up at her wimple. "Mother, why did you leave me?"

Her eyes shone with tears but she breathed deeply and told him about his father and the dangers they faced.

"Tell me more about my father."

She told him all she knew. It was not a long story because their married life had been cut cruelly short.

"Kiss me, mother."

Her heart swelled fit to burst and she bent over to place a gentle kiss on his sound cheek. A strong arm emerged from under the blanket and held her tight as her body shook and tears bathed his face.

"It was my fault."

The words made her raise her head and look at him.

"What?"

"This wound. Osburh's not to blame. I dropped my guard, distracted. There's this maid…"

Cynethryth laughed and stroked his hair.

"You're more like your father than I thought! Well, thank the Lord you didn't lose that eye, you'll need them both to stare at maids! Your fortune is that there are no wenches on battlefields."

"Mother! Ought a nun to speak so?"

She wanted to reply that she and Caedwalla had had many a verbal skirmish but decided to opt for discretion. She had regained her son and there would be many an occasion to bandy words. She would restore his good looks so he could return to leering at maidens. Aethelheard closed his eye and slipped into sleep with a smile on his face. Her own lit up the room. She kissed his forehead and returned to her duties in the infirmary.

Chapter 10

Wimborne Abbey, winter 706-707 AD

Rain set in during Aethelheard's convalescence and spoilt the harvest but the wet weather did nothing to dampen Cynethryth's cheerful mood. She delighted in tending to her son and assisting his steady recovery. Each passing day brought a twofold benefit: firstly, Aethelheard's visage returned to its former handsome state as the bruising faded and the swelling disappeared. When his mother gazed upon the leonine features, heightened by the long blond hair, a sign of nobility, she might have been looking at her departed husband. Small gestures and smiles made her heart quicken and ache for the man she had lost and who she had now, in a sense, regained. Secondly, their exchanged confidences grew into trust and the settled familiarity that they had both longed for in their darkest hours returned. In the end, Aethelheard promised he would remain close by visiting the infirmary once a week.

Given the mother superior's position on segregating the nuns as far as possible from male presence, Cynethryth sought permission for the visits: a wise move that met with indulgence.

"You are out of the public gaze here, sister," the abbess said, "far from prying eyes at court. How could I deny you the occasion to meet the son you have only just found anew? You will be able to give him sound counsel and instruction in the ways of the Lord."

Cynethryth smiled into the kindly face, noting for the first time a tautness of the flesh that suggested underlying suffering.

"Mother," she said, anxiety creeping into her voice, "have you been unwell?"

"It is nothing, child. Of late, I have suffered from headaches and pains in my joints."

"Ah, it's sure to be the damp weather. It makes our bodies ache so. I'll prepare you a draught to ease the pain."

"Bless you, sister!"

The abbess was not the only patient the infirmarian needed to tend. The rain, followed by a drying autumnal sun, took a toll on the rye crop. The people harvested it as usual but gave little importance to the sugary honeydew that dripped out of the florets.

The first realisation that ought was amiss came with villagers begging admission to the abbey, to the infirmary, with a variety of ailments. Some complained of a severe burning in the legs and arms.

One man appeared dazed and Cynethryth observed his muscle spasms and tremors.

"Sister, I get these pains in my fingers and toes. They come an' they go."

"What are these pains like?"

"Awful! They shoot to the tips. Ay, that's it, shooting pains."

Cynethryth began to put these complaints together and drew on her learning from the library in Barking. She had read a treatise in the abbey near Lunden, obtained from the Low Countries, but she could not remember the cause of the illness nor the cure. She did, however, recall how the symptoms he lamented would develop in time into paralysis. The infirmarian regarded the man with pity and determination that she would not let it happen to him. To this purpose, she hurried into her preparation room and sorted through the many parchments of notes she had brought from Barking. At last, she found the one she sought, where, in her neat handwriting, she read about the dreadful cycle: rain followed by honeydew droplets that assailed the florets and then upon drying, transformation into miniscule fungi like tiny mushrooms, the fungal infection of rye and barley. Expounded here were all the symptoms of the ailment, including high fever and vomiting, tremors, hallucinations, pains, and paralysis... Cynethryth groaned as she realised the significance of her discovery. The infected crop must be destroyed, but as a consequence the villagers would go hungry through the winter. Already, a meagre diet left many of the women as thin as birch shoots. Starvation would await many if they could not make bread. On the other hand, paralysis or death would be their lot if they continued to use the infected grain.

Cynethryth rolled up the parchment and replaced it with care before hurrying into the sickroom.

"My friend," she said, "it is the fault of the wet weather. Your grain has a fungus and eating it is making you ill. You must burn the crop."

"We can't! What are we supposed to live on?"

"You have no choice. These pains you feel are nothing compared with the loss of movement to your limbs."

"But burning the grain!" There was a wildness in his eyes.

"Calm yourself. God sees everything and will provide."

"Why did he send the rain at harvest time, sister?"

Cynethryth felt helpless and did not know the answer. She knew for sure the crop must be destroyed and repeated it.

Good sense and faith in the reputation of the infirmarian prevailed and resulted in no further cases arriving at her door, but in the depths of winter, the villagers came to the abbey gates begging for a pittance – the name given to the scraps of food they clutched and bore away.

There was one other result, although Cynethryth did not associate it with a vision. Often, the villagers brought gifts of produce to the infirmary in gratitude for healing. One day, a grateful woman took a freshly-baked barley loaf from her basket and gave it to the infirmarian. Since weeks had gone by since the outbreak of the disease, Cynethryth, not making the connection, did not hesitate to accept the welcome gift. She ate several slices of the apparently wholesome loaf. She did not feel sick but somewhat giddy. When she went to Vespers, her head spun and, to her eyes, the priest's features distorted as he led the service. When she gazed at the crucifix, to her horror the red painted blotches representing Christ's wounds opened to drip and flow blood. She sank to her knees, not following the ritual, but nobody dared disturb her seeing the look of ecstasy on her face revealing her to be in a spiritual trance. After the service, Cynethryth confessed that she had had a vision of Christ in Glory and that the Lord commanded her to write down what she saw and heard. Thus it was that Cynethryth began what was later to become a large volume describing a building with many rooms, each devoted to a personage symbolising a particular virtue. Her visions continued until she had finished the loaf and although they did not recur, their startling clarity were etched in her memory so she was able to record them in their entirety. Never once did she imagine the visions were inspired not by God but by a fungus. Later, she would draw on her hallucinations for inspiration in periods of trial and tribulation.

Meanwhile, a system developed in place throughout the years to come, with Guthred in the king's counsel, who informed Rowena of everything except the most reserved details. She, in turn, brought them to Cynethryth, who used them to guide Aethelheard. Her son honoured his promise to pay her weekly visits, confiding in her and seeking advice. A mother may freely offer counsel but if the son, like his father, is headstrong and prone to rashness, it is a thankless task.

In the early visits there was none of this, hence Cynethryth was able to enjoy his presence and revel in tales of his exploits in falconry, boar hunting and, more to her taste, his efforts at rhyming and riddling. As winter progressed, the sickroom filled with patients, both lay and religious, suffering above all from the seasonal ague. However elated Cynethryth was by her son's midweek visits, when she and Sefled found themselves overwhelmed by demanding patients, these had to be her priority. To her delight, Aethelheard reacted to the lack of attention she afforded him by rolling up his sleeves, unbidden, and applying cooling cloths to fevered brows.

How much harder then, when he failed to attend a regular midweek visit. All sorts of explanations troubled her for the next two days. Had he succumbed to the ague? Had the king forbidden him to come to her? She refused to imagine worse possibilities and began to search for happier ideas – had he fallen in love and come under the spell of a beautiful maid?

Rowena came and brought with her the reason for Aethelheard's absence.

"Dearest friend, forgive me. I ought to have come two days ago as Aethelheard bade me. I have had so many matters to deal with. You must have been concerned when he didn't come but do not worry, it's the usual lot of women, we must endure the consequences of men's lust for power and glory."

"What are you saying, Rowena?"

"The King has exiled three aethelings from Wessex."

"Why did Cuthred do that?"

"Not King Cuthred – Ine!"

Cynethryth paled and wrung the cloth she held in her hand.

"My God! Aethelheard was one of these!"

"No, he was one of the princes accused, but don't fret, Cuthred protected him. He wrote to Ine saying he was prepared to swear on oath that your son had no part in the plot to overthrow the King. It seems that Ine accepted his word but sent a messenger ordering Aethelheard to be confined to court until he decrees otherwise."

"Thank the Lord! So that explains why he did not come. Oh, Rowena, why did he not tell me about his ambitions? I could have warned him to stay away from the aethelings. Who are they?"

"Guthred has named Ealdberht, who has a strong claim to the throne; a certain Oswald, who is the king's distant cousin, and one named... oh, I forget... but there *was* another. The new ealdorman expelled them from court together a week ago and they rode off to find a king who might shelter them from the wrath of Ine. They will have to ride far because there is no such king in the southern kingdoms. Ine has them or the ealdormen in the palm of his hand."

"Stupid boy! Can he not see how things truly are? Oh, how I wish I could speak with him!"

"I can get a message to him if you wish."

Cynethryth reached out and took her friend's hand.

"You are an angel in my moment of need. Tell him to speak out loud and long within the hearing of the whole court in favour of King Ine and against the aethelings. Say, even if he hates Ine, that he is to do it. Let him know it is a game like chess. There will be Ine's spies in court who will refer everything to their lord."

Rowena looked with admiration at the infirmarian, "It's sound counsel and I'll bear it to him, word for word."

Time was the key to the success of this ploy, and so it proved, for a whole moon and the waxing of another had to pass before Aethelheard arrived at her door.

"Mother," he said, when he broke free from her long embrace, "Ine," he lowered his voice to a whisper, "that son of a mangy bitch," his voice recovered its strength, "has decreed my freedom to move where I will."

"Ah, the Lord be praised!"

"Amen. And hark! My friends found shelter in the land of the Est Seaxa with Kings Swaefred and Sigeheard, who have no love for Ine."

"It's a dangerous game and one they play badly."

"Why, mother?"

"Because a move to take power can only be made when the time is right. Ine is loved by the West Seaxa for his just laws and peaceful reign. He has strengthened his position with the Suth Seaxa, whom he controls, and has struck up a firm friendship with the powerful King of Kent."

"My friends deem him a tyrant and wish to overthrow him."

"Friends, do you say? Don't delude yourself, Aethelheard. These are not true friends but *rivals*, who seek to make use of you and your father's name for their own ends."

"Mother, you do not even know them. How can you speak thus?"

Cynethryth blew out her cheeks in exasperation. She gave him a level stare:

"Because, my dear boy, I lived through more unsettled and violent times than these. I saw your father conquer the southern kingdoms and become king over the whole of the south. Do you suppose he did that by throwing in his lot with a band of desperate opponents?"

"Ah, you think you know everything! You are always the one in the right!"

Red-faced, Aethelheard strode to the door, slammed it behind him, and she heard the hoof beats of his horse as he galloped away. He had been with her for so few minutes that it was all she could manage not to shed a tear. Instead, with gritted teeth, she threw herself into her work and hoped he would come back to comfort her. But he did not. She might not know everything, as he accused her, but she did know he had the same pride and temperament as Caedwalla, so she needed to wait until he managed to calm himself.

Chapter 11

Aethelheard did not reappear until after Christ's Mass but when he did, he was contrite.

"Mother, I beg your forgiveness, pardon my bad manners. You were right and I was wrong."

Cynethryth was pleased to see her son and bore no resentment. Her heart went out to him. Her sweet smile was enough to make him sweep her into his muscular embrace and kiss her cheek repeatedly.

"Mother, I'll love you so long as the grass grows upwards and the rain falls downwards!"

"And what, pray, has brought about this change of heart?"

He released her and stepped back to regard her with a self-deprecating smile.

"King Ine!" He paused for effect. "He met with Swaefred and Sigeheard at a synod held in Brentford. He paused again and stared into space.

"Are you going to tell me or not?"

"He threatened them with invasion. Imagine that! He said he'd invade forthwith if they didn't agree to banish my frie– *er – rivals* from Est Seax forthwith. What do you think of that?"

Cynethryth smiled, "I think your opponents are in mortal danger and that you were sensible to follow my advice to speak out against them. King Ine is too powerful for the moment. If ever you are to claim his throne, it will be when the time is propitious. Only then will you move, my son."

"You are wise, mother. Henceforth, I'll heed your counsel."

'*The swine in the farmyard are more likely to take wing!*'

She did not express the thought but it made her beam at him with fondness and that was enough for him to embrace her again.

"What will become of the aethelings?" he murmured in her ear.

"They have challenged the king and there's no place to hide. They must throw themselves on his mercy and bend the knee or else leave the country and seek refuge in other lands."

"And what of me, mother? What must I do?"

"Go to King Ine and offer him your sword."

"Offer him my sword? *Are you mad!*" He spat the last three words as he pushed her away.

Cynethryth held him with her stare even as he was about to spin away from her.

"What?" he asked.

"You know what. Your vow didn't last two minutes!"

Now, he smiled, and it was a rueful one.

"You're right, of course, but I need to understand."

"You are just like Caedwalla. One day, but *not now*, I'll tell you about the shoe."

"The shoe?"

Cynethryth blushed. "Another time. But this matter of offering the sword. There can be no better moment. You must ride as soon as you have the ealdorman's blessing. He will give it, for he is no fool. God knows, I do not want you to leave – but think of this – Ine is irate with the aethelings, so, he'll welcome another aetheling, dissociated from them, who will be loyal and serve him. You'll enter into his good graces and it'll strengthen his position in the eyes of his people. He can't and mustn't know – for the time being – that you are Caedwalla's son. Let him go on thinking you are Cuthred's boy – he probably imagines you are the bastard of some serving maid!" Cynethryth came out with an earthy laugh that startled Aethelheard.

"Mother, you are an unusual nun, but a wise one. I'm off to the court to seek the ealdorman's blessing for this venture. I'm sure father would have approved."

She watched him go with mixed feelings. How naturally he had used the word 'father' when referring to Cuthred. Caedwalla had not lived to see the birth of his son, she sighed, but what a good father he would have made. She had persuaded Aethelheard to leave but had she placed him in mortal danger? Was he cunning enough to hide his loathing of Ine? She wished she had spent time warning him but he was so restless, and gone in a trice.

* * *

"Clever fellow! How did this splendid idea come to you?"

The ealdorman's, like Cynethryth's, sentiments were also mixed. Aethelheard's idea of putting his sword at Ine's service was a master stroke and he was quick to seize on it.

"Brilliant! Especially at this delicate time. What better way to prove our loyalty to the King of Wessex than to send him Cuthred's son? Ine believes this court to be a nest of malcontents and he would need little persuasion to invade and overthrow us. We've heard about his threats to Est Seax. If he believes us responsible for the menace to his throne, what's to stop him moving against us?" Deep in thought, the ealdorman stroked his beard, and stared over Aethelheard's shoulder into space. He resumed, "I'll miss you, my friend. Heed me well. Assure yourself the goodwill of the king and never let him know who your real father was – it's perilous. Let him think Cuthred adopted a bastard – Heaven knows, there are quite likely one or two of his in Wareham!"

Aethelheard almost confessed he had just received the same advice from his mother, but thought better of it. The ealdorman did not know that the Wimborne infirmarian was his mother. As far as he and the other lords knew, she was safe in an abbey near Lunden.

Aethelheard achieved the ride to Winchester with one overnight stop. He took his best friend, Osburh, with him and ten warriors of the royal guard as an escort. Travelling through forest required precautions. An unwary traveller might find himself assailed by a band of outlaws. A lone nobleman, commanding a hefty ransom, made an irresistible prey. Instead, in this way, Aethelheard arrived untroubled at his destination.

He took his letter of presentation, written before King Cuthred's demise, to the hall in Winchester, and although he obtained the audience he requested immediately, King Ine bristled with hostility. The thin face with hooded eyes stared balefully at him, and the king's first words were admonitory.

"Mmm, Aethelheard of Dorset, one who must learn to choose his friends more carefully. Here, your father states that you wish to place your sword at my service. And if I commanded you to use it to take off the head of the aetheling, Ealdberht, would you obey?"

Aethelheard fought against his every instinct and bit back his words. The supreme effort to hide his true feelings caused him to delay answering.

"Well?" Ine glared at him. "You will know, the punishment for treason is death."

"Sire, my father was and I am a loyal subject. Your wish with regard to Ealdberht, or any other, is my command."

"Ah! your father, you say? Are you not adopted? Who is your true father or are you a by-blow of Cuthred's misspent youth? by the way, my condolences."

Aethelheard's face burnt with resentment and shame. The man enthroned before him was King of Wessex, but he felt sure he would defeat him in single combat in a matter of moments. Was such a pathetic weakling deserving of kingship?

"I know not, Sire, but I believe a man's lineage is less important than the strength of his arm and I believe I can beat any man who sets against me."

"Do you, indeed? Those are fine words, worthy of an aetheling – perhaps your father is Cuthred after all."

"Cuthred was my father, Sire, and I'll slay any man who dares to doubt it."

"Steady, young fellow! Do not come to regret rash words uttered before your King. You wish to place your sword at my service, then kneel and swear fealty to Ine, rightful King of Wessex."

Aethelheard knelt at once and gave his oath and was relieved to kiss the king's hand and to be received into the court as a welcome friend and loyal subject. Within his breast was another matter, where a smouldering hatred of Ine needed little to fan it into a raging blaze. He stood back and watched Osburh swear a similar oath. Evidently, Ine's spies had been thorough, because the king subjected Osburh to taunts also regarding his friendships. But the youth was quicker-witted, perhaps because less resentful than he and replied, "Sire, Aethelheard and I have publicly dissociated ourselves from the traitors and have ridden here willingly to show and prove our loyalty to Ine, by the grace of God, our king."

The sallow, acid features relaxed into a smile.

"You are both welcome to my hall. Aetheling, you, who are of royal blood, will be a member of my council. Come at this time tomorrow and I'll present you to the lords."

Aethelheard grinned and bowed, stuttering his thanks. The odd insult aside, this had gone far better than he'd hoped.

The next day in the Council proved the wisdom of his mother and Cuthred. Introduced by Ine as the *Aetheling of Dorset*,

Aethelheard's esteem among his peers was assured. In this meeting, he learnt immediately of Ine's ambitions. These were, for the most part, aimed at expansion of his kingdom westwards across the River Tamar, where King Geraint of Dumnonia held sway. The council heard reports from scouts sent out to assess the defences of the Brittonic kingdom. Aethelheard's instincts told him the grounds for optimism expressed by the counsellors was misplaced, but as a newcomer, he did not express his misgivings. He knew that Cuthred's dealings with Geraint had been far from uncomplicated. Given the ferocious spirit of the Dumnonians, border disputes had been settled by diplomacy not by battle.

Fortunately, Ine had many matters to deal with in this period, so any attack on Dumnonia was postponed. The king's principal concern seemed to be his desire to achieve a law code for Wessex that surpassed any previous provision. Council meetings, therefore, tended to reduce to quibbling over the exact amount of a fine for a specific crime. Aethelheard, a man of action, was bored by such details although he understood the need for the people to see their king as just and interested in their welfare.

Aethelheard and Osburh settled into their new lifestyle at Winchester with ease. Their prowess at swordsmanship helped them. None of the youths at Ine's court, try as they might, were able to overcome either lad. The excellent tuition of Cuthred, himself a renowned warrior, stood them in such stead that their reputation burgeoned. Aethelheard chafed that their practice was not being tested where it counted – on the field of battle.

Another thing that helped enhance Aethelheard's standing among his peers was his fine voice. The aetheling had musical talent and ever sought to expand his collection of songs, never refusing to pick up the hearpe to entertain the company of the moment. Thus, the weeks turned to months and these slipped by until two winters had passed since their arrival in Winchester.

* * *

Yuletide festivities over, and the feasting on slaughtered beasts a fond memory, the king called another council meeting as the first crocuses and snowdrops bloomed in the nearby woodlands.

King Ine rose and addressed the assembly, "Members of my council, my patience with Dumnonia is exhausted. I have received reports that Geraint has sealed an alliance with the Wealisc and intends to strike at our lands in Devon and Dorset as soon as dry weather permits."

Aethelheard's pulse raced at these words, for his home was under threat.

"For this reason, my lords, we have exchanged messages with King Nothelm of Suth Seax and the Ealdorman of Dorset..." at these last words Ine's gaze sought out Aethelheard and rested on him as he continued, "both have promised their allegiance in the forthcoming war. Even now, they are summoning their fyrds." His eyes met Aethelheard's, "Aetheling, your father's successor promises three hundred men and *you* will lead them in battle."

Aethelheard looked around the chamber, raised his chin and said, "Willingly, Sire!" His voice boomed strongly and with pride. At last, he would prove his worth in battle. He'd prove Ine wrong not to have chosen him as his father's successor.

Ine expressed his approval, "Good. Now, my lords I expect each of you to summon your bondsmen to arms. By the next moon we must be ready to march. How many days to the moon?"

The question provoked a din of raised voices as some maintained ten, others fourteen, days until Ine raised his hand. Silence restored, he said, "It matters not: ten or fourteen. We'll say ten and stare at the sky to see who's right. In either case, by the full moon, we want the army gathered at Winchester, armed and ready to march."

The roar of approval, stamping of feet, and drumming of fists on tables at these words stirred Aethelheard's blood. The Dumnonians would be made to pay for their effrontery. But he did not have time to dwell on his thoughts. Ine was speaking again.

"...and it's my intention to build a fortress at Tantun. It will bar the road into our realm to the Wealisc from the north. If they wish to join Geraint, they will have to do so by water or leave their hides at Tantun."

The roar that greeted this speech left no doubt that the men of West Seax were keen to test their mettle.

* * *

Wimborne, Dorset, spring, 710 AD

Cynethryth gazed into the sage green eyes of her dearest friend.

"War, Sister. It's war against Dumnonia. King Ine has summoned the fyrd and Dorset must provide three hundred men. Oh, Cynethryth, it's been so many years since I had to worry about Guthred. I told him he's too old to go into battle."

"What did he say?"

"I can't repeat his words, they're too vile! I feared he'd strike me, but thank the Lord, he did not."

"So he will lead the Dorset men?"

Rowena looked stricken and Cynethryth stepped forward to comfort her but it was she who needed consoling.

"He will not! It's not he who'll lead our men, but Aethelheard."

Cynethryth gasped and her mouth dropped open, closing slowly as the words sank in.

"B-but he has no experience of battle – is Ine deliberately putting him in danger?"

"I believe not, my friend. I asked the same question of Guthred."

"And what did he say?"

Cynethryth gabbled the question in her anxiety, causing Rowena to smile, take her hand, and make her wait for the reply.

"Calm yourself, sister, or take one of your calming draughts! Guthred says King Ine has chosen well, for everyone knows Aethelheard is peerless with the sword. Is he not the son of Caedwalla? You should fear for the Dumnonians, not for your son!" She laughed and squeezed the nun's hand. "He also swore to me that he will cover Aethelheard's back."

Cynethryth smiled at last.

"You are my dearest friend, Rowena, and only you know how to comfort me. It's only natural a mother should worry. *Oh!* Forgive me – you must be worried too. How selfish and thoughtless I am!"

"I refuse to worry, dear heart – Osburh will have Aethelheard and Guthred by his side. If anything, I fear more for my husband. He's too old for war!"

"Guthred is a grizzled lion and can take care of himself, have no fear!"

In spite of all reassurances, both women fretted and as events proved, they had every reason to do so.

Chapter 12

The banks of the River Parrett, Somerset, spring 710 AD

"I don't like it, sire. It feels wrong." Aethelheard addressed King Ine as they gazed from the higher ground on the Dumnonian host below.

"Says the *boy* from the height of his experience," said King Nothelm.

"It's true, lord, I'm young and can't boast your experience but I can draw on that of my father with this self-same foe."

"Ah, your fearsome father, a man who prefers to send a boy to fight in his stead!"

"It's not in my place to trade insults with a king," Aethelheard said, fighting to keep his tone humble. *He does not know father is dead.* "All I'm saying is it feels wrong."

Nothelm made to sneer again but Ine silenced him.

Aethelheard breathed his thanks, kept challenge out of his voice and said, "It's unlike the Britons to concede an advantage, sire. Look around, to our left is the river, to our backs, wet moorland. If a force comes from the right, we are in a trap and at their mercy."

"*If* says the boy. So where is this phantom force?"

Aethelheard's eyes flashed at the arrant fool.

"Exactly, sire, where is it? I see no Wealisc ranked below us, only the men of Dumnonia."

"Mmm. You are right, Aetheling." King Ine stared at the massed Brittonic force. "So, you think the Wealisc are waiting their moment?"

"I do, sire."

"What then do you suggest?"

"Let me take my men of Dorset off along the causeway to the right and cover our flank."

King Nothelm snorted, "Surely you give no credence to this boy? Like father like son, he has no stomach for the battle and would deprive us of three hundred fighting men for the battle to come! If the Wealisc are nearby, why haven't our scouts found them?"

"The Britons are wily, sire. They know the land and how to make themselves invisible. I would ask one question of the King of the Suth Seax, if I may?" He turned to address the scornful monarch, "Is it not true, sire, that some of your scouts have never returned?"

The countenance of the king became thunderous.

"That is true, but its meaning is unclear. They might have met a party of Dumnonian foragers or been led astray by elfin magic, who can say?"

"Or murdered by the Wealisc." Aethelheard could resist no longer. "And as to me being a coward, I'll kill any man who makes such a claim," he glared at Nothelm.

"Silence!" Ine roared, "We'll have no quarrel among ourselves. The enemy is down there. It is *they* who shall feel our wrath."

"Sire, I beg you, let me take the men of Dorset to the right. If it is true there are no Wealisc, we'll return at once to the fray."

"You may go with my blessing and God be with you, Aetheling."

"I must protest, King Ine."

"Enough! You have had your say, Nothelm, I have decided. We'll not sit idly by in a trap."

"Pah!"

Aethelheard led his men along the trail they had taken before, when following the Dumnonian host.

They had been marching for less than a mile when the Aetheling raised his hand and brought his men to a halt.

"Yonder!" he pointed, squinting to see better. The weak sun, reflecting, had produced a glint of metal. "Osburh, Guthred, do you see?"

They did. The unmistakeable movement of hundreds of men, approaching.

"Shield wall!" Aethelheard cried and the disciplined Dorset men interlocked shields, the front row kneeling, behind them men on foot did the same. Satisfied, Aethelheard called, "No man is to move until they are upon us. Make the Britons pay for not staying at home!"

"Ay!" came the roar of three hundred voices to contrast the war whoops of the Britons, their faces painted with blue pigment to create fear in the enemy.

The clash of the onrushing foe, breaking like waves upon the rock of the Saxon shields, mingled with the screams of the wounded. But the shield wall held firm and Aethelheard, unused to this situation, longed to break free and fight as in sword practice.

"Not yet, lord," came the urgent reply from Guthred to his garbled request. "We must hold firm until they weaken."

The Aetheling knew good sense when he heard it and contented himself with the limited jabs and thrusts the narrow gaps allowed him. Through one of these, to his dismay, came the slash of a Wealisc weapon across the hand of Osburh, whose sword fell from his grip whilst blood turned his hand crimson. To his credit, the young warrior redoubled his effort to hold his shield position but his hand was useless. Both he and Aethelheard stared in dismay at the hand dripping red.

"Now, Lord!" Guthred's voice was hoarse with fatigue.

"Up and at them, men!" Aethelheard thundered, and setting the example, leapt up and smote the foes before him. The Wealisc ranks buckled and those who stood their ground were hewn to the ground, whilst the others fled.

Wise to the tricks of the Britons, Aethelheard boomed in his loudest voice: "Hold! Regroup!"

Their bloodlust quelled and obedience assured, Aethelheard turned his attention to Osburh.

"It's bad!" he murmured, "We must bind the wound. You're losing too much blood."

"Lord!" A veteran of many campaigns pressed forward. "Horse dung, Lord – it stops the bleeding and helps heal the wound." He pointed at a fresh pile of dung steaming on the ground behind Aethelheard's mount.

Guthred nodded his agreement. "I've seen it done many a time. It's the best cure."

They led Osburh to the horse excrement and the veteran scooped a handful and slapped it on the back of Osburh's hand. "Stinks a bit, Lord, but it works a treat." He bound a cloth cut from the hem of his tunic around the hand.

"I'll be of little use today," Osburh said and his tone was glum. "How it throbs and my head spins."

"Because you've lost blood, but you can be proud of what you did," Aethelheard patted his back. "You held the shield wall even though wounded."

"So you did," Guthred said, "good man!" his smile was that of a proud father and comrade.

The sight that greeted them on the field by the river was not a happy one. King Ine's Saxons were in full flight. The Dumnonians had broken them and were in pursuit. Aethelheard hammered his sword on his shield and his men took up the beat with their own weapons.

"Charge!" yelled Aethelheard and his men followed him down the slope. It was enough to halt the Britons in their tracks and sufficient to allow the Saxons to unite with the men of Dorset.

"By God," said King Ine, "you saved the day, Aetheling. We are in your debt."

"You showed up too late!" Nothelm sneered, "We'd have beaten them with your men. At least we have slain Geraint mab Erbin."

"Nay, you'd have been picked off in the Wealisc trap. Whilst you were losing your battle, we won a great victory."

"Ay, it's true," Guthred glared at the Suth Seaxa king. "We wreaked slaughter among the blue-painted heathen."

They watched the Dumnonians push their boats into the Parrett and cross to return to their homeland.

"If God wills it, one day we'll return and Dumnonia will fall to West Seax," Ine muttered.

"It may be so, but you'll have to choose your men better," Nothelm scowled at Aethelheard.

Ine replied in mordant tone, "At least I'll know to whom I can entrust my host." He patted Aethelheard on the arm and smiled in his face.

"Pah!"

Aethelheard shot Nothelm a fearsome glare so the king of the Suth Seaxa turned his horse and trotted away to join his men.

"The man's an arrogant fool and I can break him just as I raised him," Ine said.

King Ine, grateful to Aethelheard, felt he could not do without his counsellor, so whereas Osburh and Guthred returned to Wimborne, they did so without their friend.

* * *

Rowena came to Wimborne Abbey, whiter-faced than usual, in a state of agitation. The sight of her in this condition made Cynethryth cling to the table for support. She feared dreadful news concerning her son.

"What ails you so, Rowena?"

"Sister, it is Osburh!" Her eyes swam with tears.

"Is he, is he...?"

"No! Not slain, but wounded. He risks losing his hand for it's infected and gone bad."

"So, where is he? Why did he not come?"

"Guthred is a stubborn fool!"

Cynethryth frowned, "What has Guthred to do with this?"

"Everything!" Rowena wailed. "They smeared horse shit on the wound and my fool husband says he's seen countless men cured that way, but it's gone bad like I said. He says if horse shit won't work, there's naught to be done. He's talking about chopping off the infected hand!" Rowena collapsed sobbing into the nun's arms.

"We'll see about that! Horse dung, indeed! You tell Osburh I'll save his hand if it's God's will and bring him here as fast as you can!"

They were back before nightfall and the enraged infirmarian wrinkled her nose in disgust at the mess and stench that greeted her senses as she unwrapped the wound. She held the cloth at arm's length between finger and thumb.

"Sister Sefled, burn this at once! Rowena, fetch a pail of fresh water from the well. Osburh sit you over there by the window, I need light to inspect the wound."

Until the water arrived, there was very little to inspect but when it did, she revealed the full horror of the infected wound. She took a knife as sharp as a razor and pared away at the edge of the slash, where the flesh was rotting.

"I know. I know, it hurts," she reassured him, "but it's the only way to save the hand."

Sweat beaded on Osburh's brow but through gritted teeth he said, "What use is a one-handed warrior?"

"Ignorant men!" Cynethryth snorted, "Horse dung and maiming is all they're good for. Now, this will hurt, Osburh, I'm going to wash the wound with vinegar. I find it combats infection."

"Aaargh! It stings!"

"Better this than a chopped off hand, believe me," the nun smiled encouragingly at the grim-faced Rowena. "Sister Sefled, bring me the salve in the blue glass jar – the one on the second shelf over the table. Ay, that's it, and find a fresh, clean bandage from the chest by the door."

Cynethryth studied for sufficient cleanliness of the raw flesh and felt sure that her salve would heal it. Only one tendon was slightly severed. He'd been lucky, she mused, as she stitched it with silk thread. How much longer the wound could have gone without the dreaded black decomposition setting in, she hated to guess. In that case, he would certainly have lost the hand.

"I made this ointment myself from the comfrey plant and lavender oil. It will heal the wound, Osburh, but you must aid the healing by keeping the hand away from muck and wetness – and keep it away from knocks and weights."

"I will, Sister, and bless you for what you've done. I truly feared for my hand."

"When you go back into battle, one day for sure you will, steer clear of wounds but if you, by mischance, receive a cut, never let anyone near it with horse shit – or the faeces of any other animal, for that matter!"

"I heed your words, sister."

"Now, tell me about the battle – about Aethelheard."

"He saved the king's life, I believe, sister. King Ine's convinced of it. Thanks to your son, we didn't fall into the Britons' well-laid trap. He fought like a lion to stop the Wealisc springing the snare on our unsuspecting flank and we fought them off. It was there I got this," he waved his bandaged hand.

"Keep it still! I've only just tended to it – *humph*, men!"

Osburh grinned at her. "Then guess what happened?"

"Do not tease or next time I'll use stronger vinegar!"

"Well, Aethelheard hastened back to the river, just in time. The men of Dumnonia had broken through in pursuit. All would have been lost if we hadn't appeared. For sure, the king would have been taken or slain."

"It wasn't God's will."

Rowena, who had remained tense and silent until now, spoke, "I'll wager Guthred took it ill that the battle ended at that point. He'll be itching to fight them again."

Cynethryth smiled sadly at her friend, "Aethelheard too, if I know ought about men."

"Dumnonia will have to wait," Osburh grinned, "at least until my hand's healed. How long do you think, sister?"

"At least three winters!" She winked at Rowena and laughed at Osburh's stricken expression.

"You'll be fine by the end of summer if you follow my instructions."

"I will, I promise!"

"Come back after another ten sunrises and we'll change the binding and treat it some more."

He came back alone at the appointed date, bearing gifts of silk and oriental spices. Of these, Cynethryth was particularly pleased with the roots of ginger because she could make of them various uses in the infirmary. How much the gifts were Osburh's own idea or the fruit of Rowena's gratitude, she had no way of telling. The greatest gift he bore, however, was news of Aethelheard. Osburh had received word from his friend and brought it faithfully to Cynethryth.

"King Ine has appointed Aethelheard commander of the *hearthweru*, his personal hearth-guard, a position of great trust and honour, accompanied by a huge stipend and the best arms and armour in the kingdom."

'*Clever boy! You've surpassed my wildest hopes!*'

She beamed at Osburh, but keeping these thoughts to herself, said, "That's wonderful news. He's in the king's favour."

"There's no-one more fitted to the post, sister," the faithful Osburh replied. "King Ine has also built a great fortress at Tantun. It makes Dorset safer from attack from the north."

Unimpressed with military matters, Cynethryth said,

"Let's look at that hand."

The infirmarian unbound the wound and inspected the cut. The jagged edges of the tear were closer together than ten days before and the flesh around the slash a much healthier colour.

"Gently, now, I want you to clench your fist."

He winced as he did so but she was pleased with the result.

"Osburh, there will be no lasting damage – unclench, good. Avoid making a fist until your next visit here after another ten sunrises. Only a scar will remain to remind you of your experience in the shield wall. You are a quick healer. Look sister, how it mends!"

Chapter 13

Cynethryth, who had been catching up on writing about her visions, was weary. At this warmer time of year, thankfully, there were only routine ailments to deal with and since Sefled was reliable, she left her assistant in charge and became involved only when called upon. Last week, Sefled, out of her depths with the blacksmith's eye, summoned her from the desk and her inky scratching. A small but sharp nail had rebelled under the craftsman's hammer, taking flight and piercing the left eyeball.

For such a muscular man, the smith proved less than stoical. Cynethryth, who needed to operate with delicacy, required his complete cooperation. The fellow's anxiety, constant flinching and restlessness hindered her. She gave him a draught to calm his nerves, which helped as did the eye drops that numbed the organ but she'd later swear the brute quaked when she approached his eye with tweezers. Sefled, almost fainting, did not help either. Nonetheless, Cynethryth extracted the nail, rinsed the eyeball with a saline solution and covered the wounded eye with a patch.

"God willing, master smith, you'll not lose the eye. Sister Sefled, pour yourself and the master a beaker of mead. You could both benefit from a drink!"

She laughed and returned to finish her account of meeting Constancy in Heaven.

Was it the fatigue of the day, the stressful challenge of the smith's eye, the heat of the evening or overdoing the writing? Whatever the cause, Cynethryth's night was disturbed by a vision. This was not a repeat of the effects of the tainted rye bread but on a wholly different scale. In her dream, Cynethryth was transported into the presence of the Lord. As she blurted out, still in ecstasy the next morning, to Sefled:

"Sister, the most incredible thing…I had another vision this night!" Her face radiated joy, "I met the Blessed Virgin, Mother of Our Lord…oh, Sefled, she's *so* beautiful, kind and loving, and she took me by the hand. Can you believe it?" The earnestness of her speech and the bliss in her expression made the impressionable young nun tremble. The infirmarian, her mentor, had *seen* the Virgin! "She led me into a chamber to a bed and there lay…" her voice rose and quavered, "…there lay her son, Our Lord, *Jesus Christ*! Sefled, He was alive! Yet, His wounds were fresh and His poor mother pointed to them with tears in her eyes and she led me to a shelf – just like ours – and asked me which salves to use to ease His pain. Why ask me? I'm unworthy! She is the Mother of God."

"It is a mystery, sister. But a sign from God!"

"A sign?"

"Ay, that you are a great healer, beloved of Our Lady in Heaven."

"Do you believe that, Sefled?"

"I do, sister, and I'll tell anyone the same!"

Unbeknown to Cynethryth, that is exactly what she did, blurting the whole tale to a group of young nuns. Her intentions were good, wishing only to demonstrate the brilliance of her mentor to all and sundry, but her enthusiasm had the opposite effect. Sefled might have minded her tongue had she noticed the malicious glint in the eye of the listening Wynflaed.

The time for revenge on the infirmarian had come when least expected! Wynflaed hurried off to seek her erstwhile friend, Leofwen, now risen to the heights of sub-prioress – one in authority – to whom this must be referred.

"... and she claims to have met the Virgin and Our Lord... and heed this... pretends the Virgin sought *her* advice. If that isn't the Devil talking... well, at the very least, it's *pride* – and that's a sin! And if it's not, it's *heresy*, that's what it is! Sister Cynethryth must be severely punished!"

"That is not for you to say, sister."

"You can't just do nothing!"

Leofwen, dismayed, stared at the floor, not least because she could no longer tolerate looking at the malignity in Wynflaed's face. She was torn between love and respect for Cynethryth and awareness of her duty to refer the matter to a higher authority, because, by now, the matter was the wonder of the nunnery.

She looked at Wynflaed and said, "I am well aware, sister, of my duty and will away to inform the prioress."

"I'll come with you for I am a witness."

How could she argue with that? But Leofwen's instinct to protect Cynethryth was stronger. The sub-prioress now drew upon her native cunning, "Nay, Sister, I shall go alone to my superior, for she must not misunderstand your religious zeal – and I can convey it better to her."

"Nay, sister, I shall go alone to my superior, for she must not misunderstand your religious zeal – and I can convey it better to her."

Wynflaed stared at her with mistrust but accepted with reluctance.

Leofwen sought the prioress and referred the matter, with her misgivings, to her immediate superior, whose thoughts followed the same course taken by those of Leofwen.

"We are obliged to inform the abbess of the facts – it has become the talk of the nunnery. It's not for us to judge, Sister

Leofwen. The matter is of great spiritual importance and beyond our competence – the abbess may even have to refer it to a higher authority still."

Leofwen paled and her hand shot to her mouth.

"The bishop! I *do* hope Sister Cynethryth isn't in trouble."

"Come with me to the abbess, Sister Leofwen, and we'll tell her what's afoot."

Abbess Cuthburga listened attentively to the sub-prioress's account and when she had concluded, turned to the prioress, more stern-faced than herself, but whose forbidding exterior disguised a gentle soul.

"Sister Quenburga, what's your opinion?"

The countenance of the prioress clouded with worry, "Mother, forgive me, these are matters beyond the competence permitted by my poor preparation."

A dimple formed in the cheek of the abbess, "Sister, do not hide behind your undoubted modesty."

The nun flushed, "Forgive my presumption, Mother, but I believe our infirmarian is a good soul and would never vaunt spiritual superiority. But I fear there may be others who would accuse her of unwonted pride in that sense.

The abbess looked shrewdly at Leofwen, "By chance, does the first accusation come from Sister Wynflaed, Sub-Prioress?"

"I fear it does, Mother, but–"

"But, what?"

"The accusations are not entirely unfounded."

"Why?"

"Because, Mother, the facts were referred immediately by Sister Sefled, the assistant infirmarian."

"I know who Sister Sefled is, Leofwen!"

The sub-prioress flushed, "Forgive me, Mother."

Prioress Quenburga intervened, "If I might, I believe Sister Leofwen means to say the tale has stirred our community – for good or ill – and we cannot simply ignore it."

The abbess's brow wrinkled, "That is indeed the point, sisters. We cannot and will not! This cannot be whispered in the cloisters and behind closed doors. It must be dealt with in the open and we must hear what Sister Cynethryth has to say and also what say her accusers. For this reason, I will convene the whole community to a hearing."

The abbess appeared pensive, and continued, "Tell me, you who were her friend, Sister Leofwen, why does this Wynflaed dislike our infirmarian so?"

Leofwen looked uncomfortable and twisted her fingers in her other hand, "I believe she is jealous, Mother, of my friendship with Sister Cynethryth," the nun, as ever, flushed. The abbess favoured her with another dimple, "You will know the saying, *birds of a feather flock together*, so my sweet linnet, we have a cuckoo in the nest!"

* * *

That same afternoon, the sisters trooped dutifully to the chapter hall near the church. The air filled with excited chatter and only when the mother superior entered and stood on the dais did silence reign before her severe scowl. The sisters knew why the abbess had assembled them, so her words of explanation, rehearsed and measured, did nothing to change the general opinion that the infirmarian was on trial.

"Sister Cynethryth," the abbess called in a strong unwavering voice, "step forward here beside me and tell what happened to you in the night."

All eyes turned to the familiar figure as she approached the abbess, her head bowed and hands clasped in front of her. The majority of the congregation felt pity for her but some less noble spirits rejoiced in her discomfiture – and a few of these immediately felt ashamed.

"Mother, I make no claims..."

"Speak up, sister, we cannot hear a word!"

Cynethryth looked around at the expectant faces and wished she was anywhere but there. She was at once aware of the gravity of her situation. She risked expulsion from the abbey, her home, from the work she loved. She gathered her courage and tried, "Mother, I make no claims about what I saw or dreamt – I cannot be sure if it was a dream or a vision," – she went on to describe the scene with the Virgin and if nothing else was comforted by the awed expressions of her audience."

When her account ended, the abbess announced, "We are assembled here to take a decision, sisters. You have heard what our Infirmarian has said. We must decide whether she is blessed by God or tainted by the Devil's handiwork. I find in what our sister has said no cause for condemnation, but should anyone else be of a different mind, I would hear her now or forever hold her peace, let us be clear on this."

Sister Wynflaed hesitated. She did not like the drift of the abbess's argument but now was her moment and she would not waste it in useless hesitation. She pushed her way to the front of the assembly. Everyone peered at her, some on tiptoe, craning the neck for a better sighting.

"I, Mother, would like to say that the Bible teaches us that pride is a sin born of Satan's whisperings. I accuse our infirmarian of heeding his seductive urgings. Can she claim to be wiser than the Mother of Our Lord?"

Angry murmurings greeted these words.

Pale-faced, Cynethryth tried to defend herself, "I make no such–"

"Silence!" The abbess cried, "We shall hear the accusations first! Continue, Sister Wynflaed."

"Then there's the matter of the crucifixion. Is our infirmarian, in her wisdom, trying to tell us that Our Saviour didn't die on the cross? Heresy!" she screamed, and pointed at the trembling nun. "I say we must punish her – send her away. She's not worthy to be in a religious house…!"

"Hold!" The abbess's face showed her outrage. "How dare you, Sister Wynflaed! I asked for your accusations, not your judgment. It is not your place to judge. I'll remind you all, if you need reminding, that *I* am Abbess of Wimborne and as such, God's voice in this house."

"*S*-sorry, Mother!"

"So you should be, child. I wonder at your motives. Your accusations are most grave and cannot be dismissed out of hand but I ask you to reflect on your hasty judgment. How would the abbey manage without its infirmarian?"

Accepting lost for lost, Wynflaed plucked up her courage, "As to that Mother, everybody knows that the assistant, Sefled, has surpassed her mentor."

"That's a lie!"

All heads turned to seek the speaker.

"I'm here, Mother," Sefled raised her hand, "only last week there was an accident and our smith came to us with a nail in his eye." The audience met her words with collective gasps and groans. "Had I not been able to call on Sister Cynethryth and her vast knowledge, the blacksmith would have lost his eye as sure as I stand here. Our infirmarian, the Lord be praised, saved his sight!"

"Thank you, sister for your testimony and *loyalty*," the abbess spat the word at Wynflaed. "The time has come for me to make a decision and let it be noted that whatever I decide is the will of God, incontestable and final."

She gazed around at the upturned countenances, agog to hear her verdict, adding, "Hence there will be no more gossip or comments on this subject. I find no pride in the infirmarian's words. Quite the contrary, as she made it clear, quite modestly, she cannot distinguish between a dream and a vision. Let us say that she dreamt last night. As to that, the Bible, which Sister Wynflaed is so fond of quoting, was also subject of Pope Gregory the Great's commentary. I feel sure, sisters, you will give more credence to

Pope Gregory than to Wynflaed – he who sent Saint Augustine to bring our faith to these shores!" There was a ripple of suppressed titters around the hall and Wynflaed's cheeks flamed red. "The Pope," the abbess continued, "referring to the Book of Job, in his *Moralia in Job,* says, 'The voice of God is indeed heard in dreams, when with a tranquil mind there is quiet from the action of the world and in the silence of mind divine precepts are perceived.' Moreover, it is no heresy to say Christ didn't die *after* the crucifixion. We all believe in the resurrection, do we not?"

The abbess crossed her arms and stared around the room as if she were challenging each and every one of the sisters. "I declare that Sister Cynethryth is blameless, indeed blessed by the approval of the Lord for her calling. Let no-one dare say otherwise, lest they blaspheme. As for you miserable sinner," she pointed at the quailing Wynflaed, "I find that you are motivated by jealousy and spite…"

"*I*-I–"

"Silence! Your words have done enough harm and it's not the first time you've surrendered to the promptings of the Devil. There is no place for you in this House of God. Be gone! You are banished from Wimborne and your veil is rescinded."

This time, the gasp around the hall echoed from the rafters.

Wynflaed's visage contorted with malice and she spat like an enraged feline, "You can't do this! My father will withdraw his gold from this abbey!"

"Your father may be a nobleman but there is nothing noble about *you*!" said Cuthburga, emanating royalty. "God will provide for this abbey."

Wynflaed's thin face twisted with spite and she pointed a trembling finger at Cynethryth, "Don't think you've won! This isn't over. I'll make you pay for this, see if I don't."

Cynethryth paled at the sheer venom in the words but reflected as she watched her retreat, *what can Wynflaed do to me from outside these walls?*

As always, fear of the unknown disturbs one's faith in the future, but for the moment, Cynethryth enjoyed affection from the abbess, the prioress, Leofwen, Sefled and many others down to the humblest oblate.

Chapter 14

Returned to the infirmary, Cynethryth and her assistant stared at each other and exchanged timid smiles.

"I'm glad that's over," Sefled said.

"And I must thank you for your loyal intervention, sister."

"I only spoke the truth. Oh, how I wish I had your knowledge and wisdom."

Cynethryth pursed her lips and stared at the younger woman, "Which do you think is more important?"

"They're the same thing, surely."

"Of course they aren't! One comes from contemplation, reasoning, thoughts and learning; the other derives from the senses, observations, habits and intuition."

"I'm afraid I don't understand, sister."

At these words Cynethryth made a decision: she would repay the girl's loyalty by making her achieve all of her promise through understanding. Sefled would become a great infirmarian even if it meant her own patience, like now, would be tested. She warmed to her argument.

"Do you think you can smell like a hound can smell?"

"Of course not, sister."

"Can you see like a hawk can see?"

Sefled laughed and looked puzzled.

"Nay, but why do you ask?"

"Because I'm talking about your consciousness and what exists beyond it. Think of your perception as an endless dark field, Sefled. You have five senses – sight, sound, smell, touch and taste, do you not? Well, think of each as a small bright light that illuminates one minute corner of that field, to uncover reality. None of us ever captures the whole field."

"I'm beginning to understand."

"Good, because luckily we have the power to think, sister, and it is our way to reach into the blackness beyond the lone, isolated light cast by our senses. You see, our senses are limited but thought enables us to create knowledge."

"Do you mean thinking allows us to build knowledge, sister?"

"Ay, but the five senses allow us to create wisdom. Let me explain better. Think of our mother superior and of a fisherman. The abbess has great knowledge, does she not?"

Sefled nodded vigorously, "Indeed. Think how she quoted Pope Gregory at the hearing. She is very learned."

"Exactly, *learned* – you say well. But what of our fisherman? He can't read. But he is wise, he knows about the sea, the weather and the currents. His experience comes from mistakes and the lesson drawn from each. So now, Sefled, you are on a boat at sea and there's a storm brewing. Who would you rather be with – the abbess? Or the fisherman?"

"The fisherman would know how to act."

"True, but the abbess has faith and would pray."

"I now see the difference between knowledge and wisdom, sister."

"What you must do is apply it to your duties as an infirmarian."

"My own choice is for wisdom, sister."

Cynethryth glared at her and Sefled looked crestfallen.

"Foolish child! Have you learnt nothing? You need *both* to become a truly great infirmarian. You must shine a light on the darkness – use your intuition but also your reason and observe! We can feel our way ahead in the darkness but like the fisherman, act in harmony with our surroundings. Understand this and maybe Wynflaed will be right about one thing, sister – one day you will surpass me as an infirmarian. You are young but have time and intelligence in your favour!"

* * *

Outside the abbey walls, Wynflaed, setting aside her resentment to think calmly, came to the conclusion that she had shed her shackles. She was well aware that she had never had a calling, a vocation. Like many young noblewomen without means, she had been sent away to the nunnery in Barking as her father's convenient method of ridding himself of a burden. She was free, at last, to live her life as she pleased but under no illusions as to the hardships that faced her. What might become of a young penniless noblewoman without a home? This was the fault of the damned infirmarian! She would have her revenge if it was the last thing she did on this Earth. But that lay in the future, for now, she had more urgent problems like where to find shelter.

Her eldest brother had drowned in a storm, a shipwreck off the Dumnonian coast. Her second brother was Bishop of Worcester and no doubt would drive away a shame-faced, un-veiled nun. Her elder sister returned her hatred – as children they fought over their father's affection – and Waerburh always succeeded in wheedling her way into his good graces. Somehow, Wynflaed was always to blame for anything untoward. Now her sister, ever the lucky one, profiting from a dowry she, Wynflaed, would never have, was married to a cousin of King Ine and had given him two children. Of the possibilities open to her, only her father remained, but she feared his wrath. He had placed her in Barking Abbey and grudgingly transferred, with her, his patronage to Wimborne. She might well persuade him to use that money on providing for her. She'd offer to pray for the soul of her dear departed mother, but would he see her with jaundice as a failed nun?

She carried these thoughts with her as she trudged forth, heading for her father's estate near Lunden. Surely, he would think it much better that her righteous sisters at Wimborne continued to recommend her mother's soul to the Lord! However, where else could she go if not to him?

The answer to this came in the most surprising way, inducing Wynflaed to believe the opportunity heaven-sent. As she tramped along the ancient Roman road running eastwards, the whinny of a horse made her turn and stare back the way she'd come. A short procession of various riders, men and women, reined in to greet her. She had not cast off her wimple nor removed the wooden cross dangling from her belt so it came as no surprise to her when the first horseman greeted her as 'sister', "Sister, where are you bound? It is unsafe for a young woman to wander the land alone."

"God will protect me. I am on a mission," she replied vaguely, hoping to gain some advantage. To her immense satisfaction this ploy brought immediate results.

"As are we, sister. We are on pilgrimage, bound for the tomb of Saint Lewinna at Bishopstone."

Wynflaed had never before heard the name of the saint nor the place but a sly glint came to her eye, "The Lord be praised! He has answered my prayers! I too am bound for Bishopstone on the command of my abbess. But tell me, why are you directed there, good fellow?"

"The saint has performed many miracles and my daughter" – the man pointed to a girl on a donkey – "is losing her sight. Saint Lewinna will intercede and restore her to health. Bless the Lord, sister, now we have found you and are put to the test, and we'll not be found wanting." Wynflaed wondered what he meant but he explained. "The Lord wishes us to succour a lone and vulnerable woman and so we shall! You will ride with us to Bishopstone and share our food and lodgings. I offer this up to the Lord."

"I accept, my friend. You are a true Christian and I'll pray for your daughter's health." Wynflaed was quick of thought and knew that she might easily lose credibility, so before being exposed, she said, "My mother superior sent me out alone as a penance, but the Almighty is a loving Father and has directed you to me. The abbess told me where to go but told me naught about Lewinna. I beg you to enlighten me, brother."

The traveller, a wealthy cloth merchant, flattered by the nun's epithet for him, invited her to ride in front of him on his horse. He promised to relate what he knew of the saint as they rode. In truth, his thoughts were far from spiritual. His wife, whom he had left behind in Gloucester to tend to the household, was not with them, otherwise he would never have dared invite a young woman to ride so close. He leapt at the excuse to clasp an arm around her slender waist, and the recounting of a tale to press his cheek against her wimple-covered ear.

"The story of Lewinna is a sad one, sister. I hope not to distress you. As you know, Bishopstone is in the land of the Suth Seaxa and, until not long ago, when Saint Wilfrith converted them, they were savage pagans. The family of Lewinna was among the first to accept baptism at the hands of Wilfrith. Are you sure you can bear to hear this?" The merchant squeezed the soft waist of the nun in a false gesture of reassurance.

Wynflaed placed a hand over his invasive one in complicity, "I beg you, have no fear, I am stronger than you think, brother."

Encouraged, the merchant pressed on and pressed closer, "The heathens surrounding the family wouldn't tolerate Christians among them and one day burst into Lewinna's home. They ordered them to worship their gods but her parents refused. Lewinna begged them to spare her mother and father but by way of reply the brutes clove her head with an axe – and she but eleven winters old! This happened but thirty-seven winters ago. Ever since, the heavenly merits of the virgin martyr are daily shown, sister, for she cures the blind, the crippled and the sick. They say the walls of the church are filled with parchments in written testimony to the cures. I hope to pin my own testimony there for the curing of my dearest Eldreda."

"And so you shall, brother, I'm sure of it!"

The journey passed in pleasant conversation and Wynflaed often looked at the rough road below the horse's hoofs and thanked her luck that she was not tramping it alone. From time to time, the merchant returned to the matter of her penance but she fobbed him off by saying she could not talk of her sins with a layman. The idea of her waywardness gave him impure thoughts, made worse by the warmth of her body close to his. In spite of years of closure in the abbey, she was aware of her attractiveness to men but had no intention of wasting herself on a merchant with a paunch – however wealthy he might be, and to hear him, he was laden with gold –Wynflaed aimed higher. Her vengeful plan involved men far more noble and prominent than her current Samaritan.

For this reason, when they stopped at a wayside inn for the night, she accepted a meal paid for by him but refused to share his bed, acting the part of an outraged nun. She tempered her recitation, because she still needed him for protection, food and transport. Skilfully, she flirted and led him to believe that in the near future she might be swayed by his 'charms', although she'd far rather grasp a burning brand from the hearth.

At the next inn, in Kingsham, where she learnt the court of King Nothelm resided, she stole away from the boring company of the pilgrims because she had no wish to visit the tomb of Saint Lewinna or of any other saint. Her motives were far more earthbound and driven by revenge.

Chapter 15

Had Wynflaed paid the slightest attention to her biblical study classes, she might have been better equipped not to set off along the path of spiteful revenge. Impelled by a character formed by unfortunate circumstances, which well pre-dated her acquaintance with either Cynethryth or Leofwen, she embodied the nominated sins she had yawned through. There was a deceitfulness within her heart that wilfully hid her motives and beliefs from her conscious view. Had she not been picking at a thread at the hem of her tunic when the prioress alerted her class to Jeremiah 17:9 – *the heart is deceitful above all things, and desperately sick; who can understand it?* – she might have questioned the resentment that directed and motivated her behaviour.

When she discovered that her noble cousin, the young aetheling Cynewulf, was in exile at the court of King Nothelm, she considered that divine providence had predisposed for her to wreak vengeance. As a noblewoman and a nun, she gained easy admittance to the royal palace since at Kingsham her disgrace was unknown to any but herself.

Cynewulf was as pleased to greet his cousin as she was to see him. She was too realistic to know that she could not hope to wed the handsome young prince. Bitterly, she accepted that without a considerable bride-gift, her lot was to remain unwed. Nor could she, purporting to be a nun, hope to seduce him, but her natural cunning told her that she could exert her charms to bend his will to hers, and she had a plan.

The key to this, she believed, was to bide her time, get to know him, his ambitions, weaknesses and strengths. Wynflaed could be pleasant company when she put her mind to it – as long as nobody crossed her – as when frequenting Cynewulf, who found his pretty cousin thoroughly engaging. As a result, they spent ever more time together. Cynewulf did not begrudge the cost of the small amount his fair relative ate and drank. It was a reasonable outlay for her sparkling conversation and generous smiles. Meanwhile, she listened avidly to his conversations with his friends to learn about his desires and motives. What interested her in particular was when heads huddled, voices lowered and conspiratorial looks were exchanged. She gleaned enough to realise that Cynewulf's bosom harboured a hatred of King Ine and a desire to take his throne. The aetheling, in unguarded moments told his admirers that he had a stronger claim to rule Wessex than the king, or anyone else.

On one of these occasions, when they were alone, Wynflaed took the first step on her self-appointed trail of revenge.

"Cousin, I believe I can aid you in your quest to overthrow the tyrant."

The aetheling's expression betrayed his incredulity.

"*You?* How could you possibly do that?"

She gave him her most flirtatious smile, widened her eyes and held his interested gaze for just long enough.

"I have information that will interest you and which you can use to your advantage."

"Let's hear it, then!"

His tone was unconvinced and challenging but began to change into fascination as she revealed everything she knew about Aethelheard.

"The son of Caedwalla, you say?"

The awesome implications of her words transfixed him like a seax to the gut. There could only be one person with a better claim than he to the throne, and until today, nobody suspected that the late sainted king had sired a son.

"Are you sure of what you say, Wynflaed?"

"As sure as a kingfisher devours fish."

She went on to explain how she had come by this information.

"So, his mother is the infirmarian in your abbey. Are you sure nobody else knew about this, except King Cuthred?"

"Quite sure, well, except for the abbess and one or two of the nuns but they are closed in the abbey and have no importance."

"You know what this means, don't you? You have found me a terrible rival, who may thwart my hopes."

She looked with affected fondness at his disconsolate countenance and repeated the earlier charming smile.

"What?"

"Dearest cousin, on the contrary. If you move with cunning and stealth, you will rid yourself of both Ine and Aethelheard in one stroke."

I have him eating out of my hand and his tail's wagging!

"How can that be?"

She gave a throaty laugh at the eagerness on his face.

"I haven't told you the most important thing yet."

Now, his eyes widened as he hung on her words.

"Nor will, I," she teased, "unless you make me a promise."

His pale blue eyes clouded with concern and barely suppressed ire.

"What promise?"

She placed her tiny hand delicately over his wide knuckles and stared into his eyes until the hardness melted away.

"You must promise to take me with you to Winchester, protect me from my enemies, and allow me to guide your actions in this matter."

"As to the first two requests, how could I refuse? But the third–"

"To guide you? Well, the plan is mine and it must be subtle. It's beset with peril and requires feminine guile."

She gave him the most bewitching smile she could muster and she – for whom it was normal to be so deceived about her sinfulness that she was stubbornly unaware of her internal corruption – hastened to take the fateful step.

"Promise?"

Cynewulf sighed and joined her in this macabre dance.

"Very well, I promise. Now tell me, what is this *most important thing*?"

Wynflaed paused, looked around the tavern to be sure nobody was eavesdropping, crooked a finger to bring his head closer to hers and whispered in his ear.

Shocked, and fully aware of the import of her words, he placed his other hand over hers, pressing it between his, as if to seal a pact.

"Cousin, fate has sent you to me! The way is clear," he opined.

"It is! And we'll do it together."

"Wait!" Cynewulf's face showed his suspicion. "Why? What is in this for you, my cousin?"

She smiled for she'd been awaiting these words.

"Do you find me attractive?" She gauged his reaction and modified her approach, "Do not fret, I don't ask you to make me your queen, but as King of Wessex, you will be able to offer me what I dearly wish for."

"And what is that? Do I need to fear your ambitions?"

"Nothing that will cost you dear, my cousin, but something that you may grant with ease. We will talk about it when I've helped you become king."

He wondered what it might be but his real concern was to take the throne and if his guileful relative made good her promise, he wouldn't worry. By her own words, he need not wed her. He studied the pert upturned nose and oval face, not that she wasn't a dainty dish to set his juices flowing! As he gazed, he felt shame – she was a nun. Almost as if she could read his thoughts, she withdrew her hand and looked demure. But in her heart she felt only triumph.

She thought it better to steer him away from their plot for the moment. Aware of the dangers of a revolt, she needed to prepare their movements with great care. As far as she was concerned, the fall of King Ine was incidental. Her real aim was to destroy Aethelheard and, in so doing, break the heart of her enemy, Cynethryth. She led the conversation to safer ground, to subjects that would perhaps bore a young nobleman but that would cast a favourable light on herself. Hence she told him what she had learnt about the local martyr, Saint Lewinna, associating in his mind, she hoped, herself with the piety and steadfastness of the unfortunate virgin. Inevitably, the conversation touched upon the pilgrims and to hear Wynflaed, she had been a paragon of virtue in resisting the advances of the lecherous merchant.

"He'd better not come to Kingsham," Cynewulf said, his tone gruff, "else I'll teach him a lesson he'll never forget. A man must show respect to a noble lady and to her calling."

Wynflaed smiled sweetly and took his hand again, "Cousin, I see you take your promise to protect me most seriously."

He looked into her sparkling eyes and an involuntary shudder ran down his spine. What was it? Did he suddenly realise where this seemingly virtuous, helpless nun was leading him, behind the sweet smiles and flashing eyes? To the murder of his king! Ay, she was dangerous all right. He would tread carefully with leaden-footed steps. In this mood, with this realisation, he was happy not to return that evening to the subject of their plot.

Over the next few weeks, they spent as much time as usual together but neither raised the matter until one day Wynflaed said, "Cousin, we should begin our preparations."

The thought thrilled him but he had long accepted she would be the one – the guileful one – to set the scheme in motion.

"What must I do?"

"With great caution, you must find young men from powerful families who loathe the king. Men, who will be prepared to sustain you in your quest to seize the throne. Cynewulf, do you know any such scions?"

He stared in silence and although his gaze was upon her, he was not seeing her, but was elsewhere in thought. At last, he spoke, "Ay, I know of two in particular, but how do you counsel, cousin? Each is descended from Cerdric and claims the throne, so it would be like inviting my greatest rivals to unite with me. I fear no man but it seems unwise to tempt the wolf into the sheep pen."

Wynflaed looked unperturbed and said, "Instead, these are the men we need. You can leave them to me. They will not take the throne from you. Trust me. Can you get word to them? Bring them to Kingsham."

He looked into her shining eyes, and beguiled by her reassuring smile, agreed to send a message to Ealdberht and to Oswald, both exiled aethelings like himself. Once more, the cold feeling ran down his spine.

Intrigued by the nature of the message and reassured by the recent detachment of Nothelm from his kinsman, King Ine, the two princes came to Kingsham. Sheltering these two exiles had been the principal reason for the threatened invasion of Est Seax. Aware themselves of the need for caution, Suth Seax being so close to West Seax and doubtless full of spies, they presented themselves to King Nothelm with assurances of their peaceable intentions.

They brought this caution to their first meeting with Cynewulf. The presence of the innocuous nun, his cousin, at the meeting left them indifferent. She, however, was not aloof, and used her time with them to assess their characters. Her subtle probing did not alert them to her soundings and in a surprisingly short time, she had the measure of them both. When they took their leave, Wynflaed replied to Cynewulf's questioning.

"Ealdberht is the strong character. He will need careful handling. As for Oswald, he's ambitious but headstrong. Did you see how he chafes at being forced into caution? He will be easy to handle. What you need to do now for some months, cousin, is to win their trust. Do not mention our scheme nor give them the slightest inkling of what's afoot, but take every opportunity to speak ill of Ine and above all, encourage them to confide in you their hatred of him. Try to elicit any schemes they might have to move against the king but do not let yourself be drawn into them. I shall not be involved with them until we are completely sure the moment is right."

Cynewulf grinned into her confident face. Something of her calm conviction had rubbed off on him. The scepticism he had felt when she first mooted the plan had evaporated. Not even his respect for the physical prowess of the mighty Ealdberht troubled him anymore. Seated at table, Ealdberht still loomed menacingly. Before meeting Wynflaed, he would have thought twice about deceiving the hulking warrior. Now, instead, he had faith in the duplicity of his cousin. Becoming king had been his lifelong ambition but never had it seemed as plausible as now, thanks to this slip of a nun next to him. Her sly mind was more than a match for the aethelings. He had seen how she'd elicited information from them without them once suspecting a thing.

As he studied her visage, he mused, she was changeable like a day in March. At this moment, he saw a foxiness in her expression that had replaced the sweet innocence of earlier. There! That shiver down his back again, was it possible that it only occurred when he was close to Wynflaed?

Chapter 16

Kingsham, Sussex, late-summer, 712 AD

"My friend, what joy to see you! What brings you to Kingsham? Do you mean to stay a while or are you passing through? What news of my mother?"

Osburh looked at his lifelong companion with affection. How he had missed his restless energy, manifested now in this bombardment of questions.

"Let's begin with your last question. Sister Cynethryth, bless her, is in fine health and sends greetings and a recommendation."

"What would that be?"

"Be not rash and restless."

"What makes me think that is *your* counsel?"

The sheepish grin spoke for itself, but Osburh continued, holding out his hand for perusal, "She saved my hand, your mother, another couple of days and I'd have lost it! All I have is this reminder, thanks to her skill."

Aethelheard gazed at the jagged white scar running across the back of Osburh's hand.

"At least, you bear the badge of honour for our day's work in Somerset."

"You, instead, my friend, are commander of the king's *hearth-weru*."

His hand was still outstretched and he clenched and opened his fist several times. "See," he went on, "no lasting damage thanks to the infirmarian. I can wield my sword as before and dare say, I'd overcome you in practice."

"I'll not rise to your bait, Os," he said, touching his cheek with his fingertips, "lest I spy a pretty maid and you repeat your sly trick. It was as well my mother is so skilled. I hate to think what my face would be like otherwise. How I miss her! It seems our wyrd is to be apart. I wonder what she's doing now?"

* * *

Wimborne Abbey, Dorset, late-summer, 712 AD

In the absence of her son, Cynethryth was giving her attention and affection to her assistant, more like a daughter to her.

"Sefled, we should focus on the interrelated patterns of four."

"I don't understand, sister."

Cynethryth laughed, she enjoyed arousing her helper's curiosity by being deliberately vague. She believed it made the young woman more attentive and eager to learn.

"There are the four elements – fire, air, water, and earth – the four seasons, the four humours, the four parts of the earth, and the four major winds, are there not?"

Sefled had to agree but wondered where the infirmarian was leading the conversation. Surely there was more important work to do.

"There's an inter-balance of the four humours – blood, phlegm, black bile, and yellow bile – and it's unique, based on their correspondence to superior and inferior elements—blood and phlegm correspond to the celestial elements of fire and air, and the two biles correspond to the terrestrial elements of water and earth. This is the theory I'm working on, Sefled. It's a little vague and we must discuss it for me to refine my thoughts."

The assistant infirmarian was flattered but did not have enough knowledge about the humours to make an intelligent comment. True, Sister Cynethryth had spoken about them to her in the past and to please her mentor now, she said, "Sister, you told me about plants being the direct counterpart of the humours and elements within the human body, whose imbalance causes disease."

"Good, Sefled! So you *did* pay attention. My theory is that the disease-causing imbalance of these humours results from the improper dominance of the subordinate humours. This disharmony is similar to that introduced to the world by Adam and Eve in the Fall. I believe that marked the entrance of disease and humoral imbalance into humankind."

"In class, Sister Quenburga told us the disobedience of Eve led to all our sufferings on Earth. But please tell me more about your theory, sister."

Cynethryth wanted this reaction, for her aim was to make Sefled into a freethinking nun and not a slave to the teachings expounded by the Church and heard in this abbey. She did not for a moment believe that Adam had such a small part in the Fall as priests – men – would have them believe. But she did not mention this, she did not want to make of Sefled a rebel or a heretic, but the best possible infirmarian. She continued, "Men suffer diverse illnesses. This comes from the phlegm which is superabundant within them. Had man remained in paradise, I maintain he would not have had the flegmata within his body, from which many evils proceed, but his flesh would have been whole and without dark livor."

"Pardon me, sister, but what is livor?"

"It is the black humour. Since Adam consented to evil and relinquished good, he was made into a likeness of the earth, which produces good and useful herbs, as well as bad and useless ones. Is that not true, Sefled?"

What could she say? It was a self-evident truth. But she wanted to show her real interest in the discussion and prove her intelligence, so she wrinkled her brow and contributed, "Does the soil itself not contain both good and evil moistures?" She looked embarrassed and hastened to add, "I mean, on the way to Wareham, there's soil where good plants would die. It's boggy ground."

Cynethryth's smile was encouraging, "It's important to talk with you, Sefled, you have a quick mind and aid my thoughts. You see, just like the ground, men's bodies can be good or bad. Arising from the Fall, the first evil, flesh can be ulcerated and permeable to disease. I'm convinced these sores create a storm and smoky moisture inside men, from which the flegmata arise and coagulate, which then cause infirmities."

"Do you mean, sister, that if Adam had remained in Paradise, he would have enjoyed the sweetest health?"

"Exactly, and the best dwelling-place. So, making do with our imperfect earthly abode, my dear assistant, it must become our life's work to understand, combat and conquer these poisons and phlegm and diverse illnesses man has within himself due to the Fall."

Sefled's countenance shone with the enthusiasm the vocation of healing, albeit a calling chosen for her, always evoked.

"Sister, we two women must be like some men who are warriors, called to fight and quell the foe. Our enemy is disease."

"How best do you think we can fight this battle, Sefled?"

The young nun looked shrewdly at her mentor, knowing that the infirmarian did not start conversations idly. The answer to this question would be the point of the lesson. She took a moment, then said brightly, "We must ponder, sister, to reach into the blackness beyond the lone, isolated light cast by our senses so that we can create the knowledge needed to wield against disease."

Cynethryth was overjoyed, she clapped her hands in delight and rushed to embrace her startled assistant.

"Never did an infirmarian have such a treasure by her side! Oh, Sefled, one day, when I'm gone, you'll take my mantle and surpass your teacher."

Sefled looked fearful, "Do not say such a thing, sister, you are not planning to leave us, are you?"

Cynethryth laughed, "I'm not, but life is not predictable, sister, you must be ready for anything."

"Sister Cynethryth, I thank you for your opinion of me, but you know as well as I, there's so much for me to learn. I can't bear the thought of being without you!"

"Come then, I wish to show you a document about the humours I brought from Barking Abbey. It will interest and instruct you."

"Sit there," said Cynethryth before selecting a roll of parchment from a shelf, "study this. I'll tend to our patients this afternoon, then test your knowledge. Do not simply learn without question, make a note of your doubts or even better, suggestions...we must extend our knowledge, Sefled."

With this, she left her assistant and strode into the sickroom.

* * *

Kingsham, Sussex, late-summer, 712 AD

Having stabled the horses, the broad-shouldered youth with striking copper-gold hair knotted back, strutted into the king's hall and increased his swaggering, that of a man who must prove himself. He smiled at those staring at him with an assurance that belied his age and well-hidden insecurity.

"Aelfhere!" Osburh called and beckoned his brother to him.

"Is it Aelfhere? I haven't seen him for years," Aethelheard said. "Welcome to Kingsham! You're quite the warrior now."

"I'll be frank, Aethelheard, that's why we're here. You are commander of the *hearthweru* and I seek a place by your side for Aelfhere. He's better than me with a sword and thus, by definition, better than you!"

Aethelheard scowled then grinned, "By all I hold dear, Osburh, today you long for an urgent departure from this world!"

"Do not be offended, old friend, I merely press the case for my brother."

"You've convinced me in part."

"In part?"

"When you said he was a better swordsman, for I remember all your drubbings at my hands."

Osburh was about to reply but thought better of it – he needed a favour, so he contented himself with a grin, shared by Aelfhere, for a different reason.

"What about you?" Aethelheard frowned, "Do you not wish to join the king's hearth-guard?"

"What I wish and what I must do are two different things. I must return to Wareham. Father grows old and has been unwell of late. It was mother's idea to seek this place for Aelfhere with you."

"Very well. Come, Aelfhere, I will show you around, explain your duties and present you to your comrades. As for you, if you have the strength to lift a beaker of ale, refresh yourself." He called a servant and gave instructions, turned to Osburh and said, "See you later. Duty calls!"

* * *

Seated in a tavern in another part of Kingsham, tension was running high between Cynewulf and Wynflaed.

"It's easy for you to counsel patience, cousin, but time waits for no man. My friends are becoming impatient and as you often point out, we need them to further our plan. Still you insist the time isn't right to reveal the details to them."

Wynflaed winced at the anger in his voice but what could they do? A misguided revolt would be disastrous. King Ine had his supporters and had surrounded himself with a ring of steel organised by that fool, Aethelheard. Except that he was no simpleton – she grudgingly recognised his prowess, loyalty and intelligence. He was a dangerous foe but one she had promised to herself to destroy. The problem vexing her was how to corrupt him if they could not approach him. To make matters worse, instead of helping, Cynewulf spent his time fretting about Ealdberht and Oswald, whose impatience, at least, was justified. She broke off her musing to listen to what her cousin was saying.

"They are weary of waiting and have made contact with Rhodri the Bald and Grey, King of Gwynneth. Ealdberht says that if he can persuade Rhodri to join with King Gwylog ap Beli of Powys, who is near to conflict with Mercia, there will be strife."

"I fail to see how that helps us," Wynflaed's petulant tone irked him.

Exasperated, Cynewulf snapped, "It's better than waiting around uselessly for your scheme to bear fruit, which it never does! If Powys and Gwynneth join together against Mercia, the route to Wessex opens alarmingly. It's clear Ine would never stand for that. He'd be dragged into war and, as Ealdberht says, either he's killed in battle or he loses and will take the blame for joining in a futile war with Coelred of Mercia. Mercia has never been a friend to Wessex."

"Ah!" sneered Wynflaed, and what if they defeat the Wealisc? Have you thought of that? Ine's power will increase and he'll have a strong ally in Mercia."

They sat in hostile silence for a few minutes but Wynflaed would not surrender her plan so easily.

At last she spoke, "Why do you refuse to meet Aethelheard yourself?"

"How many times must I tell you? He mistrusts me from our days together in Wareham when he too came close to exile. Have you become slow-witted outside your abbey walls?"

Wynflaed narrowed her eyes. She needed no reminding that without the support of a religious house, she had nothing except his goodwill to sustain her. She sweetened her voice, "Dear cousin, the great prize will not fall into our lap like a ripe pear from its branch, it has to be striven for. If only I could have Aethelheard's ear, I'd convince him to act in a trice."

"I don't doubt it, Wynflaed, but his ear is given to another."

This pricked her interest. At last, she had set him on the right trail again.

"Who is this person in his confidence?"

"A warrior from Wareham, a certain Aelfhere."

"Do you know him?"

"I do not, but at the time, his brother was my friend."

Wynflaed seized her cousin's hand.

"It's clear what we – *you* – must do. Win this Aelfhere's friendship and trust, then bring him to me."

* * *

The befriending of Aelfhere proved easier than Cynewulf supposed. Mention of his old friendship with Osburh opened the way and the pretence that his skill with the sword was superior than that of his brother, led to an appointment for practice combat. The ease of speech and elegance of manner of the aetheling also induced trust in the younger man. When they met with practice swords, Cynewulf, no mean swordsman, concentrated on allowing his adversary to claim the upper hand but only after a testing struggle. In this way, he gained respect whilst letting the fellow feel superior.

To press home the positive impression he had made, along with praise and admiration, he offered refreshment in the tavern he frequented with Wynflaed. The nun could not await them seated alone in a tavern, but with pleasing timing, she arrived to be introduced by Cynewulf. Far too cunning to reveal her hand on a first meeting, Wynflaed concentrated on making herself as charming to the newcomer as her many wiles allowed.

Cynewulf smiled to himself as he watched her beguile the young man. He admired her subtlety, nothing to arouse suspicion, but a combination of gestures, smiles and interest in her *subject* – he almost thought, 'victim'. By the time she rose with the excuse of a church service, the grin on the lad's face was fixed and he couldn't take his eyes off her.

"I see you have taken a fancy to my cousin, Aelfhere."

"She's a beautiful woman," he said unabashedly. But then added, downcast, "but she's a nun and unreachable."

Cynewulf had given this much previous thought when weighing up his cousin, "Don't be so sure, Aelfhere, I see her on the verge of renouncing the veil. What might a determined man achieve with patience and kindness?" he tried an encouraging smile.

The young warrior's countenance brightened, "Do you really think so, Cynewulf?"

"I'm telling you so. She's my cousin and I should know. What say you? We could meet here tomorrow at the same time."

This agreed, Aelfhere took his leave and Wynflaed, spying from a hidden vantage point, returned to her accomplice.

"Well?" she said.

Cynewulf looked about him but the few customers, at this hour, were too busy with their dice to pay attention to his words.

"Taken the bait and on the hook. But I should warn you, little cousin, you are the bait. Beware the pike doesn't swallow you whole!"

Her tinkling laugh made him smile, "I think I can take care of myself!"

Chapter 17

The combined host of Wessex and Mercia could not have chosen a more commanding position for the forthcoming battle. Aethelheard, next to King Ine at the centre of the host surveyed the magnificent view over the rolling downs. His eyes settled on the massed ranks of the advancing foe. Bards still recounted tales of the great battle fought here, many lifetimes ago, by the great Wessex warlord Ceawlin, the hammer of the foe they faced today, the Wealisc.

Aethelheard reflected on the irony of the situation. According to his spies, here they were prepared for battle, lined up beside the very ones who had whispered in the enemies' ears to urge them to this reckoning – the people who wished to take King Ine's throne from him. How events had the habit of repeating themselves! Wasn't he standing on a burial mound? Here on Adam's Grave. Under his feet lay the bones of warriors brought to die here caused by similar unrest in Wessex. Did people never learn?

Ceawlin's nephew decided to take the crown for himself and thus fought here. That battle raged all day and they say a thunder and lightning storm broke out and the rain poured down, almost as if Woden himself had sent the storm and was watching to see who would become the victor. At the end of the day thousands lay dead and after a very close fight Ceawlin and his men were forced to retreat. They were later driven out of Wessex and into exile. Would this be the fate of King Ine today? Aethelheard prayed not, for in that case, it might mean his own death on this turf.

Morose thoughts thrust aside, he consoled himself with the advantageous position they held, from which they could hurl missiles on the approaching force of Powys and Gwynneth. In the breeze sweeping across the heights, the bright colours of their emblems fluttered as banners proudly held aloft. Provoked by the sight of the embroidered mythological beasts, Aethelheard beat his sword on his shield, Osburh and Aelfhere either side of him did the same until all the men of Wessex, following their lead, created a deafening din designed to intimidate the advancing foe. They soon had to cease in favour of extracting an upright javelin impaled in the soil and, upon command, hurl the weapon down on the mass of men striving uphill. No sooner released, the warriors of Wessex and Mercia reached for another of the six javelins they had planted in the ground and threw another dart. This second hail of steel-tipped death took a greater toll and was followed frenetically by other lethal swarms.

Aethelheard exulted in the chaos wrought on the enemy ranks. Men were stumbling over the dead or wounded or else scrambling to exchange a shield made useless by a weighty spear impaled in its wood. They achieved this without striking a blow and still the darts rained down upon the screaming foe.

Missiles exhausted, cries of "shield-wall!" brought the disciplined ranks of defenders into an awesome barrier before the eyes of the enraged Wealisc survivors. However urged on by rage and bloodlust, their disadvantage remained considerable.

"They'll never breach us!" Osburh yelled in his ear to make himself heard over the war cries of the advancing foe and the insults shouted from behind the shield-wall. This confidence was not misplaced because when the breach finally came, it was only after hours of brave fighting by a staunch enemy, whose stalwart efforts exacted a high price. The men of Wessex and Mercia finally won the day but at some cost. To Aethelheard's dismay, neither his nor Osburh's skilful and savage carnage could protect Aelfhere. Not that, in their estimation, he needed their succour, because the slaughter he'd inflicted on his adversaries had impressed them. Had they miscalculated his strength? Fighting in a shield-wall was energy-sapping and he was young. Whatever the reason, they saw him fall, but engaged with an opponent in a life-and-death exchange of blows, they could do nothing until the enemy, devastated and broken, fled down the hill. Neither Aethelheard nor Osburh joined the rout but hauled corpses off their fallen comrade to find, to their relief, that he still breathed.

Aelfhere had taken a blade to the side of his lower abdomen. The point of the weapon had pierced the thick leather jerkin protecting his body. It must have been a violent sword thrust. Osburh did not have the patience to unlace the thongs holding the garment in place but sliced through them with his seax before gently pulling aside the garment to reveal the wound. The linen tunic underneath was soaked in blood.

"It looks worse than it is," Aethelheard tried to reassure his friend, who looked paler than his wounded brother. "I don't think the gash will kill him if we can staunch the bleeding."

Aethelheard looked around him at the bodies in search of clean linen – a futile idea on a battlefield.

Nonetheless, he began to slash at the clothing of a nearby corpse and managed to obtain a sizeable piece of linen. He folded it into a pad and placed it over the slash in Aelfhere's side. "Don't just gawp, find me more cloth to bind this tight around his belly!" he yelled at Osburh.

Osburh set about the task like a man possessed and whilst he rolled bodies to inspect them for suitable clothing, Aethelheard pressed down on the pad and gazed down the hill trying to understand what was happening. Sporadic fighting continued but there were more men wearily returning than those engaged in combat. Without doubt, victory was theirs but, at that moment, Aethelheard felt anything but joyful.

"Will this do?" Osburh broke across his thoughts, waving a linen cloth like a banner.

"Cut it into strips, knot them together, we must pass it right round his body."

When Osburh was ready, he said, "Help me raise him enough to slip the bandage under him. Gently, now, steady!"

The dead weight of Aelfhere lifted, they repeated the operation twice until Aethelheard was satisfied that they'd bound the pad tight against the wound. He stood up quickly, startling what the poets called *blood-geese,* but that he called ravens, picking at the nearby corpses. He grunted in disgust and put his mind to how to remove his friend from the battlefield. They would need a litter. To this purpose he called on a group of returning warriors, plodding uphill, to recover eight javelins. These would form the stretcher poles. What he would give now for a cloak to make the bed, but warriors did not wear mantles in battle.

Osburh solved the problem by removing three leather jerkins from corpses.

"We can use the thongs to bind around the javelin shafts. They are strong and will take the strain."

In a surprisingly short time, they had improvised a serviceable stretcher and Aethelheard rounded up four of his *hearthweru* to carry their pallid comrade down the hill. Before they set off, they found the king, delighting over his trophies, four Wealisc banners, captured in ferocious skirmishes.

"These will adorn the walls of my hall at Winchester!" he gloated.

"Sire, I beg leave to take our wounded brother to an infirmary. I know the infirmarian at Wimborne is skilled with wounds, she cured my cheek and Osburh's hand."

"Ay sire," said Osburh, "here!" He displayed his scar with pride.

The king scrutinised the blood-spattered faces of his hearth-guards with fondness.

"You have served me well today, my friends. Take as many men as you need and God willing, your brother will survive. Make haste!"

They sped their progress over the nineteen leagues by stopping at a farmstead, purchasing four horses and, each rider taking an end of a pole, suspended the stretcher between them. It proved a difficult operation to maintain this formation but as they rode ahead, they were able to maintain a canter that ate up the miles.

The impossibility of travelling overnight in this or any other way and the pressing need to have Aelfhere's wound treated were irreconcilable. The only advantage of an overnight stop was that they could provide the patient with a warming fire and give him fresh water. Aelfhere regained consciousness but was obviously weak. His main emotion, whispered to Osburh, was shame.

"I'm not worthy to be a *hearthweru*, brother."

Osburh touched his brow with the back of his hand to check for fever but it was cool. Reassured, he said, "We saw you fight next to us as fierce and proud as any warrior on the field. In battle, a blow can arrive when least expected. Remember my hand?"

"Aelfhere closed his eyes but his brother was relieved to see a fleeting smile greet his words. he could not bear the thought of losing his younger brother. It was this thought keeping him awake most of the night, stoking the fire, checking Aelfhere at the slightest groan and saddling all four horses so that he could rouse his comrades to be away at the first glimmer of dawn.

The welcome sight of the abbey nestling in the valley between the Rivers Stour and Allen was never more pleasing to their eyes. For Aethelheard, the pleasure was double for he would combine treatment for his friend and reunion with his mother.

Her joy at seeing him was all too soon replaced by a brisk efficiency. She removed their temporary bandages, inspected the wound and summoned her assistant. Aethelheard was pleased to greet the young nun who had treated him kindly with his broken cheekbone.

"Warm water, Sefled, not too hot, mind."

Cynethryth looked up from her scrutiny of the wound.

"Rowena can breathe easily," she smiled, "his wound has not pierced the gut. He was lucky, the blade entered at a sharp angle, taking it away from the bowel and missing the large blood tubes. He looks so pale because he lost blood but you did well to patch him up. My task is easy now – first, to clean the wound, then to sew it up and heal it with salves."

"Mother, I swear you are the best healer in the land!"

Cynethryth stared hard at her son.

"I should say you would need to meet many healers to make that claim, Aethelheard, but I prefer you to remain far away from healers."

"These are risks a warrior runs in battle, Mother. Yesterday we won a great victory over the Wealisc."

His face clouded over.

"What is it?"

"Oh, it's that there can never be peace for the likes of us."

Had Cynethryth not been preoccupied by her patient, she would have questioned him. As it was, Sefled arrived with the water and she concentrated on rinsing the wound with as much care as she could.

"Sister, fetch me vinegar."

She took the bottle from her assistant.

"This will sting terribly," she warned her patient but, to his credit, he did not cry out but his eyes closed tight. "Now, I'm going to stitch you up but my needle will not hurt like that sword you walked into."

She used a fine silk thread and covered the wound with a salve and fresh binding.

"It's best I keep you here for at least a fortnight, Aelfhere, so I can change the dressing and treat the wound. Most of all we must guard against infection. To that purpose you must keep as still as possible in bed. I'll send for your mother, for she'll want to see you."

"Thank you, Mother, I knew you'd sort out our comrade. We must be on our way to Winchester, for the king needs his *hearth-weru* now more than ever."

Cynethryth gave Aethelheard an enquiring look but when he ignored it, she said brightly,

"So short a visit, my son. I pray to the Lord every day to keep you safe."

"He answered your prayers this day, sure enough. Farewell, mother."

She watched him leave and her lower lip trembled, but she fought back the tears. She had the consolation of her calling, and this told her to send to the kitchen for chicken broth to build up her new patient's strength.

That night as she lay on her pallet, her mind kept returning to Aethelheard's words: *the king needs his hearthweru now more than ever.* What did he mean by that? Why hadn't he answered her admittedly unexpressed query. It wasn't the only curious thing he'd said, but try as she might, she could not remember his other words. She might find out from Aelfhere. He was a *hearthweru* – as Rowena reminded her endlessly.

Chapter 18

Experience told Cynethryth that the strength of youth would bring a speedy recovery in Aelfhere. The absence of fever and a return of colour to his cheeks meant she could question without overtaxing him. She put the nagging refrain of Aethelheard's words to her patient, "Do you know why my son said the king needs his hearthweru now more than ever? Is King Ine in danger?"

Aelfhere looked uncertain, but replied, "The king is always in danger, sister. That is why we serve as his hearth-guard."

The infirmarian fixed him with a penetrating stare, convinced he was withholding something.

"What you say is true but something in particular is troubling Aethelheard and I wish to know what it is."

Aelfhere had grown up with a deep respect for the woman before him, given the tales his mother had related. Here she was, his healer, to whom he owed a debt, concerned for the safety of their king. Should he tell her? Wasn't he obliged to do so?

The dark grey eyes of the nun watched this inner conflict play out in his expression, and bringing them closer to his, said, "I think you ought to tell me."

He bit his lower lip for a moment, then with a look of resolution said, "Sister, what I have to say could put me in danger and I need to know that you will not use it against me."

"I've known you since you were a babe, Aelfhere, and your mother is my dearest friend. How could I harm you?"

"Sister, forgive me, but these are perilous times. There is a plot against the king and I've been approached by rivals for his throne. If I did what they asked of me, I would betray not only the king but also my friend Aethelheard and my brother."

The colour drained from Cynethryth's face.

"Who are these people?"

Alarmed at the effect of his words on the infirmarian, Aelfhere refused to confide further.

"I cannot say."

Remembering her main duty to her patient, Cynethryth did not press him but swore she would extract the names from him before the sun's shadows grew long.

In the afternoon, she came to a decision: either she would obtain the names from him or she would task Rowena to do so. She had still not sent for Aelfhere's mother because she was waiting for her patient's healing to be more advanced.

Returning to Aelfhere, she found him chatting with Sefled, who was sitting on the edge of his bed. When Cynethryth arrived, the nurse said brightly, "Sister, Aelfhere was just telling me he has met a nun from Wimborne in Winchester. From his description, I think it's Sister Wynflaed."

Aelfhere's face made her suspicious as it assumed the furtive expression the infirmarian had seen earlier.

"Is she one of the people whose name you would not give me earlier, Aelfhere?"

He did not need to confirm it – his manner betrayed him.

"You should know, my friend," she continued, "that this woman was cast forth from this nunnery by the abbess because of her malice and spite. Are you sure you wish to protect these people by not revealing their names? I implore you to tell me. Take my word, it will do you no harm."

Sefled stared from one to the other, mouth agape.

Aelfhere, unexpectedly, addressed the assistant, "This Wynflaed, was she as bad as the sister just said?"

Cynethryth bit her tongue and swallowed her resentment at the doubting of her word by the young warrior. It was as well she did because Sefled said without hesitation, "Much worse, I'd say. She was wicked when she was here and was one who sought constantly to create trouble. From your words, she's a greater danger outside these walls. Stay away from her if you know what's good for you."

Cynethryth did not look at Sefled but kept her eyes on Aelfhere. The effect of her assistant's words clearly had an impact.

"She seems all sweetness and is very convincing," he said at last, "but if one forgets her beguiling ways and thinks only of what she wants, it's enough to realise she's not what she seems."

Cynethryth, determined to get to the bottom of the plot, pressed him, "How did you meet Wynflaed in the first place?"

Aelfhere closed his eyes and frowned, but muttered, "Through her cousin, the aetheling."

"Is it he who wishes to become king?"

Aelfhere looked into those deep grey eyes and recognised the intelligence that lay behind them. His mother was right. This was no ordinary nun.

"Ay, sister, his name is Cynewulf and he has a stronger claim than Ine to the throne, or at least, quite as strong."

"And they wanted you – or was it Aethelheard? – through your position in the hearthweru to slay the king. Am I right?"

Throughout his recovery Aelfhere had shown no signs of fever but now beads of sweat appeared on his brow. He was clearly agitated, so it was Cynethryth who called a halt.

"Enough! You have done well to confide in us Aelfhere. It means that nought will happen to you or your family. You will have no more to do with this wicked plot. Leave it to me. Sefled, come!"

They left him to think over what had occurred. In the preparation room, Cynethryth took a quill, dipped the tip in ink and wrote a note to Rowena. It exhorted her to come to the infirmary at first light and her husband too.

"Sefled, take my horse, ride to Rowena's house and give her this message. Come back with her and Guthred tomorrow morning. It will be too dark to return tonight. We need to sort out that demon, Wynflaed, once and for all."

* * *

Winchester, three days later.

Guthred rode into Winchester with the sole purpose of finding Aethelheard and warning him of the threat posed by Wynflaed and Cynewulf. On the face of it an easy task, but not so. He rode straight into chaos. Armed men had stormed the royal palace and its doors were being stoutly defended by warriors led by... Guthred stared... ay, by Aethelheard. So, these were the famed hearthweru defending the palace. Guthred urged his reluctant mount forward, drew his sword and broke into a gallop, scything down any of the insurgents unfortunate enough to bar his way to Aethelheard's side.

The warrior-leader, beset by foes, was too occupied to welcome him, so Guthred hewed about him, his battle-trained steed rearing and crashing its steel-shod hoofs on those who threatened to attack under its muzzle. Step by step, they drove back the rebels until the hard-fought retreat turned into a rout.

Aethelheard shouted orders curtailing pursuit. As far as he was concerned, their work of preventing the king's foes from entering the palace had been a success. No point in risking the lives of his men in the narrow streets of Winchester.

Doubling the guard on the palace door, Aethelheard turned his attention to Guthred.

"Welcome old friend. Your arrival was timely, but tell me, what brings you to Winchester?"

Guthred gave a wry smile, "I came to warn of a plot against the king, but it seems I came too late."

"Leave your horse," he waved to a stable boy, "come inside and give me your news."

Guthred's eyes roamed around the magnificent hall and came to rest on three tattered banners nailed to a wall.

"Ah, the Wealisc emblems we took at Adam's Grave," he said with satisfaction.

"What do you know about the revolt?"

"Your mother sent me. Aelfhere is mending well and he told her of a plot to murder the king in his bed by stealth. This aetheling, by the name of Cynewulf, is behind it, with his cousin a disgraced nun. There was no talk of an attack on the palace."

Aethelheard shrugged and looked unconcerned.

"Our spies warned me of today's attack. It was fomented by two aethelings, Ealdberht and Oswald. They'd better flee the kingdom at once because King Ine wishes them dead. It'll be my pleasure and duty to execute them."

"The news I bring of this other matter had nought to do with today's events, then."

"I think not. But I'll have my men investigate the activities of this Cynewulf and his cousin. We can't be too careful."

* * *

In another quieter part of town, Cynewulf and Wynflaed were deep in conversation.

"I told you the time for an open revolt was not ripe," she said. "See what Ealdberht and Oswald have achieved – nothing! Except to strengthen Ine's position. The hearthweru will redouble their guardianship of him and the people will believe the king to be unassailable. But it is not so. My plan will prove that to be false. When things have settled down, bring our friend Aelfhere to me and we'll put the finishing touches to our plan."

"I haven't seen him since he went away to fight the Wealisc."

Wynflaed narrowed her eyes, "I hope he wasn't slain in battle after the work we've done on him. Can't you find out?"

"We must wait until things are quiet. It's a disaster, for I doubt we can count on Ealdberht or Oswald and their followers."

"When Ine is slain and the blame laid upon Aethelheard, the people will seek an untainted aetheling as king – you! As king, you will appoint me as Abbess of Wimborne."

'*And then I will punish the infirmarian every day.*'

"And what will you have me do with the present abbess?"

"You can send her to Boniface on a mission in Thuringia."

"You have it all worked out, don't you?

Wynflaed's expression was smug but underneath she did not feel as confident as before this inconvenient revolt. The important piece in her game of chess was missing – the black knight. When would Cynewulf be able to contact him? That worried her.

* * *

King Ine stared gloomily at Aethelheard, "No sooner do we quell one revolt than a plot to murder me rears its head, is that it? Round up this Cynewulf and his cousin and lock them away."

Aethelheard was too wise to gainsay his king but was not happy about arresting an aetheling purely on hearsay. Nonetheless, he called the best of his spies and ordered him to bring the two miscreants to the palace in irons.

However, in the state of confusion in the town, frightened by the manhunt for the two rebel aethelings and his known association with them, Cynewulf decided to leave Winchester with Wynflaed to await less turbulent times. They left on horses for Kingsham and a return to their old haunts. Ealdberht and Oswald, instead, fled farther afield, arriving in Est Anglia after several days' journey on horseback. It was a safe haven for them since King Ine had no influence over this peaceful and wealthy kingdom nor its King, Aelfwald.

Cynewulf would have fared better had he gone to Est Anglia and better still had he rid himself of Wynflaed, who never ceased her scheming. Months went by whilst Cynewulf wisely waited for a more suitable opportunity to return to Winchester. His character tended to the cautious, which infuriated Wynflaed who wanted nothing more than to gain revenge on Cynethryth. She might have been furious within but could not show it too much for fear of being cast aside by her protector.

King Ine was busy making sure that the new Mercian king, Aethelbald, did not aggrandise his territory at the expense of Wessex. Otherwise, he was occupied by projects such as the new stone church he was constructing at Glastonbury and sorrowful events like the funeral of his brother Inglid.

His subjects, apart from the few with dynastic ambitions, were content. Ine had provided peace, a stable currency and justice. In order to achieve this, he had clipped the wings of notable families and herein lay the source of their smouldering resentment.

* * *

The time had come for Cynethryth to discharge Aelfhere. She had overseen the complete healing of his body but she would not let him leave the abbey until she had worked on his mind.

"Remember, Aelfhere, the Devil's ploy is to tempt sinners with what their hearts most desire. You must always remain strong and do what is right. Satan comes to us in many guises, be it in the form of a smooth-talking nobleman or that of a beautiful woman. Beware blandishments and false smiles."

"Sister, I know you refer to the aetheling and his cousin but fear not, I know where my duty lies. My deepest thanks for the care you have taken of me and to you, Sister Sefled. I'll wear my scar with pride."

"Let it serve as a reminder of your duty," Cynethryth would not let the matter go, such was her fear of Wynflaed's guile.

* * *

She had good reason because even as she spoke to Aelfhere in Wimborne, Wynflaed, in Kingsham, was whispering in Cynewulf's ear,

"Time passes, Ine waxes and we wane. We must away to Winchester. Seek out this Aelfhere, bring him to me!"

Cynewulf would have none of this, fearing Ine's spies and believing the king's strength was too great for him to move. His own informant at Winchester had been unable to locate Aelfhere and Cynewulf grew convinced that the young warrior had fallen in battle. In that case, Wynflaed's plan was in vain because they would have no corruptible hearthweru to murder the king.

In spite of Wynflaed's constant, tiresome urging, the situation remained stalled and two winters passed until one morning, Cynewulf's informant appeared with news that he had seen Aelfhere on guard duty. The former nun was upon Cynewulf like a feral cat pouncing on a shrew. Her tenacious claws prevailed, so that the aetheling was obliged to agree to travel with her to Winchester.

Once there, he refused to lure Aelfhere to them with the excuse of caution. He wanted to be sure that their presence in the out-of-the-way inn he had chosen had gone unnoticed. With this in mind, he waited three months before contacting Aelfhere.

Three months of persistent carping from Wynflaed and his own ambitions smouldering under the surface at last induced him to move.

For his part, on receiving the invitation to meet Cynewulf to learn of something to his advantage, Aelfhere decided to comply. Whatever his true motives, he was faced with the most difficult choice of his life.

The aetheling, never once relenting his mesmerising stare into the younger man's eyes, probed for doubts or other signs of weakness. Satisfied the warrior would cooperate, he moved to his main offer, which he believed to be irresistible.

"When we have carried out our plan Aelfhere, and I am king, I mean to undo the tyranny of Ine. My first act will be to restore the under-kingships. You, my friend, will have the lands nearest to your heart. I will raise you to the position of King of Dorset, what say you to that?"

"What of Aethelheard? Surely he has a better claim than I?"

"What claim can be made from the grave, Aelfhere? This brings me to the plan we have devised. You will carry it out so there can be no error but the blame must fall on Aethelheard if you are to be King of Dorset, make no mistake."

"It can be done," said Aelfhere.

Wynflaed intervened, "How exactly will you make out Aethelheard as the murderer? It must be convincing."

"His sword is unmistakeable and he's in the habit of hanging it from a nail in the wall by his bed. I'll take it while he sleeps, use it for the slaying and leave it impaled in the king's corpse."

Wynflaed smiled and held his gaze, softening her eyes to entrance him, "It's a good plan but as it stands, too much can go wrong. We must ensure that Aethelheard doesn't waken. I'll procure a sleeping potion for you to mix into his drink. Naturally, you will be the one to raise the alarm in the morning and to accuse Aethelheard. Do this well and remember, as King of

Dorset you can have any woman you desire." She widened her eyes and tilted her head.

"It's agreed," said Cynewulf, "we'll meet at the next moon, it's but days away. Wynflaed will provide you with the potion and we'll talk over the final arrangements."

Chapter 19

Winchester, early spring, 721 AD

On his way to the Royal Palace, Aelfhere had to admit that the aetheling's pretty cousin set his pulses racing. But was that not exactly what Sister Cynethryth had warned him against? The unspoken implication by Wynflaed, communicated by smiles and gestures, that she would be his woman when he became King of Dorset, put a spring in his step. To become king and have his father as a subject, imagine that! It would show Guthred and his mother who was the better man between him and Osburh.

The cursory nod and smile from his comrade on guard duty at the hall door was enough to curtail these flights of fancy. What was he thinking? By God, the infirmarian had it right, the Devil knew how to tempt a mere mortal!

With this in mind, Aelfhere strode to the farthest end of the great room, beyond the hearth, where the women seated around it were employed in carding fleece. He ignored the hypnotic rhythm of their movements as they drew the flat-back carders and the calming sound of the fleece being pulled through the leather-seated curved hooks. As a child, he'd stared fascinated for long minutes at this activity, now as a man – a warrior – he had matters of state in his head. He strode on past sacks stuffed with freshly shorn fleece without deigning them as much as a glance. He needed to find Aethelheard and hoped he would be seated at a table poring over a rota or other kind of document the king wished him to sign.

Aelfhere was always embarrassed when he had to speak with his friend formally in front of comrades or officials. It made him awkward and overly conscious of the tone of his address.

"*Ahem*, Lord," he began, "I have uncovered a plot against the life of our king."

Little did Aethelheard care as to the manner of the communication, but its content had him on his feet and dragging the younger man to a discreet place behind the heavy drapes that separated this area from the body of the hall.

"Hush! Keep your voice down and tell me everything."

Aelfhere related every detail of his meetings with Cynewulf and Wynflaed. After due consideration, he omitted Cynethryth's advice, thinking that this element would only serve to show irresolution.

"Loyal and worthy friend," Aethelheard began, "I'd prefer to act without disturbing the king..." his face became troubled, "...but it involves an aetheling from a prominent family... come, Aelfhere, we must inform King Ine."

The narrow visage of the king, with his deep-set eyes, appeared longer than usual to Aethelheard because of the downturned mouth and sorrowful expression.

"Cynewulf, you say? I was there the day he was born. His mother is a cousin of my father. Can it be we have serpents in the bosom of our family?"

"Sire, I fear the closer the ties, the more the bonds bite."

"Aethelheard, if you were not commander of my hearthweru, with your turn of phrase, I'd appoint you court bard!" Ine's haunted features managed a weak smile. He turned to address the other man, "Aelfhere, you have done well and I'll not forget your loyalty. As to the traitors, they must be punished." His expression became irate. "Enough of these plotters! Do they believe I'm a feeble pawn in their game? Have we not just seen off another attempt to seize my throne, fought off valiantly by my trusted men?" The king directed a warm smile to the two hearth-guards. Aethelheard, I charge you with the task of seizing and executing these two unfaithful subjects. The time is come to make an example to those who dare attempt to strike against their chosen king."

"It will be so, Sire."

Aethelheard had long since set aside his earlier ambition to become King of Wessex. This was partly because the time never seemed right, as his mother had advised, and partly because he had settled into his role as the sworn protector of the king. Now, he was called upon to slay his erstwhile friend and one-time fellow conspirator against this selfsame ruler.

Withdrawing from Ine's presence, Aethelheard reflected on this and the deed stuck in his craw but he acknowledged the reasoning behind the command. The decision he reached with ease, but how to organise the counter-blow preoccupied him. Aelfhere would be the one to fulfil the royal command but he would not place his friend in peril.

"When is your next meeting with the traitors?"

"They've called it for the next moon, it's but six days hence."

Aethelheard was relieved, there was time for him to devise a plan to deal with Cynewulf and Wynflaed and when he had, he would not share it with anyone but Aelfhere. Surprise was the best weapon when dealing with conspirators. For this reason, he would not involve Osburh in the planning. At this stage, he did not need undue discussion or the slightest prevarication.

* * *

"Sister, is all well? What are you doing out here in the middle of the night?" Sefled asked.

In reality, Cynethryth was worrying about the safety of her son and the senselessness of strife. But she was not about to confess that to her assistant. Here, under the star-spangled sky, she seized the opportunity to continue the education of her protégé.

"*Contemplating*, Sister, on knowledge – on how we know, what we know, and what we should know."

Awed by the celestial canopy she rarely witnessed, for she was one of the many who avoided the darkness with its hidden malevolence, Sefled felt there was so much to learn and was in receptive mood.

"Tell me more, Sister."

"I've spent much time deep in thought in recent days and considering how we see reality. I've condensed it into three separate strands."

"Three strands?"

"The first is that we must rediscover the wisdom of the past. Consider that the ancients wrote long texts on medicine and healing. Sadly, much of this work is lost to us. Also, our forefathers and mothers knew much about curing ailments but the Church, out of fear of witchcraft and pagan practices, has suppressed it. Sefled, the past is far more experienced than our shallow awareness of the present."

"We must seek out this wisdom, Sister."

"Ay, but we need to tread carefully. There are those who would condemn such a search for truth."

Sefled's eyes roamed over the constellations and with a thrill she felt as if she was on the threshold of a fundamental vision of the world, new to her.

"And the second strand, Sister?"

"We must liberate our awareness through an active approach to life, not a contemplative one. We have to try novel and uncertain things, shed the shackles of habit and routine. Look around you, at this abbey. There is value in the contemplative life, but Sefled, we do not build knowledge and awareness by thought alone but by showing who we are, to others and ourselves, through the actions we take. Remember this, the only way to create knowledge is to step into the unknown. As I tell this to you, one day you must tell it to your assistant."

"I will, Sister. And the third strand?"

"There is a collective memory we must all learn from..."

"I-I don't understand."

"I mean, there are lessons that endure, which are sources of hope and inspiration, which we may use for our guidance."

Cynethryth looked up at the Lady's Wain constellation, below the Great Bear, and prayed her thoughts might be illuminated since she was struggling to express them in mere words. She continued, "All our ideas of morality, good behaviour and togetherness draw on this collective memory, Sister. You see, most of what we know exists outside of minds and is governed by what's around us. We experience it every day in the tolling of bells that determine our actions."

Cynethryth's expression changed into one of sorrow.

Sefled, alarmed, clutched at her sleeve, "Sister, what ails you?"

The sweet concern on the countenance of the young nun helped her recover.

Cynethryth had been momentarily discomfited by a sense of not only her own, but also a wider futility. Would Man never learn? Her arguments were directed to the knowledge of healing but equally they applied to dynastic struggles, and the safety of her son was involved. She sighed heavily. Was it a blessing or a curse that she could see so clearly?

"Nothing, dear sister, just an insignificant and fleeting thought – a mote in the infinite universe."

* * *

"Tomorrow you have your meeting with the traitors. This is what you'll do."

Aethelheard outlined his plan to Aelfhere.

"Is that clear? Remember, you must let enough time pass, neither too much nor too little."

"I understand."

The next day, at the usual corner table in the same tavern were seated Cynewulf and Wynflaed, heads close together in whispered conversation. Aelfhere unconsciously checked the dagger at his belt, a well-honed hand-seax, ideal for the murders, and strolled casually towards the awaiting conspirators. He glanced around the room and, to his displeasure, saw that there were too many customers. Were any of them Cynewulf's men? This he could not know and he must rely on Aethelheard to maintain his part of their agreement. Not the time for faint heart, Aelfhere announced his presence with, "Tonight the moon is full, I believe."

"Well met, Aelfhere, Cynewulf grinned up at him. Come, partake of an ale."

This would be his first disobedience. Aethelheard had entreated him not to drink but an ale might provide him with the courage to do the deed. He also needed to let some time go by, so what better way? The innkeeper, at Cynewulf's summons scurried over and took the order. Was it his fancy or had the rogue scrutinised him more than the mere taking of an order merited?

Aelfhere decided it was just his frayed nerves but even so, he glanced around the taproom to check for suspicious characters.

"Aelfhere, you are not yourself, today. Does the seriousness of this business weigh upon you?" Wynflaed smiled sweetly as she ended her question.

Its irony did not escape him.

"In a certain sense, it does."

He bit off further comment because the landlord placed three beakers of ale in front of them. The curtness of his reply was justified by the innkeeper's presence. Cynewulf slid a coin across the table and the unsavoury tapster withdrew.

"Here," Wynflaed passed a small vial into his hand under the table. She whispered, "A few drops in Aethelheard's drink and he'll sleep sound as a babe gorged on its mother's milk."

"Then you'll take his sword from its nail on the wall, enter the king's chamber as silent as a wraith and plunge it into his throat," Cynewulf sneered.

"Like this!" Aelfhere struck with the speed of a swooping swallow and plunged the blade into the great vein in the aetheling's neck.

Wynflaed's eyes bulged and her scream, high-pitched and fearful, silenced the din in the room.

"A-are you mad?" her voice, faltering, terrified rose suddenly, "Help! Murder!" she cried.

Aelfhere, his right arm covered in blood, had stood stock-still, ensuring the death throes ended before sliding the blade from his victim. His gaze fell upon the white face of the nun and he moved towards her as chaos ensued. Men shouted, knives were drawn, benches overturned as enraged customers leapt to their feet.

"Seize him!"

"Murderer!"

"Send for the constable!"

"Save the woman!"

Everyone shouted at once. Aelfhere stared around. Where was Aethelheard? Would he be overpowered before he arrived? There was still the matter of Wynflaed to deal with. To this purpose, he leapt at her, seax raised to strike. The last thing he remembered was her flinching with terrified, pallid visage contorted. Blackness replaced that sight when a blow to the back of his head sent him sprawling over the table, scattering beakers and ale in all directions.

A wet cloth pressed to his brow restored his senses and with blurred vision and a pounding head, he made out the concerned countenance of Aethelheard.

"You'll survive, my friend. It'll take more than a pat on that bonehead of yours to finish you!"

Aelfhere tried to speak but the effort produced blinding silvery lights behind his closed eyes. His head felt as if an ox had trampled on it. Had he been able to speak, he had so many questions for his friend. As it was, he slid back into unconsciousness.

This time when he came round, he was on a soft bed, not a hard wooden bench as before.

"Where am I?" he groaned, for the effort cost him considerable pain.

The familiar voice of Osburh replied,

"Upstairs, in the inn. You sure know how to waste good ale, brother."

Relieved to be with his sibling, Aelfhere tried to laugh, only then realising quite what a hefty blow had laid him low.

"Be still," Osburh said, "You'll need an hour or two before you're dancing a jig! You did well, brother. Aethelheard announced how the plot to slay the king had been thwarted. He arrested the villain who hit you with a barstool – a thegn of the traitor, Cynewulf. The nun got away, though. But I hardly think she'll be a menace to the king."

By way of reply, Aelfhere could only groan. He did not know himself whether he was pleased or dismayed at the news concerning Wynflaed. Would he have struck her death blow or succumbed to her charms? To this he would never know the answer.

Chapter 20

Wimborne Abbey, 721 AD

"Sister Cynethryth, your services are needed elsewhere," Abbess Cuthburga said sorrowfully.

"Elsewhere?"

A cascade of thoughts rushed through the infirmarian's mind, most of them negative, for she had so much work to complete here in Wimborne.

"My brother, King Ine, is ill and his doctors make no progress towards a cure. Your fame as a healer, Sister, has reached the court in Winchester. I wonder..." her eyes twinkled, "...whether Aethelheard might have sung your praises in the king's ear?"

"Must I travel to Winchester?"

"As soon as your escort led by Lord Guthred arrives. The king ails, child."

"But my work here–"

"Is in capable hands, thanks to your excellent teaching."

The anxiety for her brother's health, clear on the stern countenance of the abbess, breached the last of Cynethryth's resistance.

"It is as you say, Mother. Sister Sefled is more than capable of running the infirmary in my absence. I beg leave to attend to my chores."

* * *

Winchester, three days later.

The king lay weakened by blood letting, diarrhoea and nausea and he complained of dizziness. Where the sleeve of his linen nightgown had risen above the elbow, Cynethryth saw the tell-tale sign of reddish papules. She lay a cool hand on his brow, and to her relief, found no fever. A series of possibilities raced through her mind but she was disturbed by the monarch, "A nun? Who are you?"

She had expected a sharp interrogation and had worried about keeping her true identity, and above all, that of Aethelheard secret; instead, the king's ailment made him vague and confused.

"Sire, I'm the infirmarian at Wimborne and you sent for me."

What was this new expression on the royal visage? Understanding mixed with relief? Indeed, it was.

"At last," with an effort, the king raised his shoulders to look around the chamber. "Have they driven out those good-for-nought charlatans as I commanded?"

"Sire, we are alone in the room, except for two other sisters from the abbey, as propriety demands."

A thin smile crossed the narrow features of the king.

"Sister, you need not fear for your virtue in my weakened state."

He attempted a laugh but his features contorted.

"This accursed itch," he made to scratch his arm but Cynethryth caught his hand.

"We must see what ails you. The rash is only a sign, Sire. I have salves to soothe and cure it but it's the deeper malady we must conquer. Are there other signs, my King?"

With surprising force, the ruler threw off the bedcovers and pointed to his right foot. A large blister had formed there.

"Ah, it's as I thought," Cynethryth murmured.

"Do you know what ails me, Sister?"

"I do, Lord."

"How is it that a nun from Wimborne knows more than all these worthless imposters?"

"It's simple, Sire. You see, I read the works of the ancients. These doctors do not because they condemn them as pagans. I do not share these fears: all knowledge is God-given."

"Do you believe these scripts guide you to know what ails me?"

"I do, my King. In this case they were written by a Greek who practised medicine in Rome long ago, his name is Soranus of Ephesus. Do you eat much freshwater fish, Sire?"

"It is my preferred food, why do you ask?"

"Because this illness is caused by a parasite found in certain waters."

"A parasite?"

"Like the mistletoe sucks the life from the tree, so the *fiery serpent* feeds on your flesh."

"Do you compare me to an oak?"

The thin smile reappeared.

"Sire, a few days and I'll have you strong as an oak once more. Unlike the mistletoe, any man can see, the fiery serpent is hidden within your body."

The king looked anguished, fear in his eyes.

"What *is* this fiery serpent you keep mentioning?"

"It is mentioned in the Bible, Sire. It's known as the little dragon from Medina."

"Then, it's a long way from home!"

Cynethryth smiled, "It can be anywhere in the world. The name was given where it was first recognised. But dread not, Lord, *dragon* and *serpent* are but names; it's more of a *worm*. Our task is to entice it from your body." She ordered one of the silent sentinel nuns, "Sister, find a servant. We need a deep bath of water, lukewarm, not hot.

The king sat on the edge of the bed, his foot submerged in the deep basin of blood-warm water to coax out the worm. After many minutes, the blister burst and the head of the parasite emerged from the flesh. Cynethryth grinned in triumph and taking the creature between finger and thumb began to pull gently until she met with resistance. She did not insist but ordered a nun to fetch a small stick. She wound the exposed part of the worm around it. In this way, she could keep up the tension. The process of removal continued into the next day, but at last, she succeeded in removing the parasite and could concentrate on cleaning the wound. Having prepared a paste of honey and garlic, she applied it to the broken flesh to prevent infection. As she worked scrupulously, the king studied her face.

"I know you, sister! Aren't you Cynethryth? I was a youth at your wedding."

Cynethryth's heart raced and she flushed.

"I see by your face that I'm right."

The infirmarian held her breath. Would he make the connection? He would sooner or later.

The monarch, who was feeling better, had regained his quick wits.

"Which means the commander of my hearth-guard is Caedwalla's son. No wonder he mixed with the rebellious aethelings when he was younger."

"But, Sire, today there is no truer subject in your land than Aethelheard."

The king looked at the nun with genuine fondness, "Sister, do you think I do not know it? Only a few days ago, he saved me from a murderous plot. Aethelheard is close to my heart."

"If I have ought to do with it, he will ever serve you well, Sire."

"I thank you for this and for the great service you too have rendered me. How can I repay you?"

"Only by keeping my son in your favour, lord."

The monarch looked at her with respect.

"Your learning and wisdom are a credit to our kingdom, sister. You will stay with me in the coming days to tend my poor hide – an opportunity to learn from your knowledge."

To her surprise, in the days that followed, Cynethryth was admitted into the hidden sentiments of King Ine. He confessed his weariness with kingship and although she sought to persuade him that it was the result of his illness taxing him, he denied it and went on to explain.

"These ceaseless attempts to take my throne weary me, Cynethryth. I believe I have dedicated my life to my subjects but it's not enough. In recent times I've thought about giving up the throne," he scrutinised her face for a reaction and although her pulse quickened and her thoughts tumbled, she betrayed no outward sign. He continued, "What stops me is that there is so much I still yearn to achieve. I wish to extend our lands to the west, to the where the land meets the deep sea. One day, Sister Cynethryth, I long to go on pilgrimage to Rome with Aethelburg, just as you did with Caedwalla." His eyes strayed to a painting on a wooden board of the Virgin and Child. "It will surely aid our entry into heaven. Tell me about your visit to Rome, did you meet the Holy Father?"

The infirmarian recounted her experience of the capital of their faith and answered his many questions. When she had finished, the king looked around the bedchamber with a furtive air. Cynethryth could not imagine why – only herself and two young nuns graced the room.

"Heed me well, sister, I have come to a decision. You have illuminated my days. You've shown me, as I suspected, there's more to life than power and glory. I wish to enrich what remains of my time with learning. To achieve this, I too must go to Rome. The time is not right for me to surrender the throne but when I do, I mean to leave it to Aethelheard. There is no worthier man and none with so strong a claim. I'll not announce it until the last moment, for no-one knows better than I the dangers of wearing the crown.

A shrewd glint came into the deep-set eyes, "It's our secret and we will share it only with Aethelheard. Sister!" he called to one of the nuns, "hasten, fetch me the commander of my hearthweru."

Aethelheard entered the royal bedchamber and gaped at his mother. An expression of fear or caution clouded his face but he remembered his duty, "Sire, you sent for me?"

"As you see, Aethelheard, I took your advice and sent for the infirmarian of Wimborne. You omitted to mention it was your mother..."

The hearthweru stuttered, "I-I thought–"

"Let be what you thought," Ine said. "Once more you have proved the faithful servant. Aethelheard, your advice was sound. I'm well on the way to recovery. I thank you both. But I also called you here to tell you there can be no more secrets between the king and his commander. But that does not mean there cannot be secrets we keep together, understand? Good! You won't breathe a word of my decision that my successor will be... you."

Aethelheard gazed in awe from the king to his mother. *She's done this!* He knew in his heart but had no idea how she'd achieved it.

"Have you nothing to say, aetheling?"

The king's tone was sardonic but his smile was affectionate.

Confused, Aethelheard stammered inadequate thanks or, so they seemed to his ears.

'*My dream will come true after all!*'

* * *

After her brush with death, Wynflaed fled to the stable where she knew Cynewulf kept his horse. The animal already knew her and it only took two small coins to persuade the stable boy to saddle the horse and allow her to ride it away. She took the road for Lunden over the downs in the hope that the large town would provide her with the anonymity she craved.

Ever the opportunist, and fortified by her last experience with pilgrims, Wynflaed reined in her horse when she chanced upon another group. She wrongly assumed they were going to Lunden but their leader, a monk, told her they would bypass the town.

"If you wish to ride with us, Sister, we'll be pleased of your company as far as the town. We are heading to the tomb of saint Aethelthryth in Elig. They say the saint has achieved great miracles."

Wynflaed, hoping for food and lodgings from the pilgrims, as before, eagerly accepted and passed herself off with ease as a nun on a mission of mercy. Her pious exclamations and anecdotes soon found favour with the company. Before long, she received more than her fair share of smiles and compliments. By the time they reached Lunden, nobody thought it strange when she said, "I do believe I will come with you to Elig. There, I'll ask Saint Aethelthryth to intercede with the Lord on behalf of my poor cousin. The Lord brought me to you for a purpose."

Since she was so popular for her bright conversation and pious observations, nobody raised objection. It went unnoticed that she had not paid for the small amount she ate and drank or that she did not contribute to the room she shared with the two daughters of the wool merchant at their wayside inns.

The pilgrims would have been dismayed had they known her vengeful thoughts at the tomb of the saint. Wynflaed had little knowledge of the whereabouts of Elig but she had questioned

Cynewulf before the day of his death about where Ealdberht and Oswald might have flown. He had seemed sure that they would have decided to spend their exile in Est Anglia. For this reason, when she bade farewell to her companions, she enquired about the court of the king of the Est Angles. This, the monk told her, was a distance of fifteen leagues from Elig and she must follow the road eastwards to the town of Gipeswic. It was a wealthy trading port, he assured her, and everyone would know of it.

"Obtaining directions will be easy, Sister, may God keep you safe."

Wynflaed left them with a smile on her face. Her scheme had borne fruit. What she needed now was a little luck and her wits sharp. By choosing the people from whom to ask directions with great care, she managed to obtain their pity or respect according to the story she spun. On each occasion she obtained food and drink, and twice, a sheltered place to spend the night. She managed six leagues a day so did not overwork her horse and arrived in the port on the third afternoon.

Unused to the noise and bustle of a port, at first she had the sensation of being a detached and unimportant bystander as dock workers loaded large sacks of wool aboard ships after unloading from the vessels millstones and whetstones from overseas. She was impressed by the number of pots of all shapes and sizes that emerged from workshops lining the wharf. But not even her effrontery was enough to seek information from these cursing, loud-mouthed labourers. Undecided, but in need of directions, she nudged her horse away from the port district until she found a small church with a large wooden cross in front of its entrance. Carved in swirling letters into the crosspiece of the wood were the words Saint Mary's. So, the little church was dedicated to the Virgin, excuse enough for a former nun to visit.

She found a priest inside on his knees at his devotions. Seeking his assistance, she waited patiently until he crossed himself and rose from his knees. As soon as he finished bowing towards the altar and turned, she approached him.

"Father, a moment of your time, I'm in sore need of guidance."

"My dear, how can I help?"

"I must find the king's court as soon as possible. I'm on horse-back and do not know this area at all."

"Come outside, I'll give you directions."

The priest did not ask awkward questions but confined himself to repeating the way until sure she understood. She took her leave and discovered within the hour that his instructions had been perfect. At the entrance to the royal hall, the quality of her horse and speech were enough to gain the cooperation of the guard who even called a stable-boy for the pretty lady, and he confirmed there were aethelings from West Seax at court. She would find them inside the hall without doubt and if he could be of further help – he leered – he was available.

Still requiring his permission to enter, she did not toss her head and deal him a freezing glare such as he deserved, but smiled sweetly and said she'd remember his face. Inside the impressive hall, adorned with carvings of writhing beasts and entwining plants, interspersed with embroidered wall hangings and emblazoned banners, she sought the familiar faces she had travelled so far to find.

She had imagined she would find them conversing but her gaze settled on the broad shoulders and knotted blond hair of Oswald in earnest discussion with a group of finely dressed men. His distracted eyes passed over her and although she felt he had seen her, he had not given any indication of recognising her. It was no matter, she knew where he was and would search for Ealdberht meanwhile. The problem was she could not find him and when she returned to the group where Oswald had been, he had gone. One of the men noticed her looking frantically around, and detaching himself from the group, addressed her, "Lady, you are newly come here and look more than a little lost."

"You are kind. It is so, I have travelled far in search of friends. One was with you earlier, but has vanished from sight."

"Who, pray, was he?"

"Oswald, aetheling of the West Seax."

"Oswald, ay, I know him well. Do you wish to meet him?"

She nodded fervently,

"Do you know where I might find him?"

"Come, Lady, I'll lead you to him."

The tall well-set stranger advised her to leave her horse because the aetheling dwelt nearby. In fact, they turned only two corners from the hall and her guide rapped on the door of a free-standing house with reed-thatched roof. Oswald himself swung back the door and stared into her face with a look of incredulity. This time he recognised her.

"Wynflaed! What are you doing in Gipeswic? Do you know Beonna?"

So, that was his name. She smiled into the face of her rescuer.

"No, but he was kind and brought me to you. We must talk."

Oswald grinned, stretched out a hand and pulled Beonna inside by his arm. With the other hand, holding the door, he opened it wider for Wynflaed.

"Come in, then."

Pleasantries exchanged, Wynflaed proceeded to establish whether the ground was fertile for her scheme. The first necessity was to discover the whereabouts of Ealdberht.

"Ealdberht? He'll be in the arms of some wench, I'll wager."

"So, he's here in Gipeswic?"

"Where else?"

Wynflaed smiled seductively, "And you, Oswald, do you not have a woman you care for?"

"He has many, Lady," smiled Beonna, "there's safety in numbers."

Both men laughed but she noticed astutely that Oswald's was forced and he seemed uneasy.

"I bring news from Kingsham. Cynewulf is dead."

She might as well have struck Oswald across the face to obtain the same expression.

"What! How?"

"Murdered by Aethelheard. He has wormed his way into Ine's favour, God knows how, and he rids himself of those who stand in his way."

"Are you saying that Aethelheard is bidding for the throne, Wynflaed?"

"Why else would he slay his former friend? I escaped with my life thanks to the loyalty of one of Cynewulf's thegns, but came close to death. I hastened here to warn you and Ealdberht. You will be next unless you avenge Cynewulf."

"Listen to the lady, my friend," said Beonna, "these are dangerous times and have you not spent hours telling me about your claim to the West Seax throne?"

The three spoke about the difficulties of invading West Seax until the candles burnt low. They discussed the strength of King Ine and how many friends Beonna could call upon willing to risk the adventure of overthrowing a legitimate ruler. After they had exhausted all arguments, the Est Anglian nobleman took his leave.

With the contented expression of a cat devouring a trout stolen from the larder, Wynflaed watched him leave.

"You have a good friend there," she smirked.

"Indeed, Beonna's like a brother to me."

"Can you rely on him to aid our cause?"

"I'd stake my life on it."

Wynflaed stood and drew close to Oswald, making her face as seductive as possible.

"Is it true what he said about you and women?" She widened her eyes and pouted.

"That I have many? It's just men's talk, Wynflaed."

She brought her face close to his and stared up into his strong countenance.

"Is there no-one special, my lord?"

At the closeness of the lovely visage, he weakened and murmured, "There might yet be."

With this utterance, he swept her into his arms and gave her a lingering kiss.

She thrilled at his soft lips and muscular grip.

'*Oswald will be King of Wessex and I'll be his Lady.*'

With this thought in mind, she surrendered to him and consummated their new-found alliance in his bed.

Chapter 21

King Ine, at last tired of deep conversation with the infirmarian, relented about sending her back to Wimborne. Cynethryth joined her escort at the stables with a bulging bag laden with precious medical volumes purchased for her from across the Channel by the grateful monarch. To her pleasure and surprise, Aethelheard was chatting with the men assigned to accompany her. He led her to one side away from indiscreet ears.

"Sadly, I can't leave my duties to escort you, mother, but I didn't want to miss our farewells."

"Talking of duty, did you capture Wynflaed?"

"We did not, but I have men searching."

Cynethryth bit her lower lip and frowned,

"You must catch her and lock her in the deepest cell you can find. While she's free to plot neither the king nor you are safe. You do understand, Aethelheard?" She clutched at his arm and the passion revealed by her forceful grip and that transformed her voice into a hiss, startled him. "Do not underestimate the wickedness of that woman!"

He looked with tenderness at the new lines of worry on her face. His mother was still handsome but there was no halting the advance of time. The smallest wrinkles had appeared around her mouth and was that a wisp of grey hair escaping from under her wimple? With fondness he remembered the dazzling red-golden locks in the sunlight when he was a child. He swept her into his arms and held her tight.

"Don't worry mother, I'll be wary. Thank you for what you have done for me," he whispered into the cloth-covered ear. "You're a wonderful woman!"

Sorrowfully, he watched the escort leave through the great gates. He had loved having her in Winchester for these fleeting months. How cruel a wyrd that ever kept them apart.

'*When I am king, I'll have her reside in my court.*'

At once, he pushed the thought, so long forbidden, out of his mind and strode to the royal palace. Wynflaed dominated his thoughts as he walked. He had not met her but both his mother, whose judgment he never doubted, and Aelfhere swore she was a fiend. More effort must be made to apprehend her. There were still claimants to the throne living in exile. His latest reports spoke of Ealdberht and Oswald in Est Anglia, the latter with an unknown woman – could she be Wynflaed?

He spat on the muddy road and wrinkled his brow. While they were in Gipeswic what harm could they do? Still, he must stay informed.

* * *

Gipeswic, 722 AD

The object of Aethelheard's thoughts, Wynflaed, was smiling sweetly into the troubled face of the aetheling, Ealdberht. In spite of his imposing physical presence, she manipulated him at will through one emotion to the next. Now, she sought to fan the flames of his anger.

"Cynewulf was once his friend, as he was yours. Yet, this did not stay his hand when it came to slaying him before my eyes."

"Did you see Aethelheard deliver the blow?"

"It might as well have been him." She did not meet his eyes.

Ealdberht scowled, "So, it was not he?"

Wynflaed flushed and her face became spiteful, "No, he's too much of a coward. He sent his friend Aelfhere to spring the trap. The blow was deceitful and unexpected. I escaped with my life by a miracle. As sure as trees bear leaves Aethelheard aims to become King of West Seax and he will slaughter any man, friend or foe alike, who stands in his way."

Her visage took on a querulous expression, "Go on, tell me how you are different from Cynewulf? Do you suppose Aethelheard will let you live, when you have a better claim than he?"

Ealdberht looked worried, "By God, you're right!"

"Of course, I am, you know it! King Ine is getting old and with every day that passes Aethelheard's power grows."

"But the time is not right."

Baring her teeth, Wynflaed spat like a wildcat, "Tish! That's all I ever hear from you. That refrain was Cynethryth's undoing too."

"But, Wynflaed, King Ine holds the whole of the south as far as the Kentish and Mercian borders. In need, he can call on those two great kings."

"And you can call on the Est Angles: Beonna tells me so."

"That is true, but it makes more sense to wait until Ine is weaker, either politically or more likely, in health. My spies tell me he was very ill not long ago but they brought in an infirmarian from Wimborne to cure him."

The malevolence in Wynflaed's face, at these words, startled even the great warrior. But since she did not utter another word, he shrugged and supposed he had convinced her.

* * *

The opportunity for revenge Wynflaed so craved and the political uncertainty Ealdberht yearned for had their seeds in King Ine's ambitions. He would attempt to fulfil his long-held dream of extending his kingdom to the farthermost western rocky headlands.

The seagulls swirled and swooped, mewling above the cliffs. The wind buffeted the purple-headed sea thrift and the men who trampled it underfoot. The same men were now losing their footing on the yielding turf of the cliff edge, forced backwards by the enemy into the long flight to plummet to their deaths on the jagged rocks below. The West Seaxa had been lured to this doom by a cunning and stealthy enemy who knew and loved every fold of this uneven landscape. The horror-stricken commanders of the West Seax army in the rear-guard could do nothing but gape at the carnage playing out before their eyes.

They had crossed the River Tamar two days before and, mistaking the wiliness of the foe for weakness, these same commanders had let their plunging men be lured in among the gorging precipices now devouring them. Aethelheard stared at the disaster, his mood gloomier than the seal-coloured clouds hanging low over the heaving walrus waves.

"Retreat!" he called, for they had better save as many men as possible to fight on the morrow.

As luck decreed, the bulk of the West Seax force had not been caught in the trap but the tactics of the Brittonic warriors were these, honed over generations of defending Dumnonia from the Saxons or their Wealisc cousins. Picking off steadily, sapping the heart of the adversary, this was the method and like simpletons, they had marched head down to the slaughter.

Aethelheard swore under his breath. Tomorrow would be another day and he'd show the Britons what his Saxons were worth. The first thing was to protect them from the ravenous cliffs by moving the men inland. Not that the interior proved much more hospitable and King Ine appeared to be in a stubborn frame of mind.

"Sire, we must send scouts ahead to gauge the lie of the land."

"We will not lose more men to these cowards, Aethelheard. You will only send them to their deaths, have you not seen how they fight by hitting and running?"

"But, Lord–"

"Silence! I have spoken and you will obey."

Aethelheard rode along the rocky trail with ominous presentiment. The enemy knew the contours of the land as well as those of their own hand. This was a land of rocks and tangled gorse, dips and hollows, and they were vulnerable. In the afternoon of the next day, the vanguard rounded a group of rocks and came face to face with the enemy. The panicked wail of horns warned those following of the dangers ahead.

Aethelheard cursed Ine under his breath – *if only the fool had heeded me!* And an oath escaped aloud when his horse rounded the crag. The battlefield the nimble enemy had chosen was cramped so they might not take advantage of their greater numbers. There could not have been a more artfully chosen place in Dumnonia to favour the smaller, more mobile hostile army.

'*Now we pay for your stubbornness, my king.*'

Courageous and seasoned as the West Seax warriors were, the slaughter was relentless owing to the cunning enemy tactics. Only when the shadows grew long, and the men of Dumnonia, bloodlust slaked and the battle clearly won, decided to withdraw, did the massacre cease.

Aethelheard with his hearthweru grouped around the king and surveyed the carnage with sorrowful eye. In his heart, he knew it could have been avoided but what use were recriminations, which in this case would veer dangerously close to treason? He and his best men lived to fight another day, hopefully anywhere else but here, among the blue-painted faces of the Britons.

They buried the dead under stone cairns as there were plenty of rocks and little soil in this wilderness. They found a defensible site for the night and in the morn, King Ine decreed withdrawal back over the Tamar. This they achieved without further loss, the only sight of the enemy being a lone figure on a hilltop brandishing a spear in mocking triumph.

"What a disaster!" Aelfhere said to Aethelheard in a voice too low for anyone but him to hear.

"One that might have been avoided," the aetheling growled in reply.

He had been faithful to his king for years but this wilful obstinacy had cost them dear. How much longer would he be prepared to follow a pig-headed leader? Such thoughts tormented him on the return to Winchester.

Yet, Ine would not surrender his ambition of westward expansion. Taking only the time to raise more men to replenish his weakened host, and they were on the march once more into the part of Dumnonia known as Cornwall. This time, lesson learnt, Ine heeded the warnings and to Aethelheard's gratification, sent proper scouts ahead. As a result, they fought the battle on the banks of the River Hayle on ground of his choice and victory ensued, securing the whole of Devon for the West Seaxa thenceforth. In truth, King Ine did not achieve his dream of forcing the borders of West Seax forward to the westernmost rocks. The cost of this campaign was high enough and he withdrew to face other more threatening problems at home.

Chapter 22

Kingsham, 722 AD

Ealdberht waited in the corner of the tavern hunched over an ale, mentally bemoaning his stature that stood him in such good stead on the battlefield. His massive frame made him stand out in any gathering and now, when he wished to remain inconspicuous, it drew attention to him as a gumboil draws attention to the sufferer's face. The delicate nature of his proposed encounter, to coat the name of treason with honey, made secrecy essential. Trying, in vain, to blend with the wall at his back, Ealdberht kept an eye trained for the Mercian ealdorman Wyflaed had courted assiduously for the past ten days.

Ealdorman Leofwig found Ealdberht a companionable young man, but if he were to succeed with his plans, he could not let himself befriend the aetheling. The message received from Æthelbald needed all his inventive skills to deal with it. What he was asking was too much for the efforts of one person. However demanding the king could be, he was equally generous. This comforting thought spurred Leofwig's creativity as he waited for Ealdberht's reaction to a suggestion he had just made. The delay proved positive since it provided time for inspiration to goad his thinking. Why not combine all the elements of Æthelbald's request into one master plan? Ay, that was it!

The ealdorman smiled at the hesitant aetheling and said, "I see you do not like my suggestion and, in truth, after further consideration, I too can see its faults."

"What am I to do?" the young pretender sighed. He lowered his voice to a whisper, "Ine is gathering men around him as we sit here in futile discussions."

"Futile? Not so, the best ideas are like a good ale, the product of fermentation! What about taking your warriors to the fortress of Tantun? I was there a while ago, and to my eye, it is nigh on unassailable. Think on this. That stout stronghold stands near the southern borders of Mierce. It is a small step for King Æthelbald to make to unite his forces with yours."

The aetheling stared at Leofwig with a troubled expression.

"Do you really think King Æthelbald will come to my aid? Why would he do that?"

"I have told you. The king is tired of Ine thwarting his progress in the south. He wishes for new blood – an energetic ally, with whom he can work in harmony. He has great hopes of you, Lord Ealdberht."

"I shall take my men to Tantun without delay. Will you come with us, friend Leofwig?"

"Not at once. I will join you as soon as I can. But first, I have tasks to complete in Winchester to confound and weaken Ine."

Leofwig rose from his seat and held out a hand that the aetheling clasped with ardour. The Ealdorman of Grantebrycge bestowed his most charming smile upon the muscular figure, so different from his own.

Who knows, I might be dealing with the next king of the West Seaxa?

It was possible, but in his callous heart, he doubted such an outcome. Grasping this hand, he felt like treacherous Judas Iscariot receiving his silver. If his plans matured to perfection, Ealdberht was disposable.

Wynflaed watched the ealdorman leave from the vantage point of the dark corner opposite, where she had taken the precaution of extinguishing the single candle lighting the angle. She threw back the hood of her cloak that covered her luxuriant dark locks, free for many months of its restraining wimple. There was no longer need for her to act the part of a nun. Instead she wore the long, flowing hair of a noblewoman – that station she would never resign. Decisively, she strode over to the aetheling. It mattered not if they were seen here in Kingsham together. They were by now a regular sight. The losses incurred by Ine in Dumnonia meant that it was now much safer to stay in among the Suth Seaxa. It was crucial not to have been seen with the Mercian, as tongues were only too eager to wag and Ine's spies were sure to be watching Ealdberht. Keen to know the outcome of the meeting, she asked,

"Did the Mercians promise their support?"

She could not keep the eagerness out of her voice, so much was riding on their aid.

"As good as. I must ride for Tantun and Beonna and his men will join me there. King Æthelbald is as weary as are we of Ine. If I make a stand there, he will lend his forces too. King Ine's days are numbered, my dear. Will you tell Oswald or will I?"

"I told you, Oswald is gone to Dumnonia to treat with the King of Cornwall. When you are successful, you will take the throne, make him King of Devon and have allies to the west."

Ealdberht smiled darkly, "Ah, I had forgotten that he would not share in my glory. I'm used to having him by my side."

"It's important that rivals like Aethelheard cannot call on aid from other West Seaxa families and their allies."

"You're right of course, Wynflaed. You're a scheming little wildcat!"

'You have no idea! Once this is over, Oswald will slay you and I'll be his Lady.'

She contented herself with an innocent smile of satisfaction in his shaggy-bearded face – for the time being.

* * *

Winchester

Within the week, Ealdorman Leofwig stood before Queen Æthelburh. His plan to see the king had gone awry, since Ine was indisposed. The lady's flowing gown, embroidered in gold thread, did not conceal her lithe muscularity. So, the tales that reached him of her prowess as a warrior might be true, after all. The amber-flecked hazel eyes stared at him with disconcerting intensity. He told himself not to be distracted by her charms.

"My king urged me to lend any help that Mercia can provide to you and your husband, the king. Hence, I came with information of the plotting of the rebel Ealdberht as soon as it came into my possession."

"And we thank you, Ealdorman. What is it you have for us?"

"It is not a casual choice that Ealdberht is planning to hide himself in Tantun."

"I told Ine that fortress would bring trouble. It is too distant to control," she hissed.

"My informants tell me that Ealdberht is in contact with Dumnonia that seeks revenge for recent defeats," he lied without so much as a blink. "Emissaries have crossed the Saefern to enlist the aid of Gwent. It is but two steps from Gwent to Tantun. They are sure to come to assist their British cousins. I fear a trap like a vice." His voice was as smooth as honey.

The queen swallowed the untruth as a hungry carp takes a baited hook.

"Not if we move with all haste," she clapped her hands and a servant hurried to her side.

"Tell the workshops to distil as much resin of the pine as they can, by the morrow!"

A thrill coursed through Leofwig. If the queen had ordered turpentine, it meant she intended to burn Tantun to the ground. His plan, in that case, had worked beyond expectations. King Æthelbald would be gladdened and that meant glory for Leofwig.

One week later, he stood in the shadow of the fortress of Tantun. Twelve years before, King Ine had overseen the construction of earthworks, now forming the ramparts above them. Queen Æthelburh studied the solid palisade looming above, built of tree trunks brought from the Selwood.

She turned to Leofwig, "What do you say, Ealdorman. How can it be breached?"

"Not through the walls, my lady. It must be the gates."

The queen concurred. To his surprise, she ended the conversation before it had begun. Turning to a warrior beside her, "The gates, we must burn them down. Have the men drag wood, branches and straw up to them. Soak them in the liquid we brought and set them alight. Shields above their heads, mind."

The defenders hurled weapons, rocks and insults on the attackers but could not impede the assault. Within half an hour, the conflagration had begun. The turpentine ensured a raging blaze and although the solid wooden gates were slow to catch fire, they succumbed in the end. Ealdberht's force was no match for the might of the queen's army. The slaughter was merciless and Leofwig, not a warrior by nature, contented himself with defending his person by cowering behind a shield. He let the eddy of battle sweep him into backwaters where blows were not being exchanged. From his vantage point, he was able to admire the lady of the West Seax, whose ferocity matched that of her warlike warriors. He watched her dispatch two foes with her flashing sword and noted how she inspired the men around her to redouble their striving.

Leofwig stayed in the fortress to observe the destruction of the palisade and the buildings within the walls. Choking black smoke filled the air for three days until there remained nothing standing of the stronghold. Queen Æthelburh, however, allowed her temper to show when she discovered that the body of Ealdberht was nowhere to be found. He had escaped her wrath through a small postern door and fled to safety in the forest to the south. She need not have worried, for although she could not know it, his wyrd would lead him to his death. This would take place in the lands of the Suth Seaxa, but this event was in the future.

As for Leofwig, he hoped to enter further into the good graces of the warrior queen. But his first task was to send a report to his own king.

* * *

King Ine lay on his bed and his restless eyes, in contrast to his immobile head, sought out the face of his infirmarian. Cynethryth once again had responded to the royal summons. The monarch had taken a tumble from his horse whilst hunting. He probably did not know how fortunate he had been, especially at his age, not to have died of a broken neck. The temporary paralysis that gripped the ruler for some days after the fall had induced him to panic and summon her with all haste. Careful examination had revealed to Cynethryth bruising and swelling at the back of his neck and she, too expert to move him, bound his neck to keep it rigid.

"A few weeks and you will be able to resume normal activities, Sire. The important thing is to let the fractured bones heal without damaging the nerves."

The king ground his teeth.

"Am I to let my wife lead the army as she wishes? She behaves too much like a man as it is."

"Is that a real question Sire, or is my King merely stating his displeasure?"

"This fall could not have come at a more inconvenient moment, when a threat to our borders and my throne has occurred."

"What makes you think a woman is unfit to lead the army? The queen is known for her resolve."

"I will not send my hearthweru with her. I need them here whilst I'm unfit to move."

By chance, at that moment, Aethelheard begged leave to enter the royal bedchamber and permission was granted. He gave a summary nod to his mother and addressed the monarch directly.

"Sire, my informants believe they have found the reason for this rebellion. Ealdberht has been seen in Kingsham meeting with a dark-haired woman and both with the Mercian Ealdorman from Grantebrycge who begged leave to meet with you."

"Then what Æthelburh tells me is true. Ealdberht plans to seize Tantun and from there launch his challenge for the throne."

"Sire, give the word and I will lead our men against him."

"Nay, Aethelheard, I wish for you and your men to stay here to guard the royal vill. The queen will take our host to Tantun and put an end to the rebellion."

"Well said, Sire!" Cynethryth surprised them both.

"But–"

Ine cut off Aethelheard's protest.

"My decision is final."

"The raven-haired woman is bound to be Wynflaed," Cynethryth said, "I warned you about her."

"I have raised a search for the pair of them," Aethelheard replied. "Let's pray that the queen destroys Ealdberht and the witch once and for all."

That this prayer went unheeded became apparent upon the return of Æthelburh. She wished to translate her distress at allowing the rebel to evade her guards into the action of pursuit, but King Ine would not hear of it. For the moment, as he explained, he wished to be fit again to consider the safety of his border with Mercia now that his wife had reduced Tantun to a smouldering pile of ashes. With his desire for expansion, he told his commanders King Aethelbald was the greatest threat to West Seax. Aethelheard would bear this in mind in times to come.

Chapter 23

Naked, next to Wynflaed, Oswald sat up in bed, heart pounding. A sudden rush of fear drove off his drowsiness and he leapt out of bed. The battering against the door continued as he groped for and drew his sword. Conscious of his vulnerability and undecided whether there was time to dress, he pulled on his breeches. They offered no armoured protection but, in a curious way, served as a shield to his dignity. The terrified woman whimpering in his bed further strengthened his resolve. Whoever these ill-intentioned intruders were, he would exact a heavy price on them. At the instant of this thought, the lock gave way and the door swung back to reveal two armed men, weapons drawn.

"In the name of King Ine, lay down your sword and come with us!"

"Never!" Oswald placed himself between the door and the bed. "Do you know who I am?"

This feeble attempt to assert authority met with a derisory laugh.

"Ay, you're the traitor who treats with the king's enemies."

The speaker rushed at the aetheling and as the steel clashed, Wynflaed screamed. Aghast, she looked on as the second assailant rushed forward to rain blows on the frantic parries of their prey. Casting her eyes around, Wynflaed spied Oswald's hand-seax in its sheath, hanging from a belt over the bedhead. Stealthily, so as not to draw attention to her movement, whilst Oswald fended blow after blow, she drew the seax. Step by step, the attackers drove the aetheling back towards the bed. Soon, his stout resistance wheeled his opponents round so that he was no longer between her and the door.

This was her chance. Mortal danger made her oblivious to the fact that she was naked and she launched herself from the mattress like a springing feline onto the back of one of the warriors. Before he knew what had hit him, she had drawn the seax across his throat with a determination born of desperation.

At the same time, taking advantage of the distraction, Oswald dispatched the other assailant with a neat strike to the heart. Panting, he leant on his sword, oblivious to the blood swirling over his bare feet.

Regaining presence of mind, he hurried to the door and closed it, dragging a heavy cupboard against it. Next, he hurried to the window, opened it, put his head out and gazed in both directions on the street below. Satisfied, he withdrew into the chamber and turned to Wynflaed.

"My mountain lynx, I have you to thank that I'm still in one piece. Thank God there are no more of them and that I had the sense to lock the door. They will know to send more men next time so we must leave, but where to go?"

Wynflaed patted the bed next to her and gazed with horror at the crimson imprint the gesture left on the white linen.

"As to where," she said, "there is a place. Hark! If Ealdberht had been stronger, King Aethelbald of Mercia would have backed him against Ine. The Mercian king is envious of West Seax and tired of the old rulers in the south: Ine, Nothelm and Wihtred. Mercia frets to expand and to have a strong claimant to the West Seax throne as a friend..." Wynflaed's voice trailed away and her hand trembled. Oswald noticed how her eyes strayed to the corpse of the warrior whose throat she had slit. He took her in his arms and shielded the gory sight from her eyes with his broad shoulders.

"Lie down," he ordered, kissing her and stroking her hair. When she was settled with her head nestling in his cradling shoulder, he continued, "Would you have us ride to Mercia?"

"Not exactly," she murmured.

"Speak plainly, Wynflaed."

"The fortress at Tantun is no more. The northern border of West Seax is open to any foe who chooses that route – Mercia, Gwent or Powys."

"How does that aid us?"

"Of course it does. The border is with Hwicce, and as you know, there, Ealdorman Aethelric is underking to Aethelbald. We could reside in Hwicce, and gain the king's favour, without being in his grasp. And if there's one thing we've learnt from Ealdbert's failure – it's that Ine is too strong for the moment. We must await his death. He does not enjoy great health and can't live forever. Meanwhile we can enter Aethelbald's good graces."

"It's a good plan, and as you say, the way into West Seax is open. We leave at dawn. Any ideas that might help take our minds off those unwanted guests on the floor?" he smirked.

* * *

Winchester, 723 AD

The absence of Osburh in Dorset caused Aethelheard to confide more in his friend's younger brother. Thus, Aelfhere became a firm companion of his commander. When news of the death of two informants in Kingsham reached him, Aethelheard raged against the obtuse initiative they had taken against the quarry.

"They disobeyed orders, Aelfhere. They should never have moved alone against Oswald and his woman. What possessed them to do such a thing?"

"I'd guess they felt sure they had them in a trap and feared losing them to inaction."

"But now the birds have flown."

"Like a cropped coin, they are bound to show up again."

Aethelheard laughed but it was on a bitter note.

"Sure enough, then we'll deal with them ourselves. Aelfhere, I much prefer to face the foe on the field of battle to this sly business of plotting and counter-conniving."

As it turned out, Aethelheard's dislike of scheming was given respite for two years. This period consolidated Ine's conception of kingship, one of responsible statesmanship that Aethelheard hoped to emulate should he succeed to the throne. Ine had successfully blended ancient custom with new laws into an elaborate body of law. In so doing, Ine brought his clergy and nobles into deliberation and Aethelheard admired him for it.

* * *

The South of England, 725 AD

A series of unfortunate events combined to destabilise the south beginning with the death of King Nothelm in Sussex and rapidly followed by that of King Wihtred of Kent. Thus, the triumvirate guaranteeing stability in the south for three decades was gone. When Nothelm died, Ealdberht emerged from hiding in the great Andersweald. Once more, the forest had provided leafy refuge for an outlaw. He marked his reappearance by playing on the ancient rivalry between the West and Suth Seaxa. At once, he laid claim to the vacant throne and began to gather an army to defend the borders.

King Ine, who had been instrumental in raising his kinsman Nothelm to the throne of Sussex, and whom he fondly called Nunna, flew into a towering rage. In front of his counsel he declared,

"I will not accept this! We cannot have Ealdberht on our doorstep casting envious eyes upon our throne. We cannot allow him to consolidate his position. We invade Sussex at once!"

This declaration was met with roars of approval and stirred Aethelheard's blood, who, if truth be told, was tired of inactivity.

While others summoned the host, his job was to organise and ready the hearthweru for war. They formed the king's select guard, deployed around him and his standard in battle. Each man was hand-picked by Aethelheard and provided with intensive weapon and formation training. Surveying their compact ranks as they marched out of Winchester filled him with pride and confidence. As they crossed into Sussex, King Ine drew his horse next to his commander.

"Aethelheard, after your success in Cornwall, I wish to entrust our battle plans to you."

"Sire, as you wish. I have sent scouts ahead in the hope of locating Ealdberht's forces. I doubt he'll wish to skulk in the great forest. It's likely we'll meet him on the downs."

The first sighting of the enemy by the scouts confirmed this impression. They had espied the foe some leagues to the north of Kingsham, encamped on top of an ancient earthworks complete with serpentine defensive ditches.

"We can't risk a frontal attack on such a position," Aethelheard opined while King Ine nodded sagely. "We must find a way to lure them out, otherwise it will be a long siege. I want a map of the exact lie of the land," he told the ten scouts he'd assembled.

Poring over pieces of parchment placed edge to edge by his scouts the next day, he gained a complete picture of the land that lay ahead, and formulated a plan.

Separating only a third of his total force and uniting them with the king's own guard around the standard, the remaining two-thirds he hid in a hollow invisible from the commanding position of the enemy. With his reduced force, he advanced on the fortification and brought them to a halt beyond the range of javelins. With utter faith in the discipline of his stalwart warriors, he had them form a shield-wall, beating a challenge upon their shields with their weapon hilts. As expected, faces appeared to assess their strength and as hoped, shortly afterwards the enemy, deceived, poured out of the hill fort. Downhill they charged, loosing javelins that either passed harmlessly overhead or fell short. Some caused problems by burying themselves in the defenders' linden shields but caused no real harm.

Aethelheard let the foe rush into the serried shields and although desperately outnumbered, the strong trained arms held resolute. After three minutes of frantic resistance, Aethelheard blew three sharp blasts on his war-horn and waited. The arrival of the bulk of his army, so unexpected and ferocious, had a devastating effect on the men of Sussex. Their discipline, already shaky, wavered and they succumbed. Aethelheard had no difficulty in identifying Ealdberht – the aetheling and would-be king stood head and shoulders above his men under the blue banner of Sussex with its six golden martlets.

Aethelheard thrust and hacked his way towards him, closely followed by Aelfhere who had understood his friend's intent. Together, they attacked Ealdberht and marvelled at the brute strength of the man. It was not enough to save him against the united skills of two practised warriors. The attempts of his own men to succour him were in vain since foes from the West Seax shield-wall poured into the fray. Aethelheard and Aelfhere inflicted three deep wounds before the valiant Ealdberht swayed and crashed to the ground, blood gushing from his mouth. Aelfhere, at a nod from his commander, delivered the merciful, fatal blow. The death of their leader saw the end of Suth Seaxa resistance. Those who could disentangle themselves from the fighting fled downhill, some threw down their arms and surrendered, others fought to the death.

The beauty of the sward-mantled downland contrasted strongly with the carrion scattered on the battlefield and Aethelheard wondered at life wasted by ambition. Hadn't King Ine tried to lead his people by example along a better, more lawful and peaceable way? Aethelheard was world-weary enough to know that there would always be men lusting after power. If he looked into his heart, was he not one such himself? And yet, he felt sure a time would come when men would live side by side under one banner. But then, would a threat not come from other lands? Such were his thoughts as he organised the stripping of the dead and the burial mound.

At last, he reflected, one of the main threats to King Ine's throne lay dead. As a result, his own hopes for succession had been strengthened. His successful leadership in battle also marked him out as a potential ruler. Two of the three great southern kings had gone but the one who occupied the throne he coveted, the throne his father had held, was still firmly ensconced.

Chapter 24

Wimborne Abbey, 726 AD

Sefled, whose demeanour was unhurried, surprised Cynethryth by skittering into the preparations room like an untethered foal.

"What's amiss, sister?"

Sefled flushed and looked guilty: it was in her character, in spite of her impeccable conduct.

"Oh, sister, it's the prioress–"

"What? Is she ill?"

"No, not her. The prioress sent me with a message."

Cynethryth's exasperation overcame her fondness for her assistant.

"Well, out with it, girl! I don't have all day for your nonsense."

The assistant infirmarian blushed again and stammered, "S-sorry, sister, but Prioress Quenburga sends word that our abbess has taken to her bed."

"The abbess?"

"Ay. The prioress says she's been badly for three days."

"Three days and she didn't send for me! I must go to her at once."

Cynethryth had not entered the abbess's bedchamber before and was surprised at the bare and comfortless room. The air hung heavy with the smell of sickness and the infirmarian rushed to the bedside of the frail figure. The familiar pleasant, dimpled face was drawn and grey and Cynethryth feared the worst.

"Mother, what ails you?"

"She complains of pains below her stomach."

The disembodied voice from a dark corner of the room made Cynethryth start.

"Prioress Quenburga! I did not see you when I came into the room."

"That much is clear, Sister. Hadn't you better see to your patient?"

Ignoring the acid tone, Cynethryth turned her attention to the abbess.

"Mother, what is it you feel?"

"Cynethryth? Is it you? Pain. It comes and goes but it's seated here below the navel. It's agony when I relieve myself and there's blood in the urine."

Cynethryth pressed with her fingers, "Does it hurt here?"

Cuthburga gasped and nodded weakly, "It spreads right across to my hips and my back aches so."

"I can give you something to ease the pain, Mother."

"*But* there is nought you can do to cure me. Not even you, Cynethryth. The Lord has measured my days and each one is numbered. Listen, child, when I'm gone, I wish for you to be my successor."

The gasp that came from the corner of the room was far louder than Cynethryth's own, followed by, "Pay no heed, these are ramblings induced by the ailment."

"The abbess has no fever, Sister."

"Yet the malady impairs her judgment. It's clear she can't be thinking straight. It is normal for a prioress to succeed an abbess, not a mere infirmarian."

"We should discuss this outside, Sister. I must hasten to fetch medicines to comfort our mother superior."

Outside the chamber, Prioress Quenburga seized Cynethryth's arm.

"Don't you dare!" she hissed, "Cuthburga and I are the king's sisters and of royal blood. What right have you to claim the abbess's throne?"

"I have never thought of such a thing till today, *prioress*, but if it comes to that I have been a *queen* not a *mere* king's sister. Now by your leave, I will fetch the medicines."

Eyes narrowed and lips tightened, the thin features of the prioress's visage became harsher, "Wait! You know what ails my sister, do you not?"

Cynethryth considered her reply and decided on honesty.

"I do, it's what Hippocrates named *carcinos* and it has afflicted the bladder."

"I-is there no cure?"

Moved by the first display of humanity in the face of the severe prioress, whose eyes brimmed with tears, Cynethryth took her bony hand and marvelled at its coldness.

"In a younger woman, an attempt might be made with a knife but I fear at the mother's age, it would be folly. She said so herself, her days are numbered. I'm truly sorrowful."

The numbing effect of the potion restored a little colour to the cheeks of the abbess, and with a gesture, she brought Prioress Quenburga to her bedside.

"Prepare a litter for I wish to address the sisters in the chapter hall."

The prioress looked sharply at Cynethryth, "Is this wise? Surely you cannot allow this?"

"If it's the mother's wish," Cynethryth mumbled, assailed herself by doubt.

"It is my command," came the weak voice.

"Very well, but–"

"And fetch the sub-prioress to me."

Several minutes passed until the prioress returned with her deputy. She said, "Mother, I have done as you wished. Even now, the sisters are gathering in the chapter hall."

A weak smile crossed the abbess's face, who pointed and crooked a finger at Leofwen.

The nun bent forward so her ear was close to the mouth of the abbess and she heard, "Sister Leofwen, you will be my voice and refer all my words to the sisters faithfully – exactly as I pronounce them."

"I understand, Mother."

Cynethryth oversaw the gentle transferral of the frail patient to the litter. Assuring herself the covers were warm enough and well-ordered, she brought the four waiting monks into the chamber and instructed them to carry the abbess to the chapter hall.

Cynethryth did not expect the intake of breath that echoed from the high rafters above her head as the vulnerable figure was carried to the dais at the front of the hall. Until this day, none of the sisters could have imagined that the benign figure-head who had guided their cloistered lives since the first day the gates opened might not be permanent. The unthinkable was about to occur – change.

Sister Leofwen sat cross-legged beside the litter and, inclining her head towards the abbess, listened intently. A moment later, she declared, "Sisters, I speak the words of our abbess to you, for she is too frail to address you directly. Here is what she says:

"Sisters, I have gathered you here today because the Lord is calling me to Him. Before long, I shall see His shining face and I beg each and every one of you to pray for my soul."

A collective groan filled the hall amid sniffles and sighs. Leofwen leant forward again to heed the abbess's next words.

"Soon, sisters, you will need a new mother superior, and as is custom, I will announce my successor. It is my will that the abbess after me will be..." Leofwen's countenance was radiant as she looked around to seek out the face of Cynethryth and smile at her, "our beloved infirmarian, Sister Cynethryth."

The sub-prioress bent close to the abbess once more and as she did so, Cynethryth's eyes sought out Quenburga. She found her pressing a hand against her brow, looking pale and drawn, and staring with intense rancour at her.

'My God, what's happening? Am I dreaming this?'

Her thoughts were interrupted by Leofwen continuing, "Sister Cynethryth has the attributes to fulfil the role as the Holy Spirit intimated to me. I'm confident that she will carry forward my work here to the greater glory of our house and of the Almighty. In the name of the Father, Son and the Holy Spirit, Amen. Go in peace."

Cynethryth ignored the smiling faces and well-wishing to hurry to the litter. She needed to ensure her patient had not overtaxed herself. Before she could speak, the abbess clutched her hand with a frozen claw-like grip.

"Be strong, child!"

Then, she closed her eyes and spoke no more.

The health of Abbess Cuthburga declined with the fading year. The increasing pain caused by the incurable disease tested her spirit and also challenged Cynethryth's skill in alleviating the abbess's suffering.

Several days before the celebration of Christ's Mass, once again Sefled rushed into the infirmary.

"What is it, sister?" Cynethryth stared in alarm at her assistant. She expected bad news at any moment regarding the abbess. But this was not to be the dreaded day.

"Prioress Quenburga has called us all to the chapter hall for another reunion, sister."

"What reason can she have?"

"I asked around and no-one seems to know, but we'd best get along."

The infirmarians hastened to the chapter hall and stood at the back of the congregation. They were just in time to hear the prioress silence the assembly.

The prioress's voice was as harsh and cutting as her rigid character. She was a well-respected but unloved authority figure.

"As you know sisters, our abbess lies dying. At a previous meeting, she expressed her wish that our infirmarian, Sister Cynethryth, should succeed her. It is to talk about this *singular* fact that I have convened this assembly. There are some aspects of this decision that need clarification. Firstly, custom dictates that upon the passing of an abbess, the next incumbent should be her deputy. In this case, that office falls to me. In exceptional circumstances, of course, the custom may be waived. However, there are no exceptional issues to consider here. I put it to you, were it not for the fact of her serious illness, our mother superior would never have made such a preposterous utterance. I say..." here, she paused and glared intimidatingly around the hall, "...I say, she cannot have been in her right mind when she made her declaration. It was the Devil though his malevolent disease that put the words in her mouth. I implore you, in the name of God to reverse this wicked decision."

Sister Leofwen, the sub-prioress, stepped forward, took a deep breath and said, "Sisters, we all know that the abbess is God's voice in this house. How can we ignore her express wish? I, for one, I believe that God, not the Devil, spoke through our mother superior. We must be obedient to her desire and accept Sister Cynethryth as our next abbess."

Prioress Quenburga stepped over to Leofwen, seized her by the shoulder and pulled her round to thrust her face into hers.

"This is disobedience to your direct superior! How dare you?"

She turned to face the gathering.

"There's another matter to consider. We all know of the skill of our infirmarian. How come, then, she cannot or *will not* cure my sister? Her face contorted in fury, "Is it that curing her will thwart her ambitions? The Bible instructs us, in the words of the Apostle Luke, *'For what does it profit a man if he gains the whole world and loses or forfeits himself?'* – or *herself* in this case!"

Before Cynethryth could react, Sefled cried, "Wait!" and she rushed to the front of the hall through the nuns who separated to let her dash between them.

When she reached the front, the prioress said, "What is the meaning of this?"

Sefled glared at her and pointed an accusatory finger, "You should be ashamed to make such false accusations against a good and noble woman! You quote the Apostle and accuse her of ambition but the apostle Matthew says, 'Whoever exalts himself will be humbled, and whoever humbles himself will be exalted,' – or herself," she ended with a flourish.

"You – you–" the prioress bit her lip and thought better of whatever she was about to blurt.

Cynethryth spoke and, in a rustling of cloth, the sisters all turned to seek her face.

"Sisters, I did not ask our mother superior to name me as her successor and it's vile to accuse me of not curing her disease. I confess, I do not know how to cure it, and sadly, I cannot save her. But as God is my witness, I have tried. Sister Quenburga, I forgive you for your unconsidered words and extend my hand to you in sisterhood. Together we can carry forward the work of our beloved mother–"

"I will *never* work with you, sister Cynethryth! If you take what is rightfully mine, I will leave this house and even this land to take the Word to the heathen as did our sister Leoba and others from Wimborne."

Before Cynethryth could reply, the sub-prioress cried, "God Bless Abbess Cynethryth!"

Sefled took up the cry and hundreds of voices followed their example:

"God Bless Abbess Cynethryth!"

"God Bless Abbess Cynethryth!"

"God Bless Abbess Cynethryth!"

Cynethryth held up her hand and the echoing cry died away.

"Sisters, I thank you, but this is wrong! There can be no other abbess whilst our beloved mother, Cuthburga, is alive. May the Almighty give her the strength to celebrate Christ's Mass with us."

"Amen!"

It was the acid voice of the prioress. But the word was repeated by all the assembled sisters.

Cynethryth waited for the gathering to disperse and then wandered over to the prioress.

"There is no need for us to be enemies, sister."

"Isn't there? We'll see what my brother has to say about this."

"I'm sure the king will do what he believes right," Cynethryth smiled. "Meanwhile let's celebrate this festive season in the spirit of love and sisterhood. I will of course, accept the king's ruling. I ask only one thing of you, Prioress."

"And what is that?"

"That you believe I'm doing everything I can to cure your sister. Alas, her disease is incurable or leastways, my skills insufficient. I pray for her health every day."

The prioress gave her a thin smile, "I believe you, sister. When I'm abbess, we'll work well together, as you said." *'The king is deep in my debt – we'll see!'*

Chapter 25

"What's going on in West Seax, Leofwig?"

King Aethelbald's instincts told him that here was an opportunity to further his ambitions too appetising to miss.

"Sire, King Ine has thrown the south into turmoil. He means to give up his throne and embark on a pilgrimage to Rome."

"Ha! With Wihtred dead, the Suth Seax in foment and now Ine playing the devout Christian, the way is open for me to regain Lunden for Mercia. But I'll need to move carefully. What do you advise, old fox?"

Ealdorman Leofwig, who owed his wealth to the king's appreciation of his wits, smiled grimly.

"Sire, it's not the might of Mercia that will win the day," he did not fail to notice the flicker of wrath in the royal countenance at these words, "but the *threat* of the might of Mercia."

"Explain!"

The ealdorman, heartened by the monarch's quickening interest, proceeded, "Ine has chosen his successor. Did you know Sire, that the wife of the great king, Caedwalla, bore a son soon after his death? She kept the child hidden away for years but he's emerged as a great warrior to compare with his father. They say that he alone is responsible for Ine's latest victories."

"What name does he go by?"

"Aethelheard, Lord. I believe it would be unwise to make an enemy of him but the situation is complex."

"Speak your mind, Leofwig."

"Well, Sire, Ine summoned the witan and announced his intentions. He declared Aethelheard his successor to general approbation, but as ever in West Seax, there is a faction that wishes to promote its own family."

"Does this family have a candidate?"

"It does and he resides in Mercia, in Hwicce to be precise."

"Name?"

"An aetheling, rebellious to Ine, by the name of Oswald."

"To whom should I give my support?"

The ealdorman wanted to look pityingly at his monarch but, not daring, instead risked a grin at the leonine countenance scrutinising him.

"Neither and both, Sire."

"Leofwig!" Aethelbald bellowed in frustration.

The ealdorman flinched, "Forgive me, Lord, but it is a clever game you must play. Aethelheard holds the upper hand for the moment and Oswald seeks support. It would be easy enough to let him believe in your forthcoming aid but, at the same time, Aethelheard will be aware of the danger from Mercia and will seek reassurances. These will come at a price if you follow my drift, Sire."

"By Thunor, I do!"

* * *

Wimborne Abbey, three days before Christ's Mass, 726 AD

The canvas-covered cart pulled by two oxen trundled through the abbey gates flanked by two armed riders. The mud-splattered beasts plodded stoically to halt by the infirmary. Osburh and Guthred dismounted and led their tired horses to the drinking trough that Cynethryth generally used as a source for watering her herb garden.

The short journey from Wareham, on this occasion, had seemed far longer than usual owing to the muddy state of the road. Rowena, sheltered from the cold inside the covered waggon, had heard a string of curses from husband and son each time the cloying mud had sucked the cartwheels into immobility. How glad she was to have arrived, especially as the bearer of joyful news in this season of goodwill.

Guthred unlaced the canvas flaps and offered his hand to his wife to help her descend from the cart.

"I can't wait to see her face," he grinned at Rowena.

"I beg you, husband, let me be the one to tell her."

Guthred smiled his assent and told his son to tend to the oxen and the horses. He led the way to the infirmary door with Rowena battling to keep the hem of her tunic off the ground.

"Guthred! Rowena! What a wonderful surprise!"

Thus Cynethryth greeted them but, in her enthusiasm, failed to detect the roguish twinkle in her friend's green eyes.

"Cynethryth, it's about Aethelheard–"

At the nun's anguished expression, she regretted her mischievousness at once.

"I-is he...is he hurt?"

Rowena relented, smiled and replied,

"No, he's king!"

Cynethryth could make no sense of this and gazed at her friend as though she'd taken leave of her senses.

"What is the matter with you, Rowena? Are you ill?"

Guthred stepped forward and stared accusingly at his wife.

"I knew this was a bad idea," he muttered, and in a louder voice, said, "Cynethryth, King Ine has given up his throne and named your son as his successor. The witan has accepted. We have King Aethelheard!"

Tears of joy welled in Cynethryth's eyes and she sprang into Rowena's embrace. She could scarcely believe her dream had come true.

"Tell me I'm not dreaming," she whispered in her friend's ear.

"It's true, Cynethryth, Aethelheard has the crown once Caedwalla's. Everything is as it should be."

At that moment, Osburh walked into the infirmary, wrinkling his nose at a pungent medicinal smell.

"Queen Cynethryth," he bowed with a satisfied grin, "isn't that how one addresses the mother of the king?"

Reality began to strike home and Cynethryth turned to face Guthred.

"Is my son in danger, old friend?"

Guthred gave her a level stare,

"Of course, Lady. When is a king not in danger? There are those who would wrest the crown from him. It's ever thus."

"Which is why he will need sound advice. You must go to him in Winchester. I will write a message to him, stating how you helped his father."

"My lady, I'll willingly do as you ask. I'm tired of skulking in Dorset and so is Osburh, aren't you lad?"

"Father, I think King Aethelheard has little need of advice. They say he outwitted the Suth Seax in battle."

Cynethryth tut-tutted and scowled, "Men!" she smiled at Rowena, "As if the answer to everything is the sword. By the way, what made King Ine give up the throne? He was a king who understood the needs of his people, and Aethelheard will need guidance to be just as wise." Without waiting for a reply, she dashed into the preparations room, where Sefled, the originator of the pungent odour, was mixing a potion. "I'll write that note," she called over her shoulder.

"Sefled, my son is our new king," she announced.

After a moment taken to absorb the news, a triumphant light came into the assistant's eyes.

"Good, that's settled Quenburga once and for all!"

Cynethryth's mouth dropped open. She hadn't had time to think through the implications of the startling news for Wimborne. But what Sefled had grasped so quickly was true. Without Ine, she no longer need worry about any challenge from Quenburga. Only the king could countermand the decision of the abbess, ratified by the chapter – and what son would oust his own mother?

* * *

Winchester, Christ's Mass, 726 AD

King Ine, with Queen Aethelburg at his right hand and King Aethelheard at his left, presiding over his last great feast, was well into his cups. Giving up the throne had not been a hard decision for him, since as he had announced to the witan it was time for a younger man to lead the kingdom. He was weary of endless rebellion and strife and his health was not robust. If he were to fulfil his dream of a pilgrimage to Rome it had to be now.

For the fiftieth time, he raised his drinking horn to Aethelheard, in whom he had found a worthy successor. As king, Ine had been unable to hold on to Caedwalla's, this young man's father's conquests. Surrey and Sussex were now openly rebellious and although he had pushed as far as Devon, Cornwall still spoke Brittonic. His old allies and friends were dead and their passing had drained his desire to continue: he lacked the energy for new challenges. Although Aethelheard might not realise it yet, a new threat was forming in the north in the shape of Mercia, whose ambitious king was expanding his borders in every direction.

* * *

Ealdorman Aethelric, otherwise King of the Hwicce, stared into the lovely oval face of the raven-haired woman and tried not to lose himself under her thrall.

"My dear lady," he said, "how am I to convince you that the decision is not mine? If I accede to your request, I would be laying myself open to a charge of treason. Heaven knows, there are enough rivals eager to be predators and feed off my corpse."

"Surely, Sire, your word is law in these parts," she fluttered her lashes and widened her dark eyes, "and what would it matter if you offend the King of Mercia when you have the King of the West Seax as your friend?"

"How little you understand. The King of Mercia is powerful and his land encircles mine. He is also overlord to my people, many of whom would follow him if forced to choose. Your aetheling is not yet the king of the West Seax but when he becomes the monarch, I am sure we'll be friends. Also, why did he not come to speak with me but send your charming self in his stead?"

"Oswald is across the border in West Seax gathering support for his rightful cause. He has also moved to garner support from Gwent, with success."

A shrewd expression crept into Wynflaed's face. She continued, "Ealdorman, you are quite right not to risk the wrath of King Aethelbald. It would be folly but what do you think about convincing the king to take the part of the aetheling? I feel sure Oswald could be guided by us," she gave him her sweetest smile, "to make concessions to Mercia and to Hwicce. This is too good an opportunity to miss. Oswald can raise a mighty host and with the men of Hwicce and Mercia to swell his ranks, Aethelheard, the usurper, will be destroyed. Once this happens you and Aethelbald will receive your dues. What do you say?"

"You interest me, Lady. I will take your proposal to Tame Weorth and feel sure the king will be of the same mind."

Wynflaed left the palace in Worcester in buoyant mood, which contrasted strongly with her temper of three days before when Oswald had told her of Ine's abdication. The knowledge that the son of her greatest enemy had been nominated King of West Seax had whipped her into a seething fury. Oswald's state of mind matched her own but since he had been working for months to gain support *when the time was right* – always those words – he was now well placed to call upon his allies. She felt sure that she had charmed Ealdorman Aethelric enough to gain his support. There would be a price to pay, when wasn't there? But, she smiled secretively, anything was worth becoming the Lady of the West Seax.

'*When I rule in Winchester, then you will pay Cynethryth!*'

* * *

However foxy Wynflaed felt she had been, an older, slyer fox exerted more cunning. Ealdormen Leofwig and Aethelric, seated at a table in the Royal Hall of Tame Weorth, considered the circumstances with King Aethelbald.

"Sire, the aetheling's woman was right about one thing only: this is too good an opportunity to pass over."

The king's wide brow furrowed, "How can we best exploit it, Leofwig?"

"I suggest, Lord, that the ealdorman here leads the woman to believe your aid will be forthcoming. It will buy us time to see how strong Aethelheard really is. Meanwhile, Sire, do you recall the land grant you proposed to enact at Abingdon?"

"Indeed, what of it?"

"We can use it to test the waters with Aethelheard. He is new to kingship and will not know how to move for best. If you were to call upon him to witness the charter at Abingdon, you will be declaring to the whole land that he is subservient to you. By signing, he'll admit as much, but if he refuses to participate, he'll risk your wrath and support for Oswald."

"By Thunor, Leofwig, you are the sly one! You'd put Aethelheard in an impossible position."

"It's a clever move," Ealdorman Aethelric conceded. "It will work, Sire."

* * *

Abingdon, Oxon, six weeks later.

Aethelheard cursed under his breath as he entered the hall. At the far end, a group of men huddled around a table. They did not see him enter as their attention was fixed on a document – the one he was supposed to put his name to. He absorbed the five mitred figures in their bishops' regalia, the tall, shaggy-haired individual with the gold circlet on his head, King Aethelbald for sure. Grudgingly, he admitted, the King of the Mercians knew how to manipulate power.

'*He's outwitted me. Damn Oswald! If not for him I wouldn't be in this situation.*'

Finally, his presence was noted and King Aethelbald strode up to him.

"King Aethelheard, welcome! It's good to clasp the hand of friendship between our peoples."

Aethelheard murmured equal words of circumstance, pointless pleasantries. He wanted to get this over with and exact what he considered his entitlement.

As customary procedure demanded, Aethelbald, for first, took the quill from the cleric and wrote his signature on the parchment with a flourish. Aethelheard was next. Dispassionately, he watched the cleric dip the pen in ink and remove the excess. He took the plume in his hand and bent over to read the transaction in Latin which he was about to witness.

He translated: *'Aethelbald, King, to St. Mary's Minster, Abingdon, confirmation of lands and grant of 27 hides at Watchfield and 10 by Ginge Brook, Berks., with further confirmation by Aethelheard, King of West Seax.*

Underneath the fresh signature *Aethelbaldi*, he wrote *Aethelhardi, regis*. As he straightened and handed over the quill, his eyes met the satisfied gleam in Aethelbald's.

Next, the five bishops led by Daniel added their signatures, and ceremony finished, Aethelbald ordered servants to fetch food and drink. Aethelheard sat next to the King of Mercia and after the usual exchanges of little importance, Aethelheard went to the heart of the matter.

"I am pleased, King Aethelbald, that I can consider us as friends."

"Indeed, the pleasure is mine."

"If ever you need the support of West Seax, call upon me."

"That may be necessary," said Aethelbald, his eyes staring unfocused up to the rafters.

Aethelheard was surprised because it seemed from his tone as if the king of Mercia had some venture in mind. This encouraged him to press on, "Word has come to me that a rival to my throne is in Hwicce."

"Fear not, my friend, he will not have my support or that of my underkings."

With that he raised his drinking horn and toasted, "To our friendship."

"To our friendship."

'A rather one-sided friendship, but it will have to serve for now.'

Chapter 26

The demise of Abbess Cuthburga was prolonged and harrowing for the holy lady and those who nursed her. Cynethryth calculated the dosage of narcotic potions with great care but was helpless to arrest the unforgiving malady. It tore at her heart to see such a noble spirit reduced to the tiny, skeletal figure that was its earthly frame.

One spring morning, Sefled, whose turn it was to vigil over the abbess, woke Cynethryth from her slumber. Her agitated assistant urged the infirmarian to dress and had her outdoors in minutes.

"The priest is administering the last rites, sister. I thought I should fetch you at once."

"Bless you, Sefled, you did right."

They hurried to the bedchamber of the abbess, where, upon entering, the tear-streaked faces of several nuns, including the prioress, turned towards them to reveal their anguish. A nun swung a thurible three times and a billowing plume of grey smoke added incense to the already oppressively scented air. The priest, extreme unction completed, continued with the Viaticum, reciting prayers and appropriate passages from the gospels.

Cynethryth knelt by the bed and took a claw-like hand in hers. The faintest twitch at the side of the abbess's mouth was her last communication before she expired. The infirmarian delicately closed the staring eyes and rose to address the sisters.

"Our mother's sufferings are over. Her soul has flown. Do not grieve sisters, for we believe that Jesus died and rose again, and so we believe that God will bring with Jesus our beloved Cuthburga, who has fallen asleep in him."

Cynethryth was not yet officially Abbess of Wimborne and bearing in mind the blood relationship between Cuthburga and Quenburga, she delegated organisation of the funeral and entombment to the sister of the deceased. To avoid giving the impression of being secondary to the prioress, she nonetheless took the abbess's seat in the church and concluded the funeral with a eulogy to Cuthburga.

The day after the entombment, Quenburga came to the infirmary to confront Cynethryth. Her tone was caustic.

"My sister and I founded this abbey when you were still at Barking. Can you not see that it's God's will that I become abbess after the death of my sister?"

"Who can say what is God's will, prioress? Was it He who guided me to indicate this place to the blessed Cuthburga as the site to construct the abbey?"

"I do not believe you! Cuthburga discovered it."

"Believe what you choose, prioress, but in front of the whole chapter, your sister nominated me as her successor. She was the voice of the Almighty in this house. Do you dare challenge Him?"

"I came to give you one last chance to do the right thing, Sister Cynethryth. What do you know about administering an abbey?"

"Very little, I admit, but I'm willing to learn and I'll have you to lean on."

"You will *not*. Do not think you can usurp my position and count on my support. I'll do nought to help you, sister."

"Let me remind you, Sister Quenburga, that you are sworn in virtue of holy obedience and are bound in conscience."

"Obligatorily given to the rightful abbess, true enough, as it was for Abbess Cuthburga and should be for *me*. But not to a usurper. I will fight you, Cynethryth."

With these words and her tight-lipped pinched face, Quenburga turned away and marched stiffly out of the infirmary.

Cynethryth sighed and wondered how best to deal with the rebellious prioress. She had no intention of standing aside for Quenburga because she had great plans for Wimborne Abbey. The thought of managing the administration of so large a holding without the help of the practical nun made her doubt her adequacy for the role.

One week after the death of Cuthburga, the sisters proceeded to the church for the historic ceremony – the formal benediction of the new abbess. It was hard to find a nun unfavourable to the infirmarian, whose humble character and ready smile contrasted so starkly with the austere, severe Quenburga. It did not occur that morning to any of the women filing into the nave that the efficiency of the stern prioress might be missed. Thus, the atmosphere inside the house of worship was joyful as the priest blessed the new abbess and presented her with the crosier – her staff of office – and slipped the abbess's ring on her finger. It was done!

Cynethryth looked around at the smiling congregation and her heart sang. Of course, she could not see the sour expression on the face of Quenburga, who was standing just behind her right shoulder, nor the wide grin on the visage of sub-prioress Leofwen, behind her left.

The abbess had prepared her maiden speech to the sisters and now recited it by heart: "Sisters, my aim as abbess is to be a worthy successor to our blessed Abbess Cuthburga. My aim is to make Wimborne a centre of spiritual inquiry. To this purpose, one of my first works will be the construction of a library and scriptorium. All sisters will be obliged to read the holy scriptures every day and the most learned among you will carry the Word to the heathen as your illustrious sister, Leoba, did before you, thus adding lustre to the name of Wimborne. Finally, you should know that there is not only a new abbess, but also a new infirmarian. As from today, Sister Sefled will occupy my former position. In the name of the Father..." she concluded the service.

One week later, Osburh stood tongue-tied before the abbess.

"What should I call you? I mean, how do I address an abbess...Mother? My Lady?"

"Osburh, I've known you since you were a babe in arms and you have never shown any lack of respect. I hardly think it matters, do you? Come, tell me the purpose of this visit."

The young warrior frowned and chose his words with care,

"The king needs your help, *er*, my lady. Invasion. The aetheling Oswald has crossed the borders into West Seax and declared himself king."

"How do you suppose I can help? I'm not exactly a battle-seasoned warrior."

Osburh smothered a laugh, "No, my lady, but you are Abbess of Wimborne and many manors are counted on the abbey estates. You will know that the house sends regular knights' fees to the king – well, now is the time to send the warriors themselves, and their men. I'm come to deliver this message."

"I see," this was the first administrative task for Cynethryth to expedite, aside from the daily routine of the monastery. "Of course, the abbey will fulfil its obligations to our king." Her expression changed, "Tell me, Osburh, is there danger of this Oswald defeating Aethelheard?"

"Fear not, Mother, King Aethelheard is an able commander and he has many supporters in West Seax. He has summoned the fyrd. That is why I am here."

Cynethryth sent monks to the outlying manors with orders to arms. The response, according to her messengers, was generous. Even so, she spent the next days anxiously awaiting news and filled her time by studying the abbey archives. Soon, she understood the vast unseen range of duties expected of the abbess and marvelled at the efficiency of her predecessor. The sittings of the manorial courts needed scheduling, the regular balance of the abbey books, its expenditure and income could not be neglected even for one month. She identified the important individuals who regulated the smooth running of the monastic complex and summoned them one by one to her quarters. Unable to call upon the prioress, she worked closely with her deputy, Leofwen, grooming her for the role of prioress. Without Quenburga's superior experience, Cynethryth compensated by humbly exposing her inexperience to the cellarer, the bailiffs and reeves, who were all eager to demonstrate and share their knowledge. Not one of them, if pressed, would have exchanged the efficiency of the severe Quenburga for the charm and meekness of the abbess.

News of the warfare came from the most authoritative source, in the form of the king himself.

Aethelheard presented himself ten days after Osburh's visit and echoed his friend's perplexity with his own decisiveness: "I shall call you Mother, mother! Today, I bring my thanks for your support, to which I must add many more words of gratitude throughout the kingdom. We have won a great victory. Oswald is expelled and no longer threatens the throne."

"Then does he still live?"

"He escaped our forces and fled where we could not follow, into Hwicce."

Cynethryth looked over Aethelheard from head to foot and admired the strong warrior he had become – so handsome and with a presence that reminded her of her late husband. She smiled and said, "I see this escape troubles you little."

"Mother, I have an understanding with the King of Mercia. I suspect he needs me as much as I lean on him. Oswald is no longer important. My thoughts, instead, are turned to the east. I must ensure that the Suth Seax are quiet. There has been so little time to settle my affairs. That is why," he smiled, "I am here today. It goes without saying that I will require the best possible advisers around me in Winchester. Mother, I wish for you to leave Wimborne and to come and live at my court."

Cynethryth gazed at him in amazement. Had she heard aright?

"Do not look so surprised, Mother. Destiny has kept us apart for so long. Now that I am king, there's no obstacle to our being together."

Cynethryth adopted a stern expression that would have done credit to Quenburga, "It's not a mother you need, my son, but a wife. A king must have an heir! In any case, the abbey has just lost one abbess, it cannot suffer losing another."

"Is there not a perfectly good prioress to take your place?"

Cynethryth's eyes flashed, "God forbid!" then they softened as an idea flashed across her mind.

"Hark, Aethelheard, I have a favour to ask of you. There's a priory at Wareham and I'm told the prior is a man of exceptional qualities, prime among them wisdom. Take him with you to Winchester as a counsellor and appoint my prioress in his stead at Wareham."

"Mother, I know not what you are scheming, but I owe you everything and will accede to your wishes. What will you do for a prioress here?"

"I have the perfect candidate in mind. In fact, why don't we summon the interested parties? I take it you will give me your full support."

"Rely on it."

Within a few minutes, Prioress Quenburga and her sub-prioress stood before the abbess and the king. Cynethryth smiled at the great effort the prioress was making to curb her surliness before her monarch.

"Prioress Quenburga, it is my wish and that of your king, that your vast experience in administrative and disciplinary matters together with your undoubted spirituality be placed at the service of the Church.

The arched eyebrows of the prioress shot up further, her curiosity piqued.

"Mother?"

Uttering the word clearly cost her enormous effort.

"Your desire to rule a religious house will be fulfilled. Our king wishes you to assume the role of prioress of Wareham."

The prioress stared, her countenance incredulous although her eyes betrayed fleeting satisfaction,

"*B*-but what of the Prior of Wareham?"

At last, Aethelheard spoke, "We need him in Winchester, sister. On the other hand, your suitability for the position at Wareham is irrefutable. Your two houses can work together in harmony for the good of the people of Dorset."

Another fleeting emotion passed across the sour visage but the position of power appealed to Quenburga, overcoming other sentiments.

"Sire, I am pleased to serve God and my king, it will be as you command."

"That's settled, then," Aethelheard smiled, "Mother, was there ought else?"

"Indeed! You may leave our presence, Prioress Quenburga."

No sooner had the door closed behind her than Cynethryth burst out laughing.

"Oh, what joy! Not to put up with that miserable face every day! May God forgive me, but she has tested my patience. I think it will be different with the new prioress, don't you Sister Leofwen?"

"I do not know, Mother, who is she?"

Cynethryth beamed with delight at Aethelheard, "Oh, I think you know her very well, Prioress! We'll wait until the king has left with Prioress Quenburga for Wareham and then we'll announce your appointment to the sisters."

"Mother, I do not know what to say, I'm so unworthy."

"Sister Leofwen, if there's one word that doesn't describe you, it's 'unworthy'. Your steadfast loyalty alone equips you for the position. Besides, you'll grow into the post." Cynethryth grinned, "and you have the perfect model to work from – how not to be a prioress! Although, to be fair, Quenburga has many qualities," she added, looking under her wimple at her son.

Aethelheard, used to his mother's scheming, chose to feign indifference.

"I must take my leave, Mother. There's so much to do."

"Indeed! You must restore West Seax to pre-eminence in the south. And I must add renown to the name of Wimborne Abbey, in the name of the Father…"

"Ay, or – in the name of the *Mother*!" King Aethelheard laughed.

THE END

Historical Notes

The Anglo-Saxon Chronicle informs us that the aetheling Oswald died in 730 AD, that is, three years after the end of this story. It does not specify how he died. Wynflaed is an entirely fictitious character and one hopes she found some serenity and happiness. King Aethelheard reigned over Wessex for fourteen years until 740 AD. He married Frithugyth and was succeeded by Cuthred, perhaps a relative. Aethelheard was unable to contrast the might of Aethelbald of Mercia, indeed losing the strategic royal manor of Somerton to him.

Cuthburga was later canonised and on her death it is probable that her sister Quenburga became abbess. In order to develop my character, Cynethryth, I have most likely done this personage a disservice. I imagine she was a humble and noble person in reality.

About the Author

I was born in Cleethorpes Lincolnshire UK in 1948: just one of the post-war baby boom. After attending grammar school and studying to the sound of Bob Dylan I went to Nottingham University and studied Medieval and Modern History (Archaeology subsidiary). The subsidiary course led to one of my greatest academic achievements: tipping the soil content of a wheelbarrow from the summit of a spoil heap on an old lady hobbling past our dig. Well, I have actually done many different jobs while living in Radcliffe-on-Trent, Leamington, Glossop, the Scilly Isles, Puglia and Calabria. They include teaching English and History, managing a Day Care Centre, being a Director of a Trade Institute and teaching university students English. I even tried being a fisherman and a flower picker when I was on St. Agnes, Scilly. I have lived in Calabria since 1992 where I settled into a long-term job, for once, at the University of Calabria teaching English. No doubt my lovely Calabrian wife Maria stopped me being restless. My two kids are grown up now, but I wrote books for them when they were little. Hamish Hamilton and then Thomas Nelson published 6 of these in England in the 1980s. They are now out of print. I'm a granddad now and happily his parents wisely named my grandson Dylan. I decided to take up writing again late in my career. You know when you are teaching and working as a translator you don't really have time for writing. As soon as I stopped the translation work I resumed writing in 2014. The fruit of that decision is my first historical novel, *Die for a Dove*, an archaeological thriller, followed by *The Purple Thread* and *Wyrd of the Wolf*, published by Endeavour Press, London. Both are set in my favourite Anglo-Saxon period. Currently my third and fourth novels are available too, *Saints and Sinners* and its sequel *Mixed Blessings* set on the cusp of the eighth century in Mercia and Lindsey. A fifth *Sward and Sword* will be published in June 2019 about the great Earl Godwine. At the end of April 2019, a novel about the great King Aethelstan, *Perfecta Saxonia*, will be released, rapidly followed by *Ulf's Tale*, tracing events in the tenth-century English, Danish, Norwegian and Swedish empire of King Cnut. Also in May 2019 a time-travel novel *Angenga* unites our century to the ninth.

Lightning Source UK Ltd.
Milton Keynes UK
UKHW021022161120
373486UK00004B/562